WHERE THE TRUTH HIDES

THE

TRUTH HIDES

LIANE CARMEN

ISBN: 978-0-9984247-0-5 (paperback)
ISBN: 978-0-9984247-2-9 (ebook)

Cover design by 100 Covers and Jason Brown.
Author photo by Bill Ziady. (www.matchframeproductions.com)
Interior design by FormattedBooks.com

www.lianecarmen.com
lianecarmen@icloud.com

To those using DNA to solve a family mystery or just find a piece of themselves, you have shown me the emotional highs and lows that searching can bring. I hope your journey leads not only to answers, but also to family that opens their minds and hearts to you.

To the IVF warriors who endure almost anything to become a mother, I hope I've shed light on the emotional toll of infertility. If I could, I would sprinkle baby dust on every single one of you.

For Mark, my love, for always believing in me.

CHAPTER ONE

Becky

Becky Morgan tilted her head at the sound of the muffled beep. She quickly scoured the top of her desk in search of her cell phone. Littered across the flat surface were invoices, folders, order confirmations. The boutique had been busy, but at least her desk was out of sight in the back office.

"Where are you?" she muttered as she shuffled the clutter around.

Once she located her phone, Becky glanced at the text on the screen and scowled.

Two words. *"Help me."*

She dialed and brought it to her ear. One ring. Two. And then, "Hello?"

Becky spoke into the receiver in a controlled voice. "I'm not sure where you are, but you need to leave right away. Don't even hesitate. This is an emergency."

The voice on the other end let out a stuttered gasp. "Oh my god, are you okay? No, of course, I'll be right there."

Becky disconnected the call as her business partner entered the office they shared. Tonya still looked polished even at the end of the day—not a hair out of place in her highlighted chin-length bob. The linen dress she wore was as crisp and clean as it had been that morning.

Becky knew she looked like she had spent the day running sprints through an obstacle course. Self-consciously, she tucked the hem of her blouse back into the waistband of her skirt.

"Is the front door still open?" Becky asked.

Tonya grabbed her purse from the bottom desk of her drawer. "Yeah, I was just getting ready to lock up."

"Jules should be here any minute. She's on the other side of The Village at Riley's. I had to give her the emergency call."

"Another bad blind date?" Tonya asked as she peered into her purse and pulled out a set of keys.

"I guess."

"How that gorgeous girl doesn't have a man is something I'll never understand."

Becky nodded. "I know. Everyone insists on setting her up, but I don't think she's over Tim."

"Didn't she break up with him?"

"She did."

Tonya cocked her head. "I don't understand."

"I'm not sure Jules does either." Becky knew her friend had a hard time letting anyone in. She wanted someone to love her, but she also kept her heart fiercely guarded.

"I guess he just wasn't the right guy for her." Tonya shrugged. "Hey, maybe next weekend we can make plans for dinner, bring the husbands. Ask Bryan if that works for him. By then, I'm sure Scott will be ready for a night out."

"I'm sure Bryan would love that. I feel like we've been laying pretty low lately with everything that's going on."

Their social life would soon be different. How could it not be?

Tonya and Scott didn't have any kids. Becky had been shocked to find out they weren't planning to have any, but also a little relieved. Her biggest fear was that Tonya would come in one day and announce she was pregnant. Not that she wouldn't have been outwardly happy for her and Scott. But watching her waddle around the store— damn, that would be painful.

The front doorbell jangled, indicating someone entering the store.

"Sounds like the escape strategy was successful." Tonya's gaze fixated on Becky's desk.

Becky caught her eye. "Don't worry. I'll tidy up before I head out of here tonight. By the time I leave, my desk will look nice and neat like yours."

"Okay, I'll leave you to it."

Having them both there at closing was unusual. When they first decided to buy the boutique together, they spent endless hours to get it up and running. All that hard work had paid off. After a couple of years, they'd been able to afford to hire additional help, and sometimes they were able to get home to their husbands in time for dinner.

Becky heard the two women greet each other by the front door, and as she looked up, Jules staggered in her expensive high heels into the office.

She plopped down in the chair at Becky's desk. "I'm done dating. It's just too hard." She leaned her head back, her tousled auburn hair spilling over the back of the chair.

Becky winced. "No good? Well, it's his loss. You look beautiful." Her best friend wasn't just pretty. Flawless golden skin. Hourglass figure. A dazzling smile that owned more real estate on her face than would seem aesthetically pleasing on anyone else. She was stunning. Only Becky knew the insecurity that lived right beneath the picture-perfect surface.

"Please. He spent the first hour talking about his girlfriend. Well, he says it's his ex-girlfriend, but the way he went on and on about her, I find that hard to believe. I need to stop letting people set me up. These blind dates are killing me." She glanced up at Becky with a half-hearted smile. "Thanks for rescuing me."

"Anytime." Becky reached around Jules to collect her papers and folders into a neat pile. Even the picture frame on her desk was askew. She straightened it.

Jules pointed at the photo of Becky and her husband. "I remember that night. I swear you two have some weird Pictionary ESP."

Game night at Becky and Bryan's house was a competitive matter. Their friends always insisted they needed to play on separate teams to make it fair. They never would. Becky knew all Bryan's quirks, his addiction to anything *Star Wars*, the way he could read her mind.

Even when Jules wasn't working, her photographer's eye couldn't resist the urge to capture a moment as she had when she took that photo. As Becky studied the picture, there wasn't even a hint she and Bryan were in a room full of people.

She wasn't conventionally beautiful by society's standards, probably defined more by words like "cute" or "adorable" which seemed reserved for people of her small stature. She had a heart-shaped face with full cheeks, a somewhat pointy chin, and a deep dimple in her right cheek that appeared out of nowhere when she was feeling pure joy. Her husband loved that dimple and did his best to bring it out as often as possible.

Jules shook her head as she stared at the picture. "See, why can't I find a guy who looks at *me* like that? You got yourself quite a catch, my friend."

Becky didn't mention that Tim *had* looked at her like that. "Trust me. I pinch myself every day that I have Bryan."

Fate had brought her Bryan. She believed that. A flat tire during the last fleeting days of college and her knight in shining armor had approached, his blond hair glowing in the sunlight like he was heaven-sent. And maybe he was.

Becky pulled Tonya's desk chair next to Jules and sat down across from her. "The right guy is out there for you too. We'll find him."

"Well, we better hurry up. I'm not getting any younger, and the pool of decent men is shrinking every day. With my luck, I'll finally find Mr. Right and then find out I'm related to him."

"Anything back on your DNA tests?"

Jules had been adopted as a newborn, and she'd recently become determined to find her birth parents through any means possible.

"It'll be any day now. I should probably take those little tubes on dates with me. 'Here, spit, so I know we're not related.'" Jules groaned. "Can you grab dinner? I didn't even get to eat before I couldn't take it anymore."

"I would love to, but I told Bryan I'd be home. He probably already started cooking."

"Seriously, Beck? He's handsome, *and* he cooks?"

"Wanna come over for dinner? I'm sure Bryan wouldn't mind. It's not like he didn't know we were a package deal when he married me."

"Thanks, but I think I'll grab something on my way home. I've got some proofs I need to go through tonight anyway. I just need to figure out how to sneak back to my car."

"My car's in the back. Want me to drive you?"

Jules dismissed the idea with a wave of her hand. "Nah, I've done this before. I can handle it. Tell Bryan hey for me. Call me tomorrow." She sauntered out of the office, and the bell sounded as Tonya let her friend out the front door.

Purse in hand, Becky pushed open the back door and took a quick look outside. The lot was dark, an eerie silence hanging in the air. Now she regretted not making Jules walk out with her. Crinkling her nose, she pulled the door closed.

As she stuck her head out the office door to look for Tonya, the sounds of a one-sided conversation echoed in the empty store. Elbow on the front counter and her cell phone to her ear, Tonya glanced over at Becky. Without missing a beat in her call, she lifted her hand and gave a slight wave goodbye.

Becky waved back but lingered in the doorway until it was clear Tonya wasn't ready to go. A twinge of guilt swept through her that Bryan had already waited so long for dinner. She headed back into the office. After grabbing her keys off the desk, Becky pushed open the back door again. She took a deep breath and headed out into the darkness.

CHAPTER TWO

Becky

Becky scanned the small employee lot behind their row of stores. She and Tonya had the only two cars left in the otherwise empty lot. Her gaze drifted skyward. No help there. The cloudy day had dulled the shine of what there was of the moon. High atop a pole at the entrance, a dirty globe threw off a bit of dingy light.

She frowned as the door slammed behind her. The darkness had always made her wary, set her nerves on edge. If she couldn't see into the shadows, how could she possibly know there wasn't anything there? It was irrational, yet she just couldn't escape the feeling that someone could be hiding, ready to pounce.

As a car unexpectedly made its way up the side street, she flinched. After one last look down the length of the parking lot, she was satisfied she was alone. With her keys gripped firmly in the palm of her hand, she scurried to her car.

Her teeth chattered slightly, the shiver only partly due to the temperature. There was a slight nip in the air, an unusually late cold front pushing down from the north. This brisk weather was refreshing but temporary, one of the benefits of living in North Florida.

Their house, though older, had a fireplace they didn't get to use very often. She hoped Bryan had restocked the firewood. This was a perfect night to light it, and it might be their last chance for a while. They never had much of a spring and usually went barreling right into summer.

As she glanced around her car, she pushed the clicker on her key fob and opened the door. The inside of the vehicle illuminated. She slid in, the overhead light the security blanket that calmed her racing pulse. She slammed the door, then hit the button to lock it, and exhaled.

She sent a quick text to Bryan. *Leaving store now. See you soon!*

Her phone buzzed with his response: *Home from the gym. Starting dinner.* As if on cue, her stomach growled. She didn't blame it for protesting. The day had been busy, and there hadn't been much time to eat.

She pulled out of the parking lot, then made the turn onto the side street. It brought her around to the main road in front of the store. There was no sign of Jules. By now, she was probably halfway across the courtyard back toward Riley's.

The streetlights cast a soft haze over the road, but she was the lone set of headlights. As she passed the front of the store, she glanced inside. Most of the stores on their side of The Village were dark, but the boutique was lit up against the night, on display for anyone driving by. Tonya hadn't moved, still standing at the front counter where Becky had left her with the phone to her ear. It was a good thing she hadn't waited.

Twenty minutes and she'd be home. The drive took her mostly on back roads to get to the highway for the three short exits to her house. Without the sun to keep it warm, the inside of the car had gotten chilly. She turned on the heat, a rarity for Florida weather. A stale smell wafted from the vents as they blew out a bit of warm air.

The rural road she was on was starting to show some life. As she approached the entrance to the highway, she hit her blinker and merged to enter.

After turning on the radio, she punched the preset stations one by one. As the disc jockey offered up the best hits of the fifties and sixties, she paused, her finger hovering momentarily over the next button. A dull ache filled her chest, and she leaned back in her seat. This music took her back to her childhood. Her mother's fingers flying across piano keys. The record collection her dad kept in the old wooden crate.

The first few bars of the next song were instantly familiar— one of her father's favorites. Most times when she was thinking of him, she felt like she got a little hello from Heaven that he was still looking out for her.

"Hey, Daddy, I miss you," she whispered in the dark interior of the car.

She peered down to adjust the volume. As she brought her gaze back to the road, a bright light blinded her. She gasped involuntarily.

"What the—" She winced and blinked hard. The night and the road in front of her disappeared as if she had stared directly into the sun. She crushed the brake pedal to the floor in a frenzied panic as she couldn't see where she was going—she couldn't see anything. Her heart thudded. A clammy sweat formed on her face and body as adrenaline coursed through her like a sudden flash flood.

The car skidded out of control. She didn't know how to correct it. Were there cars to the right? To the left? Was she even still on the road?

Every part of her body tensed as it braced for an impact that seemed inevitable.

Mere seconds felt like minutes as images of Bryan, her mom, her dad, and a newborn baby tumbled over each other in her mind. And then, just as quickly as the stark white light had taken her sight, the car came to a sudden abrupt stop.

The blinding light was replaced with nothing but darkness.

CHAPTER THREE

Jules

Jules wrapped her arms around herself and shivered in the brisk night air. Her heels echoed on the brick through the empty courtyard as she headed back toward Riley's. She picked up the pace and, as she got closer, she slowed down and made her way toward the brightly lit restaurant.

Her car was near the end of the street in front of the coffee shop, long since closed for the day. She glanced toward the entrance in search of her blind date, but there was no sign of him—she was in the clear.

As she headed toward her car, she paused to peer through the restaurant window to ensure her date was still inside, then caught her breath. Flutters of disbelief danced in her stomach. She blinked hard. There was no mistaking the distinctive watch on Tim's wrist as he took the menu from the perky blonde hostess. Jules had given it to him for his birthday. He was seated in one of the booths near a window, just a short distance from where she stood. She teetered unsteadily on her heels. Seeing him had caught her heart off guard.

Jules had really thought she could be different with Tim, but then he started talking about marriage. While most girls were thrilled when a relationship grew serious, it filled her with anxiety. She picked a big fight over nothing and used it as an excuse to break up. She wanted to be loved, but she couldn't believe in the fairytale and take the chance he would leave her. So she left first.

It was one of the reasons Jules had started the search for her birth parents. She had begun to think her inability to let anyone get too close was the result of feeling like the two people who should have loved her unconditionally had decided she was unworthy. She needed to know why she was given up if she could ever hope of trusting in a relationship.

Tim had adored her, but her instinct to flee had been overwhelming. She had beaten herself up for months for her stupidity in letting him get away. It was her fault they weren't together anymore. She accepted that, but it didn't make it any easier.

Since they broke up, they had never run into each other. But yet, just twenty minutes earlier and she would have been there, a few tables away from him. Her stomach lurched at the thought that Tim might be on a date of his own. She bit her lip as she considered it. She had to know.

She thought about what to do next. After a look over her shoulder at his window, she made her way to her car and scrounged around in her trunk. She pulled out her pink Southern Charm cap. Tim probably wouldn't be able to see what it said in the dark, but a hat with her photography business on it probably wasn't her best disguise. She moved some boxes of photo paper around and tucked in the back, she found a Georgia Bulldogs hat. It would have to do.

While hiding in the shadow of her car, she piled her long wavy hair on top of her head and maneuvered the cap on top of it. She grabbed a jean jacket she had in the car and threw it on over the top she was wearing. While she knew her signature heels might betray her, this was better than nothing.

In an attempt to appear casual, she strolled back toward the restaurant. It was lit up inside, but the wood blinds in the window where Tim's dinner companion was sitting were partially closed. There was no way to tell who he was with.

"Damn," she muttered. She scanned the length of the building to see if there was another spot to stand in order to see the other side of his table. She didn't want to have to go inside the restaurant where she might run into her blind date. Even worse, with her luck, Tim would head to the men's room and catch her standing there.

She trudged up and down the sidewalk, but the angles didn't work, and she was too far to see much anyway. She needed to get closer. Tapping two fingers against her lips, she stood back while she assessed the situation.

She spied a row of medium-sized hedges between the sidewalk and the windows. If she got close, she could duck down behind them and glance in from his side to see who he was eating with. There was no way she could leave now. Despite the temperature outside, she started to sweat. She'd be mortified if she got caught.

A young couple exited the restaurant and headed toward their car. Once they left, Jules covertly moved toward the bushes. She scooted down out of view behind the shrubbery, her view of the window framed by green leaves with tiny white flowers. Tim was just a few feet away.

Her heart skipped as she looked wistfully at the man who could have been her happily ever after. She inhaled deeply and drank him in as if she could still feel his arms around her. She could almost smell his cologne, taste the cinnamon toothpaste he used on her lips. God, she missed him.

Maybe he belonged to someone else now. Nausea hit the pit of her stomach at the idea. She could just picture herself getting caught by Tim and his new girlfriend while she vomited in the bushes.

After a deep breath to prepare herself, she inched up slowly until the only thing above the greenery was her ballcap and her eyes. Engrossed in an animated conversation with Tim was an older woman on the other side of the table. His mom.

Jules exhaled a sigh of relief. She felt the tension slide off her shoulders, and she stood up slightly and gave herself the luxury of one last look at him. Then he casually turned to glance outside as if he could feel he was being watched. She felt his eyes lock on hers. Had he seen her? She stifled a gasp. Before she could see his reaction, she ducked down and scooted away from the hedge.

Heels clicking against the pavement, she strode quickly down the street toward her car. Just when she had it in sight, footsteps came up behind her.

"Jules?"

She swallowed hard. A feeling of dread pushed down on her shoulders.

"Jules, is that you?"

She gritted her teeth and turned around. "Yup, it's me," Jules said to her blind date, still slowly moving backward in the direction of her escape. "I had to come back for my car to pick up my friend. She has an emergency. Needs a ride."

"So you told me," he said. His eyes narrowed as he pursed his lips. "I almost didn't recognize you with the hat." He stopped walking.

Jules placed her palm over the top of her cap. "Oh, right. The hair. It was a mess, so I needed to put it up." She was almost at her car. "I'm really sorry. I have to go." She lifted her hand in a polite wave. "It was nice meeting you tonight." Jules hesitated. Seeing Tim had made her more aware than ever about holding on tight to someone you love. "You know, you should call your ex. I think you still care about her. It would be a shame to let her get away."

Before he could answer, Jules slid into her car and slammed the door. Her hands were trembling as she put them on the steering wheel. A hasty exit was necessary. The last thing she wanted was for Tim to find her talking to another man after she'd been caught spying on him and his mother.

After starting the car, she glanced in her rearview mirror, but there was no sign of her blind date. Hopefully, he heeded her advice and took off to his ex-girlfriend. She stole a glance into the mirror again. It wasn't like she expected Tim to come chasing after her, professing his love like in some corny movie. Her pride just needed to know if he had seen her, caught her crouched down in the bushes trying to figure out if the man she had broken up with was on a date. Her cheeks turned crimson at the mere thought of it.

As she pulled away, she yanked the hat off her head and released her hair back down around her shoulders. She shook her head. Caught stalking the ex-boyfriend by the blind date she ditched. "Only me," she said as she laughed at the absurdity of it all.

She put her phone on hands-free and dialed Becky's number. Her best friend was never going to believe what had transpired since she left the boutique. She couldn't wait to tell her, but Jules didn't get the chance. Her call went right to Becky's voicemail.

CHAPTER FOUR

Becky

The sheet Becky laid on was rough against her skin and reeked of bleach. Finally, a nurse pulled back the curtain. She was an older woman dressed in navy blue scrubs that set off her silver hair. "I'm just here to get a little information for the doctor," she said as she bustled around the small area.

The nurse reminded her of someone's grandmother, the kind that hosted Easter egg hunts and baked cookies for no reason at all. She always imagined other people's families with a bit of envy. The grandparents Becky remembered hadn't been warm or kind at all.

She took Becky's blood pressure. "one-eighteen over seventy-eight." She made a note on Becky's chart.

"That's okay, right?" After her mom's issues, Becky always asked.

"Perfect." The nurse asked Becky a few questions and made notes on her chart. Then she slid open the curtain to exit. "The doctor will be in shortly."

Becky scanned the room looking for her purse. She was desperate for her cell phone to call Bryan. With a glance at the spot where the nurse had exited, she put one leg over the side of the bed. As the curtain slid open unexpectedly, she jerked it back up.

A doctor appeared wearing a white coat and an expression that said he had been running from patient to patient and needed a minute to grab a cup of coffee. "Becky Morgan, right? I'm Dr. Summers." He glanced down at the screen of the tablet in his hand. "According to the paramedics, your car ran off the road and struck a tree." His expression turned serious as he went into medical mode. "Let's take a look."

The doctor fired off questions. "Do you feel dizzy at all? Nauseous like you want to throw up?"

He took a little flashlight out of his pocket and flicked it back and forth in front of each eye.

"I did, but I think it was the smells in here. My stomach feels a little better now, though I do feel like I have a headache coming my way."

"Do you remember the accident and the ambulance ride?"

Becky sat silent for a moment. "I remember being blinded by somebody's lights. The next thing I remember was hearing a woman call 911."

Before the doctor responded, she heard Bryan's frantic voice on the other side of the curtain. "I'm trying to find my wife. She's been in an accident!"

"Yours?" Dr. Summers asked as recognition of the voice crossed her face.

Becky nodded. "Yup."

"Okay, well, that's a good sign that you know who he is. I'll let him know where you are before we have to find him a gurney."

The doctor pulled back the curtain just as the nurse was pointing in their direction.

Bryan tried to catch his breath. "Beck, are you okay? I was scared half to death when I got the call. What happened?"

"I'm not exactly sure. I was coming around the curve to get off our exit. I guess someone's headlights blinded me. I panicked and hit the brakes and skidded off the road into a tree. This could have been much worse, I think."

"Really, Doctor—" Bryan stole a look at the nametag pinned to the crisply pressed white coat. "Dr. Summers, is she really okay?"

"Aside from a little bruise on her forehead and maybe a knot forming on the back of her head that doesn't look too bad, she seems okay. But that's the outside. With car accidents, we can't be too careful. Your head is moving along at the speed of the car, and then suddenly, it's not. That's where the problems can come in."

"But I feel fine now," Becky said.

"Some people dismiss it and go on to be fine. There's also the chance you could have a concussion or develop bleeding or a blood clot if we assume all is well and don't take it seriously. Sometimes signs and symptoms may not appear until days or even weeks afterward."

Just then, a nurse pulled back the curtain to reveal an older woman. Her lips, stained a deep mauve to compliment her tan, formed a circle as she looked in and spied Becky and Bryan.

Confusion flooded over Becky. "Roslyn?"

The doctor glanced over, and familiarity registered on his face. "Ros Dubin?"

The woman glanced at the tag pinned on his white coat. "Mark Summers. Look at you. I heard you were covering at the hospital here."

Becky gave Bryan a sideward glance. "Okay, exactly how hard did I bump my head? Ros, what are you doing here, and how do you know my doctor?"

"I was on the way to meet some friends for dinner, and I saw the car wrecked against the tree. The ambulance was just pulling away, and I was frantic when I saw your personalized license plate for the boutique. I called Bryan, and he told me he was on his way here, but he didn't know how bad it was."

Becky glanced at the doctor. "Roslyn is my mom's best friend. Her family lived next to ours when I was little. I've known her my whole life."

Ros gestured at the doctor. "And Mark, I mean Dr. Summers, is the son of a good friend of mine that I used to work with many years ago. How is your mother?"

Dr. Summers smiled and bobbed his head up and down. "She's good. She misses nursing, but she's enjoying retirement. Playing a lot of tennis and you know, lunching with the ladies."

Ros threw her head back and laughed. "I'll have to call her. Maybe we can meet for a match at the club and catch up."

Becky focused her gaze on Bryan who shrugged helplessly. He cleared his throat. "So, Dr. Summers, maybe you and Ros could catch up later? Is my wife okay?"

"Right. Sorry," he said. "Small world, huh? Well, we could do a CT scan, but a negative image doesn't always mean a concussion didn't occur."

"We should do that," Bryan said with a definitive nod. "I want to make sure she's okay."

"Yes, Mark," Roslyn agreed, her expression serious. "We would prefer to err on the side of caution with Becky. We don't want to take any chances that it's worse than it seems. We both know that can happen."

Dr. Summers glanced from the husband to the wife and back again to Bryan. "Well, it does appear she may have lost consciousness and was saying some stuff that didn't quite make sense."

Becky held up her hand as she tried to protest. "I made perfect sense."

Dr. Summers offered her a half-hearted smile. "Okay, apparently, according to the notes in your file, you told the paramedics you had a tiger at the zoo to get to."

Becky crossed her arms in front of her. "Well, I do have a cat at home I need to feed. That's probably what I meant. It's practically the same thing."

Dr. Summers shook his head and continued. "Some of the bigger hospitals don't always take it that seriously, but I prefer to run the scan and then follow up again in the morning. I'd like to keep an eye on her overnight. My guess is she has a concussion, but let's make sure it's not worse."

Becky wasn't prepared to stay. She scowled in Bryan's direction, but her displeasure went unnoticed.

Her husband's shoulders relaxed, and relief flooded his face. "Thank you."

"To be safe," Dr. Summers said, "I would also suggest you keep an eye on her over the next few months for anything you'd determine as odd behavior, like changes in taste or smell or sensitivity to light or noise. Look for any personality changes, aggression, irritability, unexplained memory loss, mood swings—"

Bryan laughed and then sputtered as he tried to explain. "Sorry, none of that is funny. Really. It's just that my wife and I are trying to have a baby, and she's been taking tons of hormones. I'm just wondering if I'll be able to tell which mood swings are which."

"Ah." The doctor seemed relieved there was a valid explanation. He glanced over at the nurse. "Can you go see about getting her a room for tonight?"

Becky focused her attention on Bryan as she pursed her lips.

Bryan's brow knitted in apparent confusion. "What?" he mouthed at her.

Becky turned her attention back to the doctor. "Dr. Summers, can my husband go home and get something for me? We're in the last stages of preparing for IVF, and I really, really can't miss my nightly shot."

She glanced at Bryan and then back at the doctor. "He could go and be back in twenty minutes."

Dr. Summers turned toward Bryan and dipped his head. "Go ahead. Check in with the front desk when you get back, and they'll let you know where she is."

He gave Becky a final pat on the arm and shook hands with Bryan. "No worries, she should be fine. The nurses will keep an eye on her overnight, and I'll check her in the morning. If all looks good, she can head home. But keep an eye on her. If you see anything abnormal that doesn't feel like a normal hormonal thing, bring her back in so we can take a look."

The doctor glanced at Roslyn as he left. Taking her cue, she walked over to the bed and kissed Becky on the cheek.

"I'm so glad you're okay and that Dr. Summers is being extra cautious. Better safe than sorry. I'll let you tell your mother what happened." She turned to hug Bryan. "Call if you need anything."

After she left, Bryan grabbed Becky's hands again. "You have no idea how scared I was when I got the call. I drove over here like a crazy person. I'm lucky I didn't get into an accident too."

"I wanted to call you, but I couldn't find my phone. I'm fine. Really, I am. But our baby-to-be might not be if I don't get my shot."

Bryan leaned forward and kissed her. "Okay, okay. I'm going. Don't get in any more trouble. I'll be back as soon as I can."

CHAPTER FIVE

Becky

As Becky settled into the bed in her hospital room, she glanced at the clock. Everything with IVF was so timed and precise, but now her shot was late. She tapped her fingers on her thigh as if her drumming would make Bryan magically appear.

Voices rang out in the hallway outside her room. Small, high-pitched voices chattering to each other.

A woman's voice interrupted them. "Blake, hold Aiden's hand."

Someone whined. "But, *Mommy...*"

"Please, boys, I need to find your grandmother. Stay with me until your daddy gets here, and then he'll take you home." The woman let out an audible sigh. "The last thing I need tonight is for either of you to wander off."

Becky leaned forward just in time to see the tow-headed boys reach out for each other. Brothers. She stared with a wistful expression as they hurried to make their short legs keep up with the deliberate stride of their mother.

Becky clutched her outstretched palm against her heart as if the heel of her hand could slow the constant ticking of her biological clock at thirty-two, she'd have thought by now she'd be on her second or even trying for a third. Infertility had changed her plans.

After she and Bryan finally got married, Becky assumed when they were ready for a baby, it would just happen. And then it didn't. Month after month after month, it just didn't happen. The months morphed into one year and then two.

And so here they were. No real explanation for their inability to conceive. None that the doctor or a battery of tests could point to definitively. The fertility doctor had suggested IVF, and Becky would have scaled a mountain if there was a baby at the top. So, their baby would grow in a petri dish before it grew in her. It wasn't sexy, but she didn't care.

"What are you smiling about?" Bryan asked as he entered the room, a small bag with her things slung over his shoulder. "Is this one of those crazy mood swings the doctor warned me about?"

"Nope, all good. Just hoping the next time I see this hospital it's to deliver our baby."

Bryan leaned over and brushed his lips against hers. "It's gonna happen, babe. I know it will."

She pulled up her hospital gown to reveal her stomach and turned her head as Bryan stuck her with the needle.

"Thanks for getting my shot. We couldn't have missed it."

"I know. Oh, by the way, I fed your tiger while I was home."

"Yeah, yeah, very funny. He must have been looking for his—"

They were interrupted by an orderly with a wheelchair. "Becky Morgan? I'm here to take you for a CT scan."

Becky glanced at Bryan as she settled into the wheelchair. "Go get something to eat. I'm sure you're famished. Can you also call Tonya and tell her I probably won't be in tomorrow?"

"Sure. Do you want me to call Jules?"

"Nah. She said she had some work to do tonight. I'll fill her in tomorrow."

Bryan placed a soft kiss on her forehead. "Okay. I'll see you when you're done."

When she finally made it back to her room an hour and a half later, Bryan was waiting patiently, his hand stuck in a bag of chips.

"I guess I'm done for tonight." Becky yawned loudly. "I can't imagine they won't let me go home in the morning."

"I already told my boss I'd be in late. I can stay home with you if you want."

"I'm sure I'll be fine. You can go to work. I have an appointment for a scan with Dr. Levine tomorrow." She patted her stomach. "Need to make sure the fertility drugs are doing what they're supposed to be doing."

"I don't think you'll be doing any driving tomorrow."

"Where is my car, by the way?"

"I had them tow it to the body shop. I guess you took the keys."

Becky glanced around the room. "Where—"

"Oh, good thing you reminded me. You'd never be able to reach it." Bryan walked over to the closet and grabbed her purse on the top shelf. "I put it out of sight when I left to get something to eat." He unzipped the top and pulled out her keychain. "Yup, you had them."

He put her purse on the chair and sat on the edge of the bed. "Let's see how you feel tomorrow, and then if you're up to it, we'll figure out how to get you to your appointment with Dr. Levine. Deal?"

"Deal."

He leaned in, placed his hands gently on the sides of her face, and gave her a goodnight kiss.

Becky settled in under the covers. "Don't be jealous of my scratchy hospital sheets while you're enjoying the eight hundred thread-count at home."

"I don't know if I can sleep without you, but I'll try. Besides, you know Sherlock won't share your side of the bed anyway." Becky's cat was bonded completely to her but had no use for anyone else. Bryan kissed her again. "Try to get some sleep. Love you."

As the door closed behind him, she already missed him. She pulled back the covers and then slid out of bed and tiptoed to the chair that held her purse. She crawled back into bed and rummaged through it until she found her phone. The screen was black. She cursed softly as she visualized her charger still plugged in next to her desk at work.

This strange room made her uncomfortable. Outside in the hallway, there was the squeaky sound of carts rolling and muffled voices. She wanted to be home right now in her own bed instead of under this thin blanket in a room that smelled like sick people.

The nurse had already warned her that someone would check in with her later during the night. Cradling one of the understuffed pillows, she shifted in the small bed in an attempt to get comfortable. Her back to the noises in the hallway, she heard the faint click of the knob turning.

A smile crept across her face as the door creaked when it opened. Her husband had come back for one last kiss.

"Forget something?" Her voice lifted as she teased him.

Becky waited for the familiar voice to respond, but silence hung in the air. She spun around, but no one was there. Confused, she glanced around, confident she'd felt someone's presence in the room with her.

She sat up and rubbed her eyes and then tried to dismiss it. After all, this was a hospital. She missed her husband in this strange place, and it had her imagination working overtime. She settled back under the covers, but this time, she faced the hallway. Heart skipping, her eyes were wide open as she kept watch on the closed door. It was probably just a nurse looking in on her, or maybe someone had the wrong room. Either was a perfectly logical possibility.

But then why were the little hairs on the back of her neck standing up?

CHAPTER SIX

Becky

They drove home the next morning in comfortable silence, grateful that the accident hadn't been worse. As they approached their house, Bryan offered a friendly wave. Their neighbor, Mrs. Ritter, was outside tending to her flowerbeds. The older woman yanked off her gardening gloves, wiped her hands on her jeans, and hurried across the street toward their driveway. A deep crease formed between her brows as she approached.

"Becky, how do you feel? That poor husband of yours was a mess last night. Oh, dear, is that a bruise on your forehead?"

"It looks worse than it feels," Becky said, as Bryan extended his hand to help her out of the car. "Just a little sore, but I'm going to be fine." She glanced at her husband and smiled. "Bryan's recovery might take a bit longer."

They both liked Mrs. Ritter. Her children were older and married with kids, and her husband had passed away before Becky and Bryan had moved in. They invited her for holidays, and she had even tried to teach Becky to cook. With everything going on with her mom, Becky had found herself confiding more and more in the older woman.

They always found time to chat when their paths crossed, but after spending the night at the hospital, Becky was impatient to get inside. She looked toward the house longingly as Bryan made small talk. She fixed a telepathic gaze on him. He acknowledged her look with a subtle dip of his head.

"Well, thanks for everything," he said to Mrs. Ritter. "I need to get Becky inside to rest."

As they entered the house, Becky's anxiety eased a bit. A familiar, happy chirping sound headed toward her. She bent and scooped up Sherlock, her orange tabby cat.

She carried him into the bedroom and dropped him on the bed next to her as she laid down. "Momma's home. I missed you, little buddy."

As she ran her hand from the top of his head to the tip of his tail, Sherlock's entire body vibrated. He rolled on his side so she could rub his soft striped belly, gazing at her through partially closed eyes of contentment.

One last scratch behind his ears and she glanced around for where she had deposited her purse. After plugging in her cell phone, she grabbed one of the pillows and laid down on the bed. Bryan took the spot next to her as the cat jumped off.

"Sherlock, was it something I said?" he asked and then turned his attention to his wife. "Maybe you should get some rest. I'll call my boss and tell him you're not ready to be home alone, and I'll spend the day with you."

Bryan had been with the ad agency for almost ten years, since right out of college. He had started as a graphic designer. While he still handled some of their more significant creative projects, mostly his boss left him alone to secure new business and manage the creative staff.

"Nah, go to work. I'm just tired. I didn't sleep that well last night. I know it was only one night, but I missed you." She was sure she hadn't been alone in that hospital room. An icy chill still prickled her neck when she thought about it. "The doctor said I'm not supposed to drive for at least twenty-four hours. I guess I also don't have a car."

"I'll stop by the body shop to see when they can get to it. They can have my key to your car. In the meantime, I'll call the insurance company, and we'll get you a rental car. But if the doctor said no driving today, then no driving today, even if you think you feel fine. I mean it, Beck. We still don't know what happened."

"I do have my appointment with Dr. Levine today, and I really need to go so he can check everything out."

"I'm not even sure I want you leaving the house, but I know the doctor's appointment is important. I'm sure Mrs. Ritter would take you."

"Okay then, Mrs. Ritter it is, and if she can't take me for some reason, I'll call an Uber. Would that make you feel better?"

"Yes, it does. But I'm serious about you getting some rest today."

She walked with him to the front door, and he turned to kiss her goodbye. "Call me after your appointment and check in."

"Don't worry. I'll be fine." She took in the stern expression on his face. "Okay, okay. I promise I'll call you."

As the door shut behind Bryan, Becky soaked in the silence. She glanced down at the feel of soft fur on her ankles. The low rumble of Sherlock's purring echoed upward as he wound himself in a figure-eight around her legs. He paused to meet her gaze, his amber eyes fixed hopefully on her.

"Wanna go out?" she asked.

He meowed in response, and Becky opened the sliding door off the kitchen to let him onto the screened-in porch. Most days when she was home, she left the door open for him just enough so he could come and go as he pleased.

Becky went back to her cell phone to check in at the boutique.

Tonya answered, the concern evident in her voice. "Are you okay? Bryan called last night, and I told him everything was fine when you left the store. What the hell happened?"

Becky recapped the details of the previous night and reassured Tonya it wasn't as bad as Bryan had made it sound.

"I'm sure I'll be fine by tomorrow. I could come in today, but Bryan wasn't having any of that."

"Well, if I know you, you won't be able to stay away long. If you're up to it, come on in, and if you're not, don't worry about it. Really. Anna's working tomorrow too. The delivery is coming from Kara, the new jewelry designer, so I want to get that all set up when it comes in."

"Oh, I love her stuff. Okay. My plan is to come in tomorrow and help, but if anything changes, I'll call or text you." A chime rang throughout the house. "Gotta go, the doorbell's ringing."

Becky opened the door to find Mrs. Ritter on the front porch holding a small wicker basket with a gingham napkin folded over the top. The sweet smell of ripe bananas and toasted walnuts wafted in her direction and made her mouth water.

"Just wanted to drop these off. Good for what ails you, honey."

Becky took the offering and felt the muffins were still warm. "These could cure anything. C'mon in."

Mrs. Ritter followed Becky into the house. "I didn't want to disturb you. Bryan said you're supposed to be taking it easy today."

"Well, I'm supposed to be resting today," Becky said as she set the basket on the counter. "But first I have an appointment with the fertility doctor for my scan." Becky sat at the kitchen table, and Mrs. Ritter took the seat across from her. "I also want to check with the doctor about last night. Need to make sure none of the hormones I'm taking could have affected my vision while I was driving."

"Oh, dear. Do you think that's what happened?"

"I have no idea. It's not a side effect that I can remember, but I need to ask the doctor."

"Well, I agree. That could be quite dangerous."

"I don't have my car since it's at the body shop, and Bryan wasn't about to let me take his. He's not too keen on me driving quite yet. Do you think you could take me?"

"I agree with that husband of yours that you shouldn't be driving yet. Of course I can take you. But you promise you'll come home afterward and take it easy?"

"I promise, and really, I do feel fine now. My appointment is at eleven-thirty."

As Becky's cell phone on the table rang, Mrs. Ritter pushed her chair back from the kitchen table. "I'll leave you to answer that. I'll be back to get you at eleven."

CHAPTER SEVEN

Jules

Jules paced back and forth in her kitchen with the phone to her ear. Just when she thought she might get voicemail again, there was an answer.

"Hey, I was actually just about to call you," Becky said.

"I need a little pep talk. You have time?"

"Of course. Everything okay? Is the blind date chasing you after your escape from Riley's?"

Jules let out a snort. "No. I tried to call you last night after I left. When I went back to my car, I ended up stalking Tim at the restaurant and then got caught by the blind date."

"Wait, what?"

"Yeah, Tim was at Riley's for dinner. I'm not sure, but I think he caught me lurking in the bushes. I was trying to see if he was on a date, but he was with his mom. And then, when I tried to flee, the blind date caught me."

"Only you, Jules."

"I know! That's what I said, but right now I have more pressing matters."

"What's wrong?"

"My parents are on their way over." Jules let out a nervous sigh. "I decided I need to tell them about my DNA tests."

"Oh." There was a moment of silence on the line. "How do you think they're going to take the news?"

"Not sure. I hope I can make them understand this has nothing to do with them. They're amazing, and I love them. It's just..." Jules's voice trailed off. Her parents had been nothing short of wonderful, and yet she still felt she needed to know where her story had started. "This isn't anything they did. You know I never lacked for anything from them, least of all love."

"True. Your parents were so obsessed with everything you did. I mean, who can blame them? I'll never forget when your mom sat in the front row during the kindergarten play and mouthed all your lines to you, and you kept stopping the play and complaining, 'Mommy, I can't hear you.'"

Jules's lips curved up at the memory. "I need to have answers, and it'll never make me love them any less. But you know, they're getting older. It kills me to do anything to hurt them."

"I'm sure it will be okay in the end, but I get how they feel. You're like the sister I never had. Is it bad to say I hope you don't find a sister to replace me?"

"Like I could."

As little girls, Jules and Becky had met at the park, almost colliding in the tunnel of the jungle gym that led to the slide. Instead of arguing over who got to slide first, they had decided to go down together. With that, they became the best of friends. They both had older mothers and were only children, and before long, they spent all their time together, bonding over Barbies and tea parties for two.

In second grade, they had been assigned to different teachers. When the bell rang one day for recess a few weeks after the school year had started, Jules had run to their designated meeting spot by the swings. She waited, but Becky didn't appear as she had every day before. Confused, Jules had scoured the playground, but there had been no sign of her best friend.

As Jules headed back to her classroom, she snuck a peek into Becky's room. Her desk sat empty. Even the name tag taped to the front of her desk and her books were gone. When she got home that day, Jules's mom had broken the news that Becky and her family had moved away.

"The happiest day of my life was finding you on my porch when you moved back," Jules said, her tone serious and sincere.

"I'm back," Becky had announced with a grin the summer before their senior year in high school.

The two girls had picked up where they left off, and it was like they had never been apart.

Jules was still searching for the love of her life, but she firmly believed women could have friends who were soulmates. Becky was hers. Other women were sometimes intimidated by her looks. Becky knew that underneath the swagger Jules presented to the world, insecurity lurked. And Jules knew that despite having a husband who adored her and a successful business, Becky would never feel complete until she was a mother.

Jules always felt they were bonded like a magnetic force was pulling them together. There was a reason their friendship had been given a second chance.

"So, are you home?" Jules asked. "I thought you had to work today."

"Well ..." There was a pause before Becky continued. "I had a little accident driving home from work last night."

"Seriously? After I left you? Beck, I feel terrible. How could you let me go on and on about my stuff? Are you okay? Why didn't you call me?"

"Apparently, I ran my car into a tree. I don't have a great excuse except that I guess someone's headlights blinded me, and I couldn't see. They made me stay at the hospital last night. I guess you have to be careful when you have a head injury. It was just a precaution. I'm fine. Oh, and Ros showed up and knew the doctor."

"Oh, wow. Between Ros and Bryan, I'm sure they wanted the doctor to swaddle you in bubble wrap."

"Pretty much." Becky let out a short laugh. "The doctor told Bryan to watch out for memory loss, mood swings, personality changes. Naturally, my husband found it funny when the doctor told him that. Said he wasn't sure he would be able to tell whether my craziness was from the hormones or the accident."

"Well, Bryan's hilarious. How are the hormones going?"

"I'm starting to think this is like PMS on steroids. I have an appointment with Dr. Levine today to check my levels and get my scan. Of course, now my car is being held hostage at the body shop waiting to be fixed."

Jules glanced at the clock. "What time? Do you need me to take you? I'm not sure how this will go with my parents, but I should be around later."

"No, I'm good. Bryan went to work, but Mrs. Ritter said she would take me."

"Well, okay, let me know if anything changes." The sound of the doorbell chimed up the narrow staircase to the kitchen table where Jules sat. "My parents are here. Wish me luck."

"Good luck. Let me know how it goes."

Jules's townhouse was three floors with the kitchen and living room on the second floor and two bedrooms on the top floor. She had converted the entry level into a small office and photography studio. Most times she went to the client or their event, but specific projects required she provide the space for the shoot. This setup worked perfectly for her.

When her mother was done bustling around her small kitchen to make a pot of coffee, Jules sat them down at the kitchen table, her lips set in a straight line. Her mother cast a nervous glance at her father.

"Is everything okay? Julianne, what's wrong?" Only her mother called her by the legal name she had been given when she was adopted. Julianne Stacy Dalton. Jules suited her better. Becky had coined the nickname when they were younger, and it had stuck. Maybe her birth mother had given her a name too. A name buried in a dusty old file or typed on her original birth certificate.

"Nothing's wrong, Mom, but I do have something to tell you both." Jules sucked in a deep breath, and she could feel her heartbeat quicken as she forced herself to utter the words. "I've decided to search for my birth parents."

Her mother's lips parted and then closed. She put down her coffee cup and turned her head to exchange a pained look with her husband.

Jules's gaze drifted between her mom and dad. "It has nothing to do with both of you. It's something I've been thinking about for a long time. I just feel like—" She didn't know if there was anything she could say to make them understand. "I just feel like I need to know where I came from."

Her mother stared down at the table, her shoulders sagging as if this news had placed a weight on them. When she looked up, her eyes were wet. "We don't know anything, Julianne. We never met your birth parents. It was a closed adoption."

Jules had asked her parents when she was in high school if they knew why she had been given up. She had gotten this same answer all those years ago, and then her mother had quickly changed the subject.

Her mother glanced at her father as she straightened her posture. "The agency handled everything, and they aren't even in business anymore. I heard the building flooded during one of the hurricanes, so I doubt anyone even has access to the old files."

"Actually, Mom, I'm using DNA testing. Even if neither one of my birth parents tested, the odds are that someone they are related to will show up as a match to me, and then I can follow the trail to them."

Jules's dad frowned. "DNA testing? That seems sort of extreme, don't you think?"

"It's pretty simple. You just spit in a tube and send it in. Dad, you're a financial advisor. Mom taught first grade. I can't even balance my checkbook, and can you just imagine me all day in a classroom? Maybe my love of photography came from one of my birth parents. I mean, I could even have siblings." Jules offered a half-hearted smile to try to lighten the mood. "Wouldn't it be weird if we actually had stuff in common? Maybe they hate mushrooms on their pizza too."

An uncomfortable silence hung in the air. Neither parent would look her in the eyes. Jules had always felt like the subject of her adoption was off-limits, and now she was convinced that wasn't just her imagination. Years of emotions just beneath the surface had bubbled up and spilled out into the open for all of them.

Jules bit her bottom lip. "I'm sorry—I'm not trying to make you both uncomfortable, but I didn't feel it was right not to tell you."

Finally, her father cleared his throat. "We always knew this day might come, but after all these years, you never mentioned it again, so we sort of thought maybe you didn't need to know."

Her mom's voice shook as she wrung her hands over the table. "But, sweetie, why do you need to know? What does it matter?"

It mattered to Jules in a way she wouldn't be able to explain to them. Did she get her laugh from her birth mother? Did her birth father even know she existed? She was tired of endlessly searching the faces of strangers for something—anything—that looked familiar. Finding her birth parents would be like opening the door to reveal all the things that made her who she was, the mannerisms and hobbies and interests that simply didn't come from the parents who raised her. Suddenly, it would all make sense. *She* would make sense like she finally had all her missing puzzle pieces. More than anything, she needed to settle the feeling she had been abandoned, unwanted.

Jules knew she couldn't say any of this to her parents, so she said instead, "I've been thinking about searching for a long time, but it always seemed impossible. Now, it seems like I might be able to find them using DNA."

Her mother clasped her hands around her father's upper arm as if they'd be a united force if they were connected. "Julianne, *we're* your parents. We were the ones at your school functions—the ones who taught you how to ride a bike and took you to get your ears pierced. We're the ones who cried when we dropped you at college and cheered you on at graduation." Her voice cracked. "Now it seems like none of that was important. *We're* not important simply because I didn't give birth to you."

Jules flinched as if she had been punched in the stomach. She had expected her parents wouldn't love the idea of her search, but this was worse than she had imagined.

"Mom, that's not true." Jules's voice had escalated, and she took a moment to regain her composure. "You will *always* be my parents. This is just something I need to do. For me. I didn't fall from the sky. I came from somewhere. Most people know where they started. It just doesn't seem fair that I have to feel guilty about wanting to know where my beginning happened—and with who."

"As far as we're concerned, it began with *us*," her mom said, her voice barely above a whisper.

Jules closed her eyes for a moment and took a deep breath. "Mom, you know what I mean."

Her mother shook her head. "I guess I don't—"

Her dad interrupted. "Jules, I think this has just come as a bit of a shock to us today. We just need a little time to process this, okay?"

Jules slouched back in her chair feeling defeated. "Okay." She glanced at her mother. "Mom, I wasn't trying to upset you." Jules was starting to second-guess her plans. The look of betrayal on her mother's face had knotted her stomach.

"Julianne, we love you. As far as we're concerned, you've always been our daughter. I guess—" Her mother's eyes welled up. "I guess I'm just afraid of losing you."

Jules's face softened. "Mom, I'm not trying to replace you. But if DNA can give me a little piece of my history, wouldn't you want me to find out if it's important to me?"

Before her mother could answer, her father held up his hand and offered Jules a small smile. "When we adopted you, DNA testing wasn't even a thought. It takes some getting used to."

"Do you want me to explain how the DNA test works?" Jules asked, hesitation in her voice.

Her mother shook her head. "I'm sure it's more complicated than I could understand." She reached over and put her hand over Jules's. "It will probably be hard to figure out, so I hope you won't be disappointed if you don't find anything. Besides, I've heard those tests aren't even very accurate. I'm not sure they prove anything."

CHAPTER EIGHT

Becky

As Becky sat on the examination table waiting for Dr. Levine, she rubbed her arms to generate warmth.

Some days, it felt surreal to be in the midst of the IVF cycle that could result in her finally getting pregnant. The relief she felt when they decided to do IVF was replaced by panic when Dr. Levine had walked them through the whole process.

Bryan had squeezed her hand as they sat side by side in the consultation. "You can do this, babe. We're in this together."

Becky had snorted in nervousness. "We're in this together, but I'm the one on the pointy side of the needle."

"This is Kim," Dr. Levine said as he gestured at the nurse that had sat in with them. "She'll be with you every step of the way through your egg retrieval."

Kim had pulled up a chair next to them. "I'm your partner in this process, so if you have any questions, you can call me." She had directed her gaze at Becky. "It's up to you how caught up you want to get with the internet. Some patients like to chat with other women for support, which is fine if it helps you. Just don't get sucked in."

"Yeah, I'm not really one to do that," Becky said. "I got off social media a few years ago when everyone I knew was posting pictures of their babies." She gave Kim a small shrug. "I couldn't handle it. I don't have much free time, but I also feel like I'm better off not knowing any of the horror stories. I'm nervous enough."

Kim had been there, as promised, to answer all her questions. Becky had thought about calling her after the accident, but she felt this needed Dr. Levine's expertise.

Becky cupped her hands and blew warm air into them. Just as she shivered again on the table, she heard the familiar tell-tale rap on the exam room door. She gave the all-clear.

Dr. Levine greeted her as he grabbed her folder from the slot on the door. "So, how're we doing today?" He rubbed his bald head as he scanned her folder.

Becky hesitated before responding. "Well, I had a little accident."

He glanced up from the notes in her file to scrutinize her. She filled Dr. Levine in on the events of the previous night, and he pushed back her hair to see a bruise forming. Becky had conveniently parted her hair so that it was hidden as she swept her thick bangs over it.

"Could the drugs I'm taking have anything to do with it?" she asked.

Dr. Levine thought for a moment and then shook his head. "I have seen cases of women who have some vision problems, though usually it's blurred vision and not really what you described."

"I mean, I feel fine now. No problems at all with my vision."

"Well, it could also have been some bozo with his high beams parked on the overpass where he shouldn't have been. The good news is you're okay. But, if anything else happens, I need to know. Got it?"

Becky nodded as Dr. Levine called out on the intercom for Kim to join him for the exam.

"Everything looks perfect," he said as he finished up her scan and made notes in her folder. "You're progressing right on schedule."

After she dressed, she found Kim waiting for her behind the front desk. "So, good news today. Are the shots becoming easier?"

"Yeah. We're getting through it. When I see Bryan coming at me, I remind myself it's a means to an end."

Kim nodded and offered a small smile. "Right. Did you print out the calendar from our website? It makes it a little easier to keep track of everything."

"I sure did. It's on the refrigerator, and I take great joy in drawing a big red X at the end of the day. I'm racking up those red marks, so I have to be getting close."

"You are." Kim handed Becky her appointment card. "We'll see you the day after tomorrow."

There was always the chance IVF wouldn't work for them, but Becky believed in the power of positive thinking. If she did everything she was supposed to, she'd be pregnant. This had to work. She couldn't even imagine how devastated she would feel if it didn't.

CHAPTER NINE

Becky

Mrs. Ritter insisted on dropping Becky in her driveway despite her protests that she could walk from across the street. She entered the kitchen and dropped her purse on the table. "Sherlock, Momma's home."

"Want to go outside?" she asked when the cat appeared.

Becky poured herself some juice and grabbed one of Mrs. Ritter's muffins as her stomach growled. She unlocked the slider to the porch, and they both went out to enjoy the afternoon sun.

After lowering herself into one of the overstuffed chairs, she texted Jules. *How did your parents take the news?*

The phone buzzed, and she crinkled her nose as she read the message. The thumbs-down emoticon, followed by: *They're still here. Fill you in later.*

Becky wiped a line of sweat that had formed on her forehead. The slight chill of the morning had given way to glorious sunshine set in a cloudless blue sky.

She pulled herself out of the chair and strode through the open sliding door into the kitchen and then to the bedroom. Sherlock was at her heels. She rummaged around in the dresser drawer to find something cooler and pulled out a favorite T-shirt.

As she turned to leave the room, the cat leaped off the bed and darted in front of her. With a backward glance at her to ensure she was following him back to the porch, Becky watched as he stealthily crept up to the edge of the screen to resume his surveillance.

It was then that Becky noticed the screen door to the backyard had blown open. She frowned as she pulled it shut. It wasn't even windy out. She stood for a moment and then reopened the door.

She stepped out into the backyard and studied the trees that lined the property behind the house. Had she seen a shadow protruding from one of the trees? As she squinted into the sunlight, she scanned from one end to the other, looking for movement or a flash of color. There was nothing. She glanced around the side of the house where she could see through to the street. In the distance, she saw Mrs. Ritter's front yard, but she wasn't outside.

Becky's gaze traveled the length of the backyard again. She was sure she smelled cigarette smoke, but there was no one around. She glanced into her neighbor's backyard, but it was empty.

Shaking her head, she closed the door and lowered herself back into her chair. As she drank her juice and finished her muffin, she contemplated what to do with the rest of the day. The accident had left her sore. She considered a hot bath might make her feel better, but when she stood up, she found herself teetering, her legs wobbly underneath her.

She staggered back into the house through the kitchen, stopping to use the table to hold herself up. She hadn't gotten much sleep in the hospital, and Dr. Summers had told her she could potentially feel a little dizzy for a few days.

With the sun streaming through the big picture window, she laid down on the couch and felt much better. An oversized yawn took her by surprise. She couldn't even keep her eyes open, so she closed them for just a minute, her promise to call Bryan forgotten.

***

Becky blinked several times as she tried to bring her view into focus. As the fog lifted, Bryan's face loomed over her.

He smiled and kissed her on the cheek. "You were out cold. You said you'd check in, and I didn't hear from you. When you didn't respond to my text messages, I got worried and sent Mrs. Ritter over to check on you. She reported back that she could see through the window that you were taking a big ole' nap in front of the TV."

Becky yawned and stretched. "I'm sorry, babe. I guess I was just exhausted from the night at the hospital." Sitting up, she glanced out the window. "Wow, it's dark out."

Still somewhat groggy, she trudged into the kitchen. As she peered through the opening of the sliding glass door, she flicked on the porch light. Sherlock wasn't out there, so she brought in her glass from earlier and shut the door.

Over Chinese take-out, Becky reassured Bryan she was feeling much better. If she mentioned she was dizzy and seeing and smelling things that weren't there, he would have her back at the hospital. Clearly, she had needed sleep. There was no need to worry him over nothing.

"Mrs. Ritter took me to my appointment." Becky gestured toward the banana muffins on the counter. "And look. Banana muffins. So good."

"And what did Dr. Levine have to say?"

"Oh, sorry." Becky took a bite of her eggroll and finished chewing before updating him. "I'm right where I'm supposed to be, and he didn't think the hormones could have caused that kind of issue with my vision. I'm supposed to tell him if I have any more problems, but for now, everything is right on schedule."

"Well, that's good news. I called the shop. They said your car shouldn't take too long to fix once the parts come in. I'll leave you my car tomorrow morning. Dave from work said he'd pick me up and run me over to the rental car place at lunchtime. You need to meet me there."

"We'll rent me something fast and furious, right?"

He gave her a hardened gaze. "Don't push your luck. You'll be lucky I don't make you rent a tank."

Later, they crawled under the covers together, and Bryan clicked the button on the remote. The light of the television cast a soft glow over the bedroom. She laid her head on Bryan's chest, the soft vibration of Sherlock's purring against her back.

While she could hear the steady thumping of Bryan's heart, her own seemed to be skipping all over the place. Unable to ignore the anxiety quivering through her insides, she sat up and turned to Bryan in the darkness. "Do you think—"

His eyes were closed and his mouth slack as he took in deep, even breaths. He was sound asleep. With the nap she had earlier, she wasn't even the least bit tired.

Becky took in a deep breath. She brought her hand to her neck, but her emotions were caught in her throat like she wanted to cry but had no idea why. It was probably her nerves over the IVF and the accident. Maybe it was the overload of hormones in her system wreaking havoc on her emotions.

Carefully, she slipped the remote out of Bryan's loose grip and turned off the television. After laying back down, she crossed her hands over her stomach and stared at the ceiling.

Her thoughts turned to her mother. Roslyn often visited her mom but had said she wouldn't tell her about the accident.

For a long time, Becky hadn't wanted to admit something might be wrong. Her mother's behavior had started to change in the last few years, and she tried to reassure herself that it was just old age. The scolding she'd get for not calling her mom when they had just spoken. Complete meltdowns over things that just really weren't that significant. Conversations with her mother that led to arguments because Becky didn't understand what she was trying to say. She took out her frustration on Becky sometimes and was mean. That wasn't like her mother at all.

Becky never knew what to expect. Some days her mother had seemed perfectly lucid, and she convinced herself that her fears were unfounded. Then, her mother would hold the remote to the television as if she had no idea what to do with it. Deep down, Becky knew it had to be more than just old age.

Her greatest wish was that her mother would be able to meet her grandson or granddaughter while she still understood what was happening. Her mom still had lots of good days, but occasionally a bad one would creep in, and Becky was reminded they were on borrowed time.

She'd visit her soon to check in. There was no need to tell her mother about the accident. Becky was fine, so there was no reason to worry her.

CHAPTER TEN

Felicia

The first thing Felicia Williams saw when she opened her eyes was the sign her daughter had made for her. *Don't be scared, Mom. This is where you live now. I love you! Becky* Felicia pulled back the covers. She had been under her comforter from home, white with pink flowers with little green stems. Becky had brought it along with some other personal items from her house. What would happen to the rest of her things? Anxiety would buzz through her when she thought about it.

After sitting up slowly, she swung her feet over the side of the bed. Feeling around on the floor with her feet, they slid into the terrycloth slippers by the side of the bed. Shoes weren't always that easy, but these she could manage.

Someone knocked, and then a flash of movement caught her eye as the door to her room swung open. Ellie was a beautiful Filipino woman with glossy black hair and perfect porcelain skin. She had a tray perched on her flattened palm. Felicia's breakfast. As the smell wafted toward her, her stomach churned.

"Good morning, beautiful." Ellie's voice was light and cheerful as she flashed Felicia a genuine smile.

"I'm hungry," Felicia said as she scanned the area around her. She found her robe on the end of the bed and slipped it on in slow motion—one arm in and then the other.

Ellie made room on a small table for the tray. She seemed to keep a watchful eye as Felicia put on her robe but didn't move to assist. It took several tries, but Felicia was finally able to get her hands to tie the sash loosely around her. She offered Ellie a satisfied smile as she lifted herself off the bed and ambled toward the table, step by slow step while she got her bearings.

"Maybe Becky will come visit me today," Felicia said as she sat in front of her breakfast.

"Maybe she will." Ellie handed Felicia a napkin. "That would be lovely, right?"

Felicia furrowed her brow and looked up at Ellie. "She's okay, right?"

"Yes, of course she is."

Felicia searched Ellie's warm brown eyes for reassurance. "I would do anything for Becky." Her voice shook.

"There, there." Ellie patted her shoulder. "I know you would."

Felicia grabbed Ellie's sleeve. "She's my little girl. I can't lose her."

"Your daughter loves you. Miss Becky's all grown up now, but she's not going anywhere."

Felicia sat silent a moment and finally nodded. She repeated Ellie's words out loud, "Becky's all grown up."

"She sure is." Ellie handed her a spoon. "I had them put your scrambled eggs in a bowl. They should be easier to eat now."

Felicia glanced down, surprised to see the tray. She had forgotten her breakfast was there. She took the spoon and carefully scooped up the eggs and then brought them to her mouth. There might come a day when someone had to feed her, but she wasn't there yet. Not if she could help it.

"You're doing beautifully," Ellie said as the corners of her mouth turned up. "Oh, today's going to be a good day. Do you know what day it is?"

"Wednesday?" Felicia was unsure. Sometimes all the days seemed the same.

Ellie patted her hand. "That's right, and we have exercise class this morning. Do you remember yesterday? You were dancing in the music room."

Felicia closed her eyes for a moment. "Elvis," she said as she opened them. Sometimes all her memory needed was a little nudge.

"That's right!" Ellie said with a grin. "You do love Elvis."

A wistful expression crossed Felicia's face as she remembered the old crate of records and the way her husband would spin her around the living room. "We both did. Ken loved him too." She hesitated as her eyes watered. "I miss him."

"I know you do, honey."

"It's not fair. We were supposed to grow old together." Felicia's bottom lip quivered. "He didn't deserve to die so young."

"Nobody does, honey."

"He was a good man. He would have done anything for Becky and me." Felicia lowered her voice until it was barely above a whisper. "Sometimes, I think it was my fault." They had thought finally they were free, but then it was too late. He was gone.

Ellie's face grew serious. "Miss Becky told me your husband had a heart attack. That was not your fault. You can't blame yourself."

Felicia gave a small shrug. She'd never be convinced Ken's death wasn't caused by the stress of what they had gone through. She had made the decision for them both, and he had paid the price.

"Eat your breakfast," Ellie said as she turned on the small television and found a channel with the morning news. "I'll be back in a bit to fetch those dishes from you."

Felicia glanced at the TV, but it was just noise. She didn't live in the world they talked about anymore.

She was grateful she could still close her eyes and recall her life with her husband, their time together, Becky's childhood. Her biggest fear was that she might lose the ability to remember how his love had felt. That terrorized her. Some memories she wished she could erase as if they never happened. She wanted that more than anything, but not if it meant losing the memories of Ken and Becky.

The last fifteen years had not been exciting, but she had finally found a certain kind of peace. Over time, she had noticed herself becoming more forgetful and confused about even the simplest of tasks. Lists littered the house as she left notes to remind herself. "All old people forget things," she would tell Becky when her daughter looked concerned.

But it was the day she went out by herself and found herself lost and confused at the supermarket down the street that things had changed. She didn't understand how she had gotten to the store, didn't remember getting in the car and driving there. Bewildered and scared, she didn't know what she was there to buy. In frustration, she just stood in the front of the store, between the express check-out and the display for buy-one-get-one-free mini-muffins and sobbed.

The manager, a nervous, somewhat disheveled, middle-aged man didn't seem equipped to deal with a crying woman. Taking her by the arm, he tried to steer her off to the side where she wasn't in front of the check-out lines. Felicia didn't like him touching her. She didn't like that at all.

A neighbor had observed the commotion and offered to take her home.

The front door to Felicia's house wasn't locked. After they went inside, the neighbor had walked around aimlessly and seemed to be looking for something, anything that would tell her who to call.

Felicia had pointed to the shopping bag hanging over the back of the kitchen chair. "My daughter owns that boutique."

When Becky arrived fifteen minutes later, she thanked the neighbor for helping and hugged her mother tight. "You scared me half to death, Mom!"

Her daughter had taken her to the doctor. He told them about the silent strokes that had damaged parts of her brain, used the word dementia, which had made Felicia's blood run cold. Becky told her she would need to move, someplace where she would be safe.

It hadn't taken long. Becky had moved her here to Tranquility, her new home, where nothing was familiar, things smelled odd, and the pleasant woman brought her breakfast.

CHAPTER ELEVEN

Jules

Jules stared at her laptop, her fingers frozen on the keyboard. The confidence she felt when she started this search for her birth parents was wavering.

The conversation with her parents had left her feeling awful, but she knew this was something she had to do. She just prayed they'd come around and understand.

She had done the research, joined the adoptee and DNA Facebook groups. Despite what her mom had said, you *could* find someone with DNA. There were lots of members who would testify to that. The groups said if you were adopted, you should fish for matches in all the pools. Jules had sent in DNA tests to three different companies.

One set of results was in. Day after day, she had just stared at that email. It was crazy, she knew, this trepidation she felt. She'd been checking fervently, waiting. Now that her results were here, her heart was in her throat. Her DNA matches could hold the key to answering all her questions. It was the unknown that was petrifying. She couldn't imagine if she found what she was looking for and her birth parents didn't want anything to do with her. It would crush her. More than once, fear tried to convince her to abandon her search altogether.

Loading up the home screen for the DNA site, a brooding expression crossed her face. She had planned to work on Becky's family tree too.

Jules had gone about it all wrong. She knew that now. She'd just been so excited about all this DNA stuff and wanted to share it with her best friend.

"Since you're starting a family," she had told Becky, "your baby needs a family tree. Maybe you're descended from royalty. I mean, you do kind of look like a princess. Who else but someone your size could have worn those teeny tiny glass slippers anyway?"

Becky could fit the family she had on the head of a pin. Both sets of grandparents were gone. No cousins she ever mentioned. The DNA test would help Jules find all her missing second and third cousins and build up her family history through her great-grandparents and even further back if she could. Maybe she'd also find a relative that would have a piece of Becky's history. She already had a vision of the framed gift she would present once the baby was born and she could add his or her information to the bottom of the tree.

She'd thought the idea was clever, and working on Becky's tree would take her mind off her own. The idea wasn't lost on Jules that most people took for granted they could build their family tree from people they knew were relatives. At this point, Jules didn't have a single person she could add to her biological tree.

Becky had looked less than enthusiastic at the idea, but Jules had tried to reassure her. "When I'm done, your baby will know everything there is to know about both sides of his or her family tree. I ordered a test for Bryan too. You don't have to do anything but spit in the tube and tell Bryan I'll be back for his. I'll handle it all, and I'll work on your family tree as my gift to the new baby.

Besides, I'm going to need a break from all the searching for my unknown family. Yours will be easy."

But the DNA test in the little gift bag with the baby rattle on the front had made Becky uncomfortable. "We just met with the doctor—I mean, I'm not even pregnant yet," she had stammered. "I've waited so long. The idea of a baby gift before..." her voice had trailed off. "I don't know. It just feels like bad luck."

Jules's face must have revealed her disappointment. Searching for her birth parents felt like one of the most important decisions she had made in her life. She wanted her best friend to be part of it with her.

Despite her misgivings, Becky had agreed. She'd even spit in the tube and given it to Jules to send in, even while the red blotches on her neck had given away her discomfort.

Jules shouldn't have pushed her. Of course Becky would do anything for her best friend, but it was clear she thought it might jinx her chances to get pregnant. Jules knew how important this baby was to her and Bryan, but a little spit in a tube wasn't going to change anything about the IVF process. Becky's test was just to help with her family tree. Jules was the one who had good reason to be nervous.

She could still remember the voicemail Becky had left. *The more I think about it, the more I can't ignore that I think it's bad luck to work on a baby gift before I'm even pregnant. I'm being silly, I know. I'm here to support you in your search, but can we just wait on my test and the family tree? Besides, I'll still be royalty after the baby gets here, right?*

Becky had apologized profusely the next time they spoke. Jules quickly dismissed it. If Becky thought the test and her family tree were going to affect her getting pregnant, Jules didn't want to do anything that would give her friend any more angst. The IVF would be successful, and Jules would just wait to deal with her test until Becky told her she was pregnant. Or maybe, to be safe, she'd wait until the baby was born and everyone was healthy and happy.

For now, she would just worry about her own search. Jules took in a deep breath, and with her finger shaking, she hit the button to open her results.

CHAPTER TWELVE

Becky

Bryan was on his laptop at the kitchen table waiting to be picked up when Becky strolled in, fully dressed to head to the boutique.

Bryan looked up from his computer. "Beck, you sure you're up to working today? You think you can handle the shop and the driving?"

"I'll be fine, and I'll take a break to meet you at lunch to rent the car."

Bryan scowled. "I'm not so sure—"

"The doctor said no driving for twenty-four hours. It's been more than twenty-four hours. I'm okay."

He wagged his finger at her. "You're very stubborn, you know that?"

"But I love you." She grazed her lips over his. "Text me later when you head to the rental place."

Ready to walk out, Becky paused by the bowl where she usually tossed her keys. She frowned and turned back to Bryan. "Hey, do you know what happened to my keys?"

"They're not in the bowl?"

"If they were there, I wouldn't be asking." Frustration turned her tone more brusque than she intended.

She had them when she came home from her appointment with Dr. Levine or she wouldn't have been able to get in when Mrs. Ritter dropped her off. Mentally she tried to retrace her steps from the day before.

She dumped the contents of her purse on the kitchen table next to Bryan and sifted through the pile, but there was no sign of them. She rifled through the little basket on the kitchen counter they used as a catch-all for small bits of junk that had no other real home. Not there either.

After stomping back into the bedroom, she checked the dresser and shoved aside the contents of her little desk. Grabbed the laptop and looked behind it. No matter how hard she tried, she couldn't visualize where she had put them when she came in the day before.

As she rubbed her temples, she trudged back to the kitchen. "Seriously, you have no idea where they are?"

"I'm sorry, babe, I haven't seen them. But, listen—"

"What the hell would I have done with them?" She felt her emotions threatening to escalate.

Bryan stood from the table and approached her, then put his arms around her. She flinched, but he held her until she relaxed into his embrace. As the fight went out of her, he stepped back.

"It's okay. Listen, they must be here someplace. You said Tonya's working this morning, so you don't need any of the store keys." Bryan pulled his car key off his keychain and handed it to her. "You don't need your key for my car. You can use mine. You'll be in the rental car coming home. I should be home before you, or if you beat me here, get the spare house key from Mrs. Ritter." He placed his hands on her shoulders. "I'm sure you don't need to go by your mom's today, so you don't need any of her keys, right?"

"No," she reluctantly agreed. "I guess I don't."

"Okay, then. We'll find them later when we get home. It's not like they're going anywhere." He offered her a small smile. "I'm not even sure I want you to go to work, but since you insist, you don't need anything else to worry about today. Go to work and lose yourself in scarves, pretty dresses, and purses."

Bryan had a way of putting things into perspective. "You're right. I can survive the day without them. I'll find them later."

Bryan was right. The boutique was her happy place.

Distracted by work, Becky forgot about the incident with her keys. Her makeup and hairstyle covered the bruise enough that no one seemed to notice.

As Tonya promised, the new jewelry had come in. Anna, one of the salesgirls who had been working for them for almost two years, was there to help.

As Becky headed back to the office to pay invoices and settle the receipts from the day she had missed, she heard Anna's voice as she unpacked the boxes. "Dibs on this one. Look how pretty."

Around dinner time, Becky emerged from the office for the day and found Tonya. "Hey, I'm heading out." They watched Anna at the register with a customer. She was already ringing up several necklaces they had just put out.

"I told you." A satisfied smile slipped across Tonya's face. "Her stuff is stunning. This order is going to fly out of here."

"Well, damn, then. I'd better pick something out for myself before it's all gone. I'll look tomorrow. See ya in the morning."

As she drove home in the sensible gray sedan Bryan had made her rent, she glanced at the spot where she had gone off the road. The tree had a chunk of bark missing, but it had fared better than her car. Off to the side, the grass told the story of her car skidding out of control.

Her eyes drifted up to the overpass that went above the exit. Maybe Dr. Levine was right and someone had just been somewhere they weren't supposed to be. At this point, it was all she had to explain what had happened.

Bryan's car was in the driveway when she pulled in. She turned the knob to the front door. He had remembered and left it unlocked for her.

Tiptoeing into the kitchen, she came up behind her husband while he stood at the stove. Leaning her body against his, she wrapped her arms around his waist. The hair at the nape of his neck was still wet from his shower after the gym.

"That cherry red Mustang would have been a lot more fun to drive home," she said as she rested her cheek against his soft T-shirt.

Bryan turned around and pushed her hair off her forehead. He studied her bruise for a moment. He turned his attention back to the stove as he spoke over his shoulder at her. "You're lucky I let you leave the house at all after the scare you gave me the other night."

Becky laughed even though she knew he wasn't entirely kidding. "Dinner smells amazing. Have I told you today how wonderful you are?"

He turned back around to face her, and she leaned in for a proper hug. Her body relaxed as the warmth of his body flowed into her. "I missed you today, but it did feel good to be back at work. I felt fine."

"I'm glad to hear that, but remember the doctor said that some of the symptoms could be delayed. No headache? Dizziness?"

"Nope, nothing. Did you find my keys?"

"They were on the desk in the bedroom by the computer. I put them in the bowl by the door for you."

Becky pursed her lips. "Really? I know I looked on the desk this morning. They weren't there. I'm positive."

Bryan threw some chopped garlic into a pan. "Maybe you missed them. Happens to me all the time. The good news is we found 'em."

"I guess."

En route to the bedroom to change, Becky stopped in the doorway. She couldn't put her finger on it, but something didn't feel right. She glanced around until finally her gaze stopped.

Their wedding picture on the dresser was not in its usual spot next to her jewelry box. She wandered over to inspect it more carefully. With all her appointments and the distraction of the IVF process, she hadn't been an efficient housekeeper these past few weeks. From the impression left behind in the dust, it was evident the frame had been moved. It now sat on the other side of the dresser, perched next to the oversized trophy Bryan received when his company softball team won the championship.

The dust also clearly showed a circle where she had placed a brand-new candle she had gotten from one of their suppliers. Her gaze traveled the length of the dresser. The candle was gone.

She scanned the room until she got to her antique rolltop desk where Bryan had found her keys. On the other side of the computer sat the candle. The sooty ends of the wick confirmed it had been lit.

Becky ran back to the kitchen. "Were you looking at our wedding picture recently?" It seemed a silly question even as the words came out of her mouth, but she had to know.

Bryan turned around to face her. "I don't need to look at the picture. I have my beautiful bride right here." He tipped her head up for a kiss, but her lips were pinched shut.

"What about the new candle on the dresser? Did you light that and leave it on my desk?"

He turned his attention to the stove to stir his sauce. "You probably lit the candle and just forgot."

Becky didn't respond. He spun around and studied her. "You okay?"

She offered a tenuous shrug. Something wasn't right. The picture had been moved, and neither one of them had done it. She knew she hadn't lit that candle, and she would never have left it on her expensive, antique desk.

Someone else had been in their house.

CHAPTER THIRTEEN

Becky

Becky stared into the full-length mirror that stood in the corner of the bedroom. From where she was standing, she could glance into the mirror and see into the bathroom where Bryan was shaving over the sink.

He watched her while he shaved, finally rinsing his face and patting it down with a towel. "Everything okay, babe?"

She groaned. "Yeah, I'm fine, but I'll be lucky if I don't bust a button on this dress at work today. I guess it's the hormones, but I feel huge."

He exited the bathroom. "Did Dr. Levine say anything about it at your follow-up appointment yesterday?"

"It's to be expected. I told you last night that he said everything is on schedule. In a few days, I'll be ready for the trigger shot, and then I can get all these eggs out of me."

Bryan came up behind her at the mirror and put his arms around her. "How's your headache?"

"Better. And before you go worrying it's from the accident, it's also a side effect of some of the hormones."

"I just worry about you, that's all." He gave her a gentle squeeze as they stared silently for a moment at their reflection.

"Well, worry about me busting out of my clothes and embarrassing myself at work. That's a distinct possibility."

Taking one last look at herself in the mirror, she used her hand in a futile attempt to smooth down the front of her dress. She rolled her eyes at her reflection.

Defeated, she walked back into the kitchen for the remains of her coffee. She stood at the kitchen counter, mug in hand, staring off at nothing as Bryan pulled his phone from the charger.

"I hope we have enough to freeze," she said.

"What?" Bryan was checking email messages on his phone. He glanced up at her. "What?" he asked again.

"The embryos. I hope we have enough that we can freeze some."

"Oh. Let's just focus on getting one healthy baby. If we get some to freeze, it'll be a bonus."

"I know." She ran her fingers through her hair. "I just want to be pregnant, so I don't have to wonder anymore if it's going to work. It would be nice to have an embryo or two frozen, so I wouldn't have to go through all these shots again if we want to try for another."

"Let's keep thinking positively. We're in the home stretch." He took a swig of orange juice from the carton and put it back in the refrigerator. His wife's scowl aimed in his direction did not go unnoticed. He often drank right out of the package but usually did his best not to get caught. He avoided her stare as he used a dish towel to wipe his mouth and grabbed his briefcase and cell phone.

Becky glared at him. This was all so easy for him. He wasn't the one with the hormones making his body do things it wasn't meant to do naturally.

"I'm trying to stay positive. Hopefully, once I'm pregnant I'll feel like myself again. Right now, I just feel like something's not right. I can't shake it. I still feel like someone must have been in the house last week."

Bryan set his briefcase down on the kitchen chair. "Because you forgot you lit your new candle? Or because the picture frame moved? Maybe Sherlock knocked it around." He gave her a small smile. "You know he doesn't like me much."

"The cat didn't move it, and I'm not crazy!"

Bryan reeled back. He hesitated as if considering his response carefully.

"I don't think you're crazy. Let's keep an eye on things, and if you have that feeling again, it won't hurt anything to change the locks. You know, there could be some related anxiety that goes along with the recovery from the accident. Or maybe it's all those hormones. Who knows?"

She expressed her frustration with a deep sigh. This had nothing to do with the accident. Anxiety didn't relocate objects or light candles. The hormones were responsible for making her short-tempered, but that was about it.

It was easier just to apologize. "The doctor did say the hormones could make me a little emotional. I'm sorry."

She knew he had hugged her goodbye as a way of punctuating the end of their disagreement. She'd allowed it to end and accepted he still thought she was paranoid. He didn't trust her feelings, and that stung a little. She'd always trusted her gut instincts in the past, but maybe he was right. All those hormones. It was possible they were contributing to the anxiety she was feeling.

Weary and tired, she went to work. They didn't fight often, but when they did, it was hard to shake off.

She parked the rental car in the spot next to Tonya's car and came in through the back door. After dropping her stuff down on her desk, she wandered into the store to see how the day was going.

As Becky glanced around the sales floor, everything seemed to be in its rightful place, yet there was an odd energy in the store. Coffee hadn't been made. The essential oils weren't being diffused. Even the soft background music they usually had playing was silent.

And where was Anna? Becky was certain she was supposed to be working this morning. Anna had said as much when Becky had left the night before. She should be here by now.

Tonya was by the cash register, and a glance around the store revealed there were no customers.

"Hey, good morning," Becky called out as she walked toward the front. "No coffee or music yet? Where's Anna?"

Tonya moved toward Becky, her mouth set in a firm line. She raked her fingers through her hair.

"What's wrong?" Becky asked.

Tonya took her by the arm. "Come in the back. I don't want to talk about this out here in case customers come in."

As they entered the office, she blurted it out. "I had no choice. I fired Anna."

"I don't understand." They had never had even the slightest issue with her. "What happened?"

Tonya summoned a deep breath. "Yesterday, I forgot my day planner. I needed a phone number in it, so I came back after hours to get it. The jewelry case with the Kara stuff was empty, and I know we didn't sell it all because we just did inventory. The cash and receipts for the night were sitting on your desk, and the front door was unlocked."

"Wait, what—she wouldn't do that. She's the most responsible person we've ever had. What did she say when you questioned her?"

"She denied it, of course. You were on the schedule to close last night, but she admitted she was the one who closed up."

"I had a terrible headache, so I went home early. She always closes. I didn't think it was a big deal." While most of the employees had keys to the store, whoever closed inserted the day's receipts and the cash into the slot on the lockbox. Only Becky and Tonya had keys to open that.

"I mean, Beck, she left the front door unlocked. Someone could have cleaned out the store. As it is, there's at least $4000 worth of jewelry missing from the case."

"But wait, this doesn't make sense. Why would she take the jewelry and not the cash? And if someone came into the store, it wouldn't make sense they would leave an envelope of money if it was laying in plain sight."

"Maybe I interrupted them, and they were going to come back, but I locked the door. Can you imagine if someone was hiding in the store?"

Becky's phone buzzed, and she subtly glanced down at the screen to find a message from Jules. *Can you meet for lunch? Big news!* She didn't dare respond to Jules's text in the middle of this conversation with Tonya.

"I know we've never felt we needed security cameras in the store," Tonya said, "but maybe we need to reconsider. It just really crushes me that someone we trusted betrayed us like this."

Becky pursed her lips. "I know, but I hate the idea that we need cameras. Our customers will feel like we don't trust them."

Tonya shook her head. "They have cameras that are hidden in clocks or are so small they're not even noticeable. You can pull up the footage right on your phone."

"I don't know." Becky rubbed her temples. "I just can't believe Anna would have done this. She must need the money. We know her ex never pays child support. Maybe you're right and you spooked her before she could take the cash."

Tonya held up a set of keys. "Well, I'm sorry, but her money woes can't be our problem. I took her door keys and told her she could come Friday to pick up her last paycheck. But Becky, we both need to be here when she comes in for her check. She was spitting fire when she left. I'm not taking any chances she becomes destructive."

"You really think she would do something to hurt the store?"

"I don't know anything anymore. You didn't see how furious she was."

The bell over the front door jangled. With no sales help on the floor, Tonya turned and left to greet the customer.

Becky slumped down into the chair at her desk and closed her eyes tight for a moment. After she opened them, she typed a response to Jules. *Stuff going on at the store but should be better in a couple of hours. Can you meet at 1 pm at Sam's?*

Her phone buzzed. *Perfect. Hope everything is okay. Can't wait to fill you in!*

CHAPTER FOURTEEN

Becky

Becky pushed open the glass door and stepped out of the boutique into the bright sunshine. Leaving the Anna drama behind for a bit was a welcome relief.

Sam's was within walking distance of the store and her favorite place to meet for lunch. As she passed the bookstore next to the boutique, she noticed a stack of books on display in the window. It was as if an undeniable force drew her in as she got closer. It seemed the universe was trying to tell her something with the stack of pregnancy books. Oh, she wanted to know what to expect when she was expecting all right. She couldn't buy anything just yet. First, she needed to be officially pregnant.

"I'll be back for you, don't you worry." Becky had her nose practically pressed against the glass. The owner noticed her from inside the store and waved. Her cheeks grew hot, and she lifted her hand in return before stepping back to scurry to the restaurant.

She'd only been sitting at the table for a minute when Jules entered and flashed her movie star smile. Faces lifted from their meals as she glided through the restaurant toward Becky. Her friend went through life like a spotlight had been erected to shine on her. Becky found it amusing that her gorgeous friend always seemed oblivious to the attention she drew out in public. As Jules sat down, her face was flush with excitement.

After they placed their orders, Becky folded her hands on the table and leaned in. "So, I'm dying to hear your news. Don't leave anything out. Did you have another Tim sighting, or did you find your long-lost mother?"

Jules shook her head. "You should have seen me hiding in the bushes. Just like those women on the true-crime shows where the creepy music plays in the background while they stalk their ex. Luckily, I came to my senses and didn't snap."

Becky laughed at the visual. "Well, at least there's that."

"But no, no other sightings. Maybe he didn't even see me. If he did, I kind of thought he might call…" her voice trailed off. She hesitated, regained her composure, and changed the topic. "But this news is about my search. One set of my DNA results is finally in. I have over four hundred relatives. People that are biologically related to me. How freaking amazing is that?"

"So, you can see actual people that are related to you?"

"Basically, you can see your ethnicity. I'm mostly Scandinavian and Irish. Who knew? And then you see a list of other members that are DNA related to you, and the site will tell you how probable it is that they're related to you and how much DNA you share. They measure DNA in centimorgans. And based on how many cMs you share, you can figure out how you might be related."

Becky listened, though she wasn't sure how all this DNA testing worked. The only thing she knew about DNA was that it was sometimes used to catch criminals.

Jules paused while the waitress delivered their drinks.

Becky took a sip of her Diet Coke. "And what if they match you to all those criminals in the database?"

"It's not that kind of DNA, silly. This is called autosomal DNA, and it's just used for determining shared DNA for family relationships and not whether you left your hair at a murder scene. But, you know, I did hear the other day that they used DNA from a cold case to create a profile for a killer. They used his matches to build a family tree of his relatives. Led them right to the killer after all these years. DNA is cutting edge, my friend."

"So, can you figure out who your birth mother is from the matches you have? She's not listed, right?"

Jules shook her head. "Nope, she's not. Right now, the closest matches I have are a bunch of third cousins and a ton of fourth cousins." She hesitated, and emotions flitted across her face. "I guess no one very close is looking for me."

After glancing around the restaurant, Jules leaned in and lowered her voice. "Part of me just has to know why she gave me up. Why didn't she want me, Beck?" Her voice wobbled. "My heart beat next to hers for nine months. Could she really give me away and never think about me? Not wonder if there were presents for me on Christmas morning or a cake on my birthday? Is that possible?"

Becky reached for her friend's hand. "I don't think so. A mother's love is a pretty powerful thing. I mean, I love my baby, and I'm not even pregnant yet. She probably has no idea she could spit in a tube to find you. I mean, I had no clue that was possible."

A half-hearted nod. "Maybe. I joined a Facebook group to help me figure out what to do with all my matches. New people are testing every day which will make the databases bigger and bigger. And there still could be a great match on the other sites. I'm still waiting for the other results."

"It sounds like you have a lot of work ahead of you to try to figure this out."

"You can't even imagine how time-consuming this all is. I keep looking at my matches and building trees trying to figure out where I fit in. I look up and hours have passed in a flash. I know I need to go to bed, but I'm obsessed. I almost get aggravated when I get a photography job, and I know I won't be home all day."

"I'm glad to see this is keeping you so busy. See, you wouldn't have had time to work on my tree anyway—"

"Jules Dalton!" A woman's voice echoed through the restaurant.

Becky looked up to see a well-dressed woman waving as she approached their table. It was rare to be out with Jules that she didn't run into someone she knew. She was like the mayor of their small town.

Jules turned her gaze and stood and air-kissed the woman's powdered cheek. "Amy, you look marvelous as always. How are you?"

"I'm just wonderful, dear. I'm here to meet the committee chair for the summer gala. We're still thinking about a *Gone with the Wind* theme. I know you're tickled about that, and you know I expect to see you there."

Jules gestured toward the table. "Becky, this is Amy Ostrau who runs the Children's Art Museum in town. Amy, this is my friend Becky. She owns the most darling boutique in The Village. Have you been there?"

"Forget Me Not? Is that the one you own?"

Becky smiled and nodded. "Yup, that's me."

"My daughter keeps raving about it. She loves your store. I'll have to make time to stop by."

Amy turned her attention back to Jules. "So, will you be bringing a date to the gala? Have you found your Mr. Right yet?"

Jules shook her head with a half-hearted smile. "Still looking."

Becky could see how painful it was for her friend to say that. It was the same way she felt when people asked her if she had kids. It stung.

"Oh, dear. How is that even possible? Well, I must put out the word with the ladies to see who we can find for you. You're much too fabulous to be alone." She glanced at the door to see her friend walking into the restaurant. She hugged Jules goodbye and waved in Becky's direction. "It was nice to meet you. Gotta run!"

Jules sat back down as the waitress delivered their salads. She grabbed her fork and dug in.

"How are your parents? Any better?" Becky asked.

Jules paused, her fork pierced through a tomato. "Not another word about it. It's like they're pretending the conversation never happened. I'm not sure how I'm going to tell them if I find answers." She brought the fork to her mouth and paused. "You know, the only thing my parents ever told me about my adoption was that they got the call unexpectedly from the agency, and they rushed to pick me up even though they didn't have a crib or a single diaper."

"Well, I'm sure they were thrilled. Your parents waited for you for a long time."

"Right. *They* were thrilled that day, but what about my birth mother? Was she sad? Relieved?"

Becky gave her friend a hard stare. "Jules, I doubt she felt *relieved*."

"Maybe she did. Maybe she was glad it was over. She could move on with her life and never look back."

"Maybe she didn't have family to help her or any money," Becky said. "Maybe her situation made it impossible."

Jules's gaze drifted down to her lunch. "Maybe you're right. I guess I'll ask if I find her." She exhaled and resumed eating her salad. "So, enough about me and my search for my long-lost family. How's the IVF going? Any emotional breakdowns yet?"

"I've had a few meltdowns. I'm convinced someone was in the house."

Jules looked up from her lunch. "Really? You mean, like someone broke in?"

"Well, there's no sign anyone broke in, and Bryan filed it under my overactive imagination." Becky explained about the candle and how their wedding picture had been moved.

"He's right. It's probably nothing," Jules said. "You have a lot on your mind with the IVF. You probably just forgot."

"Maybe." Becky still wasn't convinced. "And then I lost my keys and my mind the other day. They turned up, but I know I looked where Bryan said he found them, and they weren't there. Poor guy. I took my frustration out on him. He has the patience of a saint, that man."

"No offense, Beck, but you're not exactly the most organized person I know. You were forever losing stuff before all the hormones. And hey, they warned you that you might go a little crazy with all those shots, but if there was ever any couple that deserved to be parents, it's the two of you."

"God, I hope so. I just want it all to be over. The waiting is killing me, wondering if it's going to work, and—" Becky went silent as her attention drifted over Jules's shoulder.

Jules shifted in her seat and followed her friend's gaze. A young couple and their baby had been seated by the hostess. While the mother fumbled in the diaper bag for a bottle, the father was holding the baby up and cooing at her. The little girl's laughter echoed through the restaurant like melodic raindrops raining down on them.

"That should be Bryan." Becky's tears threatened to fall into her salad. "He's been so patient through all this, he deserves to be a dad. Can you imagine what a great father he's going to be?"

"And he will be. This is going to work out for both of you. I know it."

Becky dabbed at her eyes with her napkin. "I hope so. I can't even think about spending all this money and having no baby at the end. I saw a story on the news last week that there was a break-in at a fertility clinic, and the only thing they stole was meds."

"So, they think they can figure out how to do it on their own, or they're a patient who can't afford it?"

"I have no clue, but I almost can't blame them. I'm thankful all the time your dad helped me invest the life insurance money from my father, but it's not endless." Becky sighed. "But even if it works this time, I'd have to try again, right? The idea of having an only child like I was—like we both were. At least when we were little, we had each other."

Jules nodded. "I know. When you moved away, it just wasn't the same. It's an odd feeling to think I might have siblings out there after being raised all by myself. So, what was the deal in the store this morning? Did you have a meltdown with Tonya?"

"No, you know I know better than to mess with her. It wasn't about me. She fired Anna this morning."

"Fired Anna? I thought y'all liked her?"

Becky's lips curved into a small smile at her question. Jules had insisted on going to college in the south. Never mind where they lived was more south than where she went. "Florida is not the *real* south," Jules had said when Becky asked. She couldn't argue that her best friend had enjoyed every minute of college life and had come back with an expertise in photography, a penchant for sweet tea, and y'all in her vocabulary.

"We did like her," Becky said with a small shrug. "She's been great, but Tonya thinks she stole jewelry from the store last night. Not only that, she left money on the desk in the office and the front door unlocked. I was supposed to close, but I had a splitting headache. I went home, and Anna closed up instead."

Jules raised an eyebrow. "Maybe she took advantage of you leaving early. But why wouldn't she take the money instead of leaving it on the desk?"

"None of it makes any sense, but Tonya's convinced she might have interrupted something when she came back after closing last night. I think she was pretty freaked out."

Becky reached for the check when the waitress left it on the table. "My treat. To celebrate all your new relatives." She retrieved her wallet from her purse, then thumbed through the compartments once and then again, her forehead wrinkled in confusion. Finally, she pulled out a wad of mismatched folded up bills. As she shook the pile gently, her credit card fell onto the table. "What was that you were saying about me not being the most organized person you know?" Becky laughed and laid her card on top of the check.

"So, Anna ..."

"Oh, yeah. She's fired, and Tonya's talking about putting up surveillance cameras in the store."

Jules polished off the last forkful of her salad and wiped her mouth with her napkin. "There are worse things, I guess, and then at least you'd know what's going on. And, my friend, you have bigger things to worry about. Like my god baby."

CHAPTER FIFTEEN

Becky

The next day Becky sent Jules a text. *I'm off today. Dr. appt later. Want to do a little shopping?*

Sorry, can't! I have to meet someone about a photoshoot. Later this week?

Becky was a little disappointed. When she had the day off, she wished other people did too. *Definitely!*

She'd use the time to go by Tranquility and see her mom before her appointment. As she got closer to the retrieval, she wanted to share the excitement. Her mom must have been so sad to lose both her parents before she had kids of her own. Becky had never even gotten to meet them. It wasn't the same, but she didn't want that to happen to her mom and her child. She needed her to understand she was going to be a grandmother.

The conversation with Jules about her family tree had started her thinking about what she did know about her father's parents. She knew her mom hadn't liked them very much. She recalled how her grandfather had once told her he wished she was a boy.

"What does 'useless to the eggacy of this family' mean?" Becky had asked on the ride home from their house, proud she remembered the words.

"Legacy?" her mother had asked, and when Becky nodded, she had pitched a fit in the car at Becky's dad.

Maybe Jules really would find royalty in her family tree when she started working on it. At least her father's parents had acted like they were. She'd laugh if they turned out to come from a long line of poor peasants.

It all seemed so long ago now. She'd heard hushed conversations between her parents when she was a teenager. Both her father's parents had died, and they didn't even go back for the funerals. "Hypocritical," her father had said. "We didn't speak when they were alive. Why would we go to the funerals? Blood doesn't make family." That hadn't meant much to Becky in the past. Now, as she wanted to start her own family and she listened to Jules's desire to know her birth family, it had taken on a different meaning.

After her mom had moved into Tranquility, Becky had stumbled upon her grandparents' will in a large envelope that bore the return address of a lawyer. The handwritten note paperclipped to the front contained no apology for the way they had acted or anything personal. It merely stated their estate would go to their only son, Ken, the last male in their family line.

Becky had been a teenager when her father died. When she saw the will, she had started to wonder if maybe the money she had inherited from her dad wasn't life insurance money after all. He'd left substantial money to both Becky and her mom. It was what allowed her mom to afford Tranquility, and Becky had used some of hers to start the boutique and now for IVF. Her grandparents had expressed no interest in their only grandchild because she wasn't a male who would perpetuate the family name. It would be ironic if their money was now funding Becky's chance to bring their great-grandchild into the world.

She pushed open the glass doors at the entrance to Tranquility. The building was a large horseshoe built around a bricked courtyard with bright flowers planted around the border.

"Hey, Janna," Becky said to the woman at the front desk. The girls all knew her, and she usually just breezed by them on the way in. Off to the right were the independent and assisted living residents. Becky headed to the left, down the Memory Care hallway that would take her to her mom's area.

Each area had a nursing station. As she approached, Ellie was sitting behind the desk, her head down staring at her phone.

"Hi, Ellie," Becky said as she approached the desk. "How's my mom doing today?"

Ellie jumped as if she was surprised to see her. "Oh, Miss Becky." She stood up. "Well, I came in a little late this morning, but Maureen was covering for me. I thought—I mean, she said—" she stammered.

Becky's expression turned serious. "Ellie, is everything okay with my mom? Is there something you're not telling me?"

"No, Miss Becky. When I came in, Maureen did say she seemed a little off. She was talking about some stuff that didn't make much sense. She seems fine now." She hesitated. "You want to go in and talk to her?"

Becky studied Ellie's face and wondered what had her so distracted. "Of course I want to go in and talk to her. I don't have too much time. I have a doctor's appointment, but I wanted to stop by and say hello to her."

The door to her mom's room was closed, but Becky peered through the small glass window into the room. She watched silently as her mom rocked back and forth in her rocker, the slippers on her feet shuffling along on the floor. The chair faced the windows, and as she rocked, her mom's gaze seemed to be fixed on something outside.

Sometimes Becky would forget to prepare herself mentally for how different her mom was now. Some days it disheartened her, like the sparkle in her mom was starting to dull bit by bit. And then out of nowhere, the mother she remembered would be back like nothing had happened.

Becky turned the knob to open the door and pushed down the doorstop to keep it propped open. The guest chair was empty and pulled up next to her rocker, so she sat down.

Her mother looked over at her. "You're back."

Becky pushed her mom's hair out of her eyes. It had started to thin, and the gray reflected her mom's disinterest in trying to color it anymore. "I know it's been a few days, Mom, but there's been a lot going on. I just stopped by to say hi." Becky sat back in the chair, careful not to play with her own hair as she wasn't going to tell her mother about the accident. It would be easier if she just kept the bruise hidden.

"I saw you looking out the window, Mom. I don't have that much time today, but maybe next time I'm here, we can go for a walk outside. Would you like that?" The doctor had told her how important it was to try to keep her mom active, physically and mentally. The grounds were beautiful, but Felicia wore a special bracelet that kept her from being able to open the doors without someone with her.

"Do you want to have breakfast with me?" Felicia looked at Becky, a glimmer of hope in her eyes.

Becky was used to the rapid change of subjects. "I'm pretty sure you already ate."

Felicia shook her head. "No, I didn't. You ate it. I'm hungry."

Becky didn't bother to correct her mother. Usually, her mom's short-term memory worsened as the day went on. She glanced down at her watch. "It's almost time to eat lunch. Make sure you tell Ellie you're hungry."

A movement outside caught Felicia's eye, and her attention drifted back to the window. Becky followed her gaze to see a small red cardinal had landed on the tree outside, its orange beak directed right at them.

"Aww. Do you know what they say, Mom? A cardinal is sent to deliver a message from heaven. I bet it's Dad coming to say hello to us. You know, I was thinking. You love the music group they have here. Maybe I could bring your record player here with some of Dad's old records. What do you think?"

"Could you bring my piano?"

Becky lifted a shoulder. "Maybe. I could ask if they would take it as a donation here. Maybe they have a place they could put it."

"I miss him. I miss him so much." Felicia's lower lip started to quiver.

"I know, Mom. I miss him too." The piano had been forgotten. Becky leaned over and hugged her mom.

"Can we go for a walk outside?"

Becky's face fell. She hated to say no to her mother, but taking her outside could make her late for her appointment. "I wish I had time, Mom. Next time I promise."

Felicia nodded in acceptance, but Becky could see her bottom lip was still not quite still.

"I'm on my way to the doctor's office. I'm hoping we're almost ready to do the egg retrieval. We're getting so close." She took her mother's hands in hers. "Hang in there, Mom. I want to make you a grandmother, and I want you to meet your grandchild."

"I do want to meet your baby. I love babies. Will you bring it here?"

"Of course, Mom. Maybe the baby will even look a little like you or Dad."

Felicia's lower lip now quivered uncontrollably as tears ran down her cheeks.

"Oh, Mom, I'm sorry. I didn't mean to make you sad. I'm just getting excited that it's so close, and I want you to be part of this with me." She hugged her and felt Felicia's breathing had become ragged. She pulled back to study her closely. "Are you all right? I didn't mean to upset you." Her mother's emotions could turn on a dime, but Becky didn't like the way she was breathing. "Let me get Ellie."

Becky rushed outside to the nurses' station where she saw Ellie huddled with one of the other nurses. Becky called out nervously to her. "Ellie, you're right. My mom does seem a little off today. She's having trouble breathing."

Ellie hurried behind Becky back into the room.

"Felicia, you okay?" Ellie bent over her and put her arm around her. "Take a deep breath. You're all right." She rubbed Felicia's shoulder, and after a few minutes, her mom's breathing steadied and returned to normal.

Felicia had a loose grip on Ellie's uniform. "I want to take a nap," she said to neither woman in particular. She was staring off at something only she could see.

Becky exchanged a glance with Ellie and then nodded slowly. "Okay, Mom. Go ahead and rest. I love you." She leaned in and placed a kiss on her mother's soft cheek. As she walked out the door, she resisted the urge to look back. If she did, she might not be able to leave.

When she got to her car, she slid in and choked back a sob. Not bothering to wipe the tears that stained her face, she put the car in gear and headed to the fertility clinic.

CHAPTER SIXTEEN

Becky

At Dr. Levine's office, Becky felt helpless to hide the way she was feeling. Hormones off the chart had her emotions at an all-time high. They were partly to blame, and she knew that. But even so, the visit with her mother had left her rattled.

If she had gotten pregnant when they first started trying, her mom would have been able to enjoy these moments. And then, of course, she had to go through all these shots and doctor visits just to have a baby. It wasn't fair. She felt slighted by the universe as she sniffled and tried to wipe the tears with the back of her hand.

She pushed open the door to the office and then checked in. It was written all over her face that she'd been crying. With the amount of hormones going through their office every day, Becky was sure the girls were used to it.

Kim wasn't behind the desk, but Connie, one of the older nurses, looked up from her computer.

Connie's brow furrowed. "Aw, honey, you okay today?"

Becky gave a half-hearted nod. "Yeah, just having a bit of a rough day."

The older woman offered a smile. "We understand. If you need anything, let me know. I'm sure Kim will be out to get you soon."

Becky sunk into one of the few empty seats in the waiting room. She picked up a magazine from the adjacent table and flipped through it. The pages turned, but she saw nothing. Tossing it back down on the table, she took a deep breath.

She craved comfort from her husband and silently resented that she was sitting there alone. Irrational, she knew, since she was the one who had told him he didn't need to come with her today.

The office door opened, and Kim stood with her file motioning her in.

As Becky changed into the gown for her exam, she hoped this would be a quick appointment. Flashes of the visit with her mom kept replaying in her head like a bad home movie. She just wanted to go home. While she waited for Dr. Levine, one of the nurses came in and drew blood. She couldn't believe she'd been so afraid of needles, and now she held out her arm like it was nothing.

As the nurse walked out, Dr. Levine came in with her file in his hand. He smiled as he said hello and then cocked his head while he scrutinized her. "You okay? Too many hormones?"

"Well, there's that." Becky paused. "It's my mom. She has dementia. I'm just sad that she can't really be part of this with me."

Dr. Levine rolled his stool over in front of Becky and sat down. "I'm sorry to hear that. My mother has Alzheimer's. I'm sure she's older than your mom. I hate to say it like this, but luckily, I think she's near the end of her journey. It's a rough road indeed. For everyone."

"I'm sorry about your mom too. Mine has vascular dementia. It's so sad to see them changing."

"It is," he said. "But they would want us to continue living our lives, don't you think? So, let's see what's going on with you today, okay? I'm pretty sure you're getting close."

Becky laid back down on the table as he called Kim in for her exam.

He was right. Her mom would want her to continue living her life, and having a baby was what Becky wanted more than anything.

After her ultrasound was complete, Dr. Levine delivered the news she'd been waiting to hear. "Based on these measurements, your follicles look ready." He snapped off his gloves and motioned for Becky to sit up.

Kim looked at Becky over his shoulder and raised her fist in a silent cheer.

"The HCG shot or the trigger shot," Dr. Levine explained, "is the final step in the maturation of your eggs so we can go in and grab them."

The black cloud that had followed her into the office quickly lifted. Becky took a deep breath, suddenly overwhelmed with a mixture of excitement and nervousness. Her mind was racing. Somewhere in the fog, she heard her name, and it brought her back to reality.

"Becky, this is really important." Dr. Levine made sure he had her full attention before he continued. "We need to perfectly time the shot so that you can be here thirty-six hours later for the egg retrieval. That means Bryan needs to give you the shot at nine-thirty tonight. Not eight-thirty. Not nine. Nine-thirty."

"Don't you worry," Becky said. "We got this. I'm a little over all the needles, but I'm not going to forget this one."

Dr. Levine winced. "This needle is a little bigger than the others, but ice will help. Make sure you get the instructions for the shot from Kim when you leave and any questions, you can call her tonight."

"Definitely call me if there are any questions," Kim said. "You need to get the trigger shot perfect. We don't want you ovulating early."

Dr. Levine rose from his stool. "Unless the blood work shows something unexpected, one of the girls will call you later to confirm your retrieval time for Thursday morning. Since you're getting the IV sedation, you won't feel anything. Most likely, you won't even remember it. When you come out of the retrieval, we'll know exactly how many eggs we have to work with. You'll have that number in writing before you leave."

"Will all my follicles produce eggs we can use?"

"Not necessarily. The important thing is we have a good amount of high-quality eggs to choose from." He smiled to reassure her and then continued. "Once I hand over the eggs, the embryologist and his lab will take it from there and add Bryan's contribution. The lab will call the next day and let you know how many eggs fertilized, and then you'll get another update on day three when they become embryos."

Becky focused on Dr. Levine. She needed to be able to relay all this to Bryan. "When the lab calls, will they give me the grading for each embryo? So I know how they're doing?"

Dr. Levine patted her hand. "Don't get too hung up on the grading. It's very complex, and it's just one of the tools we'll use. Sometimes mediocre embryos catch up and turn out to be babies and seemingly perfect embryos arrest unexpectedly."

"Arrest?"

"That just means, for one reason or another, they stop developing. Most of the time it's something genetic, and they probably wouldn't have survived if they had been transferred."

"Oh." Becky had to adjust her expectations that every egg retrieved would go on to become a perfect embryo.

"On day five, the embryologist will assess the embryos and choose the best one. I'll use a small tube and insert the embryo directly into your uterus."

Becky scowled as she looked from Dr. Levine to Kim and back to the doctor. "So, you'll only transfer one?" She didn't like these odds at all. Hell, she'd rather have twins, or even triplets, than no baby at all.

Dr. Levine glanced back in her folder and then gave a reassuring nod to Becky. "Let's see what we end up with on day five, and we'll decide then. Kim will give you the instructions you need for the trigger shot and retrieval day. I'm sure I don't need to tell you, but you still need to lay off the love at home if you know what I mean. Tell Bryan that means self-love too." He winked at Becky, told her to get dressed, and said he'd see her in a couple of days for her procedure.

As Becky stopped at the desk on her way out, Kim handed her two pages of instructions. "Don't forget. Your retrieval is surgery, so your appointment isn't here in this office. You have to go to the Outpatient Surgery entrance on the northeast side of the building."

Becky looked at her blankly.

Kim laughed. "There's a map in the package if you need it." She took one of the pages out of Becky's hand and flipped it over. "Here's my not so secret survival tips. And all that stuff on the grocery list, you want to start that today. You want to hydrate the heck out of yourself starting now, so get some sports drinks or water with electrolytes. Protein shakes. Get salty foods which will help draw the fluid out of your ovaries."

She handed the page back to Becky. "Your levels have been okay, so I don't think you have to worry about overstimulating, but we want to make your recovery as easy as possible. If you remember nothing, drink as much as you can."

"Okay, got it. Guess I'm hitting the store on the way home. How long do you think I'll feel crappy? Any chance I could go to work on Friday?"

Kim gave a noncommittal shrug. "There are women who feel fine the next day and some who are down for a week. I would play it by ear based on how you feel, but no driving for twenty-four hours or lifting anything heavy even if you think you're up to it. Be kind to yourself and your ovaries. Remember what they've been through."

Becky crossed her hands over her chest and could feel her heart thumping. "All those red X's. I can't believe it's finally time."

"I told you you'd make it through all those shots. You're a tough cookie."

Becky leaned in to hug Kim. "I couldn't have done this without you."

"Follow the instructions for the shot tonight and have Bryan call me if he has any questions. After today, I turn you over to the girls in the lab. They'll be the ones calling with your updates from here on out. I get you to your retrieval, and they make all the magic happen on the other side of the building."

Becky felt her eyes well up. "Wow. I didn't even think about that. It'll be so weird not to see you almost every day."

She smiled at Becky. "Go shopping with my list and make some nice embryos over there, would ya?"

Becky felt like skipping out of the office, which was a far cry from the way she felt walking in.

CHAPTER SEVENTEEN

Jules

Jules scanned the small café, scrutinizing the faces at each of the round tables. She was there to meet Marion, a new client who had brought her family for photos a couple of weeks earlier. There was no sign of her yet. Jules ordered a sweet tea and a croissant at the register and took it outside to settle at one of the tables in the sunshine.

She was reaching for her phone to check the time when it buzzed. Maybe Marion was running late. It was Becky.

Retrieval tomorrow! Scared and excited!

You got this. Tell Bryan I said good luck to him too.

Bryan said he doesn't need luck because he has skill on his side. LOL

Jules bit her bottom lip to keep from smiling as she typed a response. *Are you sure he should be bragging about that? Call me tomorrow and let me know how it goes.*

You know I will!

Jules pulled out the prints she had brought for Marion. Beautiful metallic prints of a gorgeous group of women. Identical smiles beaming at her camera. The family resemblance was undeniable.

Being adopted, she understood she didn't share her parents' features or bear a resemblance. But she looked so different she felt like her looks made her stand out like a sore thumb. Like a neon sign that announced she was adopted. She was fair-skinned, her mother dark. Her parents both had brown eyes. Hers were green like the color of army fatigues. Her mom was a tiny woman, and her dad wasn't very tall either. By high school, Jules had shot up past both of them.

As she reached into her tote for her laptop, Marion approached waving at her. Her three daughters were in their mid to late thirties, so Jules assumed Marion had to be in her sixties. Her dark hair didn't betray her age with a single gray hair.

"Let me just grab a quick cup of coffee," Marion said. "I've been running all morning."

In a minute, she was back. "Thank you so much for meeting me with our prints." Marion took the seat across from Jules and sipped her coffee. "So, how do they look?"

Jules passed the clear bag that held Marion's prints across the table. "They're stunning. Your family is beautiful."

Marion put down her cup to grab the bag. She pulled out the pictures and spread them across the table. "Four generations of women. Can you believe it? My mother's still doing well, but I wanted to have these while we can. Especially with my new granddaughter."

"I still can't get over how much your three girls look like you and each other. No one could ever doubt that they're sisters and you're their mother."

Marion laughed. "I know. Isn't it crazy? People always used to say I looked just like my mom too. Well, before the silver hair and wrinkles." She turned one of the photos around and held it next to her face. "Do you see a resemblance?"

Jules squinted at the photo. "I do. The eyes and smile are the same. Your granddaughter will be so lucky to have this. Her mom, her aunts, her grandmother, and her great grandmother all together." Jules's smile faded as she realized this was a luxury she would never have with her birth family.

Marion glanced up from the photos, and a line formed on her brow. "Hey, are you okay? Did I say something to upset you?"

Jules shook her head. "No. It's nothing you did. It's just—" She twisted the straw in her tea. She didn't like to tell people. She wasn't sure why, but it always made her feel vulnerable. "It's just that I'm adopted. So, when I see such a strong family resemblance, it reminds me that I don't look like anyone in my adopted family. And your granddaughter having all those generations of strong women in front of her—" She met Marion's eyes. "I guess I'm a little envious."

"Oh, honey ..." Marion placed her hand over Jules's. "I might understand better than you think."

Jules tilted her head and looked at her quizzically. "Are you—are you adopted too?"

Marion shook her head. "No, not me. But my sister got pregnant in high school, and my parents told her in no uncertain terms she was not welcome in their house with a baby. They made her put the baby up for adoption. Things were different back then. It was shameful to have a baby if you weren't married."

"Oh, I'm sorry. Does she—" Jules swallowed hard past the lump in her throat. "Does she still think about the baby she gave away?"

Marion's expression turned serious as she dipped her head. "Every day for over fifty years. She did one of those DNA tests to see if she could find him. It was so interesting that the whole family got tests for Christmas last year. I guess I've dived in the most. You know, being retired gives me more free time than my daughters."

Jules's face lit up. "I did the test too. I just got my results, but I haven't figured anything out yet. I'm not sure what to expect. Did your sister find her son?"

Marion collected the prints and inserted them back into the protective bag. "Well, no, but it's a little harder for her. You can start from generations back and build forward to try to figure out your birth mother. My sister needs her son to test or a descendent of her son's. It's a waiting game. He may not want to find her, or maybe he doesn't even know he's adopted."

"Really? I knew from the time I was old enough to understand. My adopted parents are wonderful." A heavy-hearted sigh escaped Jules's lips. "They're not too happy I'm looking."

"Oh, I'm sorry. My sister desperately wants to know her son is okay and that he had a good life. She would love to have a relationship with him, but she's not trying to take him from his adopted parents. If anything, I think she would wrap them in a big hug and thank them."

Jules snorted. "Yeah, I'm not sure my parents are there yet."

"I'm sure they'll come around. So, you got your results back?" Marion asked. "What did you find?"

"Well, it was interesting to see my ethnicity. Swedish and Irish mostly, a little English. Kind of explains why I don't look anything like my parents, I had over four hundred matches which was surreal to me. Related to all those people. That's kind of cool."

Marion leaned in. "Did you have any close family matches?"

Jules shook her head. "No. I have some third cousins and lots of fourth cousins. I've been trying to look at my matches to see who matches me but also match each other. I've been spending hours and hours building up those trees looking for their common ancestor so I can try to figure out where I fit in."

Marion tapped her index finger on the table. "You're on the right trail. Third cousins share great-great-grandparents. The lower the amount of shared DNA, the further back you have to build on their tree to find that shared ancestor."

Jules reached for her croissant and gestured to Marion, but the older woman shook her head. "It's just frustrating how many people don't have trees," Jules said as she ripped off a piece and popped it in her mouth. "I always wonder why they even did their DNA. I mean, I don't have a family tree, but that's only because I have no idea who should be on it."

"Some people just want to know their ethnicity and have no interest in the rest. I've built a thorough family tree that's public." Marion patted the package of photos on the table. "My sister's son belongs in our family portraits. Hopefully, if he does a DNA test, he'll realize he has a match to his birth mother right away. My sister's constantly checking and praying."

"I hope my birth mom feels the same way when I find her. It's just unfair that I need to go through all this to find names that already exist on a piece of paper somewhere. I mean, seriously, my birth certificate only exists because I was born." Jules's voice escalated. "How is it that I don't have the right to see it? Don't I get a say?" Jules glanced around as the woman at the next table stared. She leaned in and lowered her voice. "Sorry. It just gets me so mad." She shoved the plate with the croissant away from her and crossed her arms across her chest. "Makes me lose my appetite."

Marion gave her an understanding nod. "I know. The laws are meant to protect the parents, and here's my sister just *wishing* they would allow her son his original birth certificate with her name. My sister finally got married and had another son and a daughter. She used to tell me it felt like a betrayal when someone would ask how many kids she had. She struggled with whether she had the right to count him among her children."

Jules pressed her lips together as she considered this. "Well, of course she does. I hope he finally searches and finds her."

"Me too. Let me show you a little secret on the site. Do you want to pull it up on your laptop?"

"Sure." Jules powered it on and typed in the web address.

Marion pulled her chair to the shadier side next to Jules. She pulled a pair of glasses from the side pocket of her purse, put them on, and leaned in. As the page opened with Jules's DNA matches, Marion gripped her arm. "That's a great one at the top."

Jules glanced down and didn't even need the blue dot next to the match to tell her it was new. It hadn't been there last night. "That's brand new! 510 cMs. It says she's a second cousin."

"That's just a generality. The site now lists all the possible relationships. If you can figure out how old she is, you could probably narrow that list down."

Jules read from the screen. "88% probability that it's a first cousin once removed, a half-first cousin or a half-great-aunt. The second great-grandmother seems unlikely unless she's about a hundred years old. What's the half mean?"

"Well, half-cousins are children of half-siblings, meaning they have only one parent in common." Marion sipped from her cup. "So, for example, my sister's kids are half-siblings to the son she gave up because they have different fathers." Marion reached for a napkin. She grabbed a pen from her purse and drew a diagram as she explained. "A half-great-aunt would mean that she's a half-sibling to one of your grandparents. And a first cousin once removed would mean that your match and one of your birth parents share grandparents. They're first cousins, and one generation removed is you."

"Ah, got it." Jules reached for the plate with the croissant and smiled. "My appetite is coming back," she said as she broke off a piece. "So, if I can figure out how old she is, would that help?"

"Definitely. Does she have her DNA attached to a tree?"

As Jules pulled the match back up on the screen, Marion clapped her hands together. "Oh, she does. That's fabulous."

Jules opened the match's tree and sat silent for a moment, the realization hitting her. "It's not huge, but one of my birth parents could be in here somewhere, right?"

Marion nodded and smiled. "If she's related to you, then some of the people in this tree are related to you too. I'd recreate her tree and research as much as you can to build her tree as far back and as wide as you can. Check out the matches you share with her. You could find a surname starts to look familiar from the other trees you've been working on."

"Looks like another late night for me," Jules said as she laughed. "It's been sort of an addiction."

"Time just disappears when you delve into all of this, right?" Marion sat back in her chair and propped her glasses on top of her head. "I'd send her a message. Don't mention you're adopted. It tends to scare some people off. Just say that you're DNA-related, and you'd like to find the connection. See if she answers you."

"I will. You have no idea how much you've helped me today. I don't always like to tell people I'm adopted, but today I'm glad I did."

Marion moved her chair back to the opposite side of the table. She picked up the package of photos and placed them in her purse. "Sometimes people cross our paths at just the right moment. And thank *you*. These are lovely. I'll give you a glowing recommendation on your website."

Jules stood and Marion embraced her in a hug. She spoke softly into Jules's ear. "I hope you find your answers, honey. Most people don't realize just how important it is to know where you came from."

Jules's eyes welled up as she pulled back and dipped her head in agreement.

"Okay, get to work. You'll figure this out. Call me if you have any questions. I'm happy to help."

As Marion exited the café, Jules sat back down and stared at the screen of her laptop, her match at the top beckoning to her. She needed to figure this out. Who the heck was Lucy16?

CHAPTER EIGHTEEN

Becky

"Sleeping?" Becky whispered, her head flat on the pillow as she stared at the ceiling.

"No." Bryan sounded wide awake. "Obviously you're not either."

She reached for him in the darkness. "I can't get comfortable, and I'm ready to get this over with as soon as possible. I need to know how many good eggs we're going to have. The suspense is killing me."

Bryan turned on his side to face her. He stroked her hair and kissed her on the forehead. "I know this hasn't been easy, but you've been a trooper. We got the trigger shot perfect Tuesday night, don't worry. The retrieval in the morning will be fine. I'm sure we'll have plenty of good eggs for Dr. Levine to work with."

She felt around for his hand and put her palm in his. He gave her a gentle squeeze.

"You know, I've been thinking," he said.

"Yeah, about what?"

"Well, if we have a boy, what do you think about naming him Luke?"

There was silence in the darkness, and then she asked, "You mean as in Skywalker?"

Bryan rubbed her arm. "Okay, okay. What about if it's a girl? How do you feel about the name Leia?"

"No doubt if we have a girl, she will be daddy's little princess, but she won't be Princess Leia. I'm saying no to the *Star Wars* names, babe."

"So, Han Solo is out of the question?"

"Absolutely out of the question." Becky yawned and snuggled into him, rubbing his foot under the covers with hers. "Go to sleep."

Finally, they both drifted off until the shrill beeping of the alarm clock brought them back to reality. Becky's eyes flew open. The big day had arrived, and she felt like a kid on Christmas morning. She leaned over and rumpled Bryan's hair.

As he pulled the covers back up over his shoulders, he groaned. "Too tired," he said with an exaggerated yawn. "Go without me. Just let me know how it goes."

She whipped the covers off him. "Very funny! Come on, sleepyhead, get up. You know I can't do this without you."

As she turned to get out of bed, Bryan grabbed her playfully and pulled her back in. Sherlock flew off the bed in protest of the early morning ruckus.

"Come on, let's make a baby the old-fashioned way." Leaning on his forearms, he hovered over her and kissed her neck.

Becky giggled. "Are you nuts? Not to mention I'm about to explode."

She kissed him long and hard. "There you go," she said as she untangled herself from him and got out of bed. "Keep that in mind when they send you into the little room with the videos and the dirty magazines. At least give me a little thought. I don't want to have to tell our child they were conceived with sperm that was the result of some centerfold."

Bryan rolled back onto his pillow and let out a frustrated groan.

"C'mon, get your swimmers up and ready," she said. "We have embryos to make."

Becky dressed in the comfortable clothes she had laid out the night before and brushed her teeth using the water sparingly.

She gave Bryan an anxious look as he walked into the kitchen and found her sitting at the table waiting. "Since I'm not allowed to eat even though I'm starving and coffee is just a big no-no, I guess I'm ready," she said as she stood up.

Her husband whimpered. "So, I don't get coffee or breakfast either? Is this like the sympathy pregnancy thing already?"

She swatted him playfully on the arm. "Very supportive. Can we stop and get you something on the way? My nerves are off the charts, and I just want to get going. Don't forget, we have to go to the other side of the building now."

"I got it. I saw the map on the fridge."

Becky grabbed the bag she had prepared for retrieval day and followed Bryan out the front door. Taking a deep breath, she clicked her seatbelt into place while he started up the car.

"Wait!" She held up her hand.

"What's the matter?"

"Some mother I'm gonna be. I forgot to feed Sherlock. Who knows how long we'll be gone." She unclicked her seatbelt. "I'll be quick. I promise."

Within several minutes she was back in the car. "Okay, let me just think this through for one second to make sure I didn't forget anything." She rooted through the bag she had packed. "Okay, ready."

As they approached the building together, his hand in hers, she stopped. She summoned a deep breath.

He turned to look at her. "You okay?"

"Yeah. Everything I've ever wanted is in this building."

Bryan gave her a lopsided smile. "Well, yes, I will be in this building."

She rolled her eyes. "I already have you. You know what I mean. Okay, everything *we've* ever wanted is in this building."

Dr. Levine was talking to the receptionist behind the desk as they entered. "So, are we all ready to get those eggs out today?" Despite the early hour, he was cheerful and upbeat.

Becky nodded and smiled. "More than ready."

Walking around the desk, he looked at Becky first. "Okay, the girls are going to take you back to change into a gown and prepare you for the procedure." He then turned his attention to Bryan. "The girls will take you to a special room to do your thing."

Bryan gave him a nervous grin. "Oh, I think I can handle it, but I'm probably going to need a really big cup."

Becky groaned and rolled her eyes. It wasn't like anyone didn't know what was happening behind the closed door. She smirked at the thought of her husband freaking out in there knowing that everyone was waiting for him to produce a specimen.

Her part hadn't been easy either: all the shots, all the hormones, all the stress wondering if this was going to work. It would be worth it in the end. As she walked off with the nurse to get ready for her procedure, she had visions of a sweet baby being placed in her arms.

***

Becky's eyelids fluttered. She blinked several times and wondered why they hadn't started her procedure. Confused, she glanced around and took in her surroundings. This was a different room.

As the sedation wore off, she noticed Bryan sitting in a chair next to her. Dr. Levine had been right about the drugs.

"Wow, is it over?" Becky asked. "I don't even remember it getting started."

"Well, look who's awake. I hear you put on quite a show in there."

"Really? I hope I didn't say anything too embarrassing. Oh, hell, at this point, who cares. How'd we do?"

"Dr. Levine wanted you to have it in writing." Bryan took her hand and flipped it over. Written on her hand in black marker was the number twelve. "I guess sometimes people come out of the sedation and don't remember what they were told. But, twelve eggs, Beck. It seems like a good amount, but they'll tell us tomorrow how many fertilized once they mix them with my stuff in the lab."

He leaned in to whisper. "Babe, I was wrong. I didn't need a really big cup, but I did good too." He grinned at her, and she grimaced.

"According to Dr. Levine, it's the next three days that are the most telling. We'll know then how many embryos we have." He squeezed her hand.

It had been a long emotional morning. Per the instructions, she had told Tonya she needed the day off. She hoped she was one of those who recovered quickly. She hadn't mentioned that she could need more than one day.

They drove home with their next set of instructions to get them to the transfer. Although she had more meds to take, she was elated to learn they weren't shots—no more needles. The next five days to get to the transfer would be torturous, but she was ready to get to the next phase in the process. They were in the home stretch. By this time next week, she'd have their embryo in her uterus.

Usually, whenever they rode in the car together, she and Bryan joked around and chatted. This time as they headed home in comfortable silence, each sat alone with their thoughts.

Dr. Levine had warned her she might feel uncomfortable after the procedure and he was right. A quick bite to eat and then she wanted to lay down.

She poked Bryan in the back as she stood behind him on the front porch. "Hurry up. I'm starving."

He unlocked the front door and pushed it open. He didn't move.

"What are you doing?" she asked. "Bryan, what is it? C'mon, I want to go inside." She finally nudged him aside to see what had stopped him in the entry to the house. From the doorway, she could see into the living room.

Sitting on the couch were two oversized teddy bears, one pink and one blue.

CHAPTER NINETEEN

Becky

"Where the hell did those come from?" She whipped around to face Bryan, searching for any indication on his face that he might have been responsible. The stunned look on his face told her he was just as shocked as she was.

"Who would have put them there?" The tone of her voice demanded an answer from Bryan, although it was clear he didn't have one. "Who even knew we were going today? Who could have gotten into the house to leave them here?"

Someone being in their house was not her overactive imagination. These bears in her living room proved she was right. She wasn't crazy.

"Do you think Jules or Tonya left them as a surprise?" he asked.

"No, Bryan, no. It just doesn't make sense. Neither one of them has a key."

Bryan put his hands on her shoulders. "Okay, calm down. I'm sure it can't be good for you to be this upset. Let me check with Mrs. Ritter." He hesitated. "Think about it, Beck. She knows most of our friends. She wouldn't have thought twice if one of them said they were leaving something for you as a surprise."

Several minutes later, Bryan jogged back to the house.

He took a deep breath. "Okay, so she doesn't know anything about it. No one has asked for the spare key, and the only people she's seen coming or going from the house are us."

"Remember when my keys were missing? Maybe someone took them and made a copy of our house key?"

Bryan shook his head. "Except they weren't missing, just misplaced. Besides, who would want the keys to our house so they could leave teddy bears on our couch? There has to be a more logical explanation than that."

"You can try to figure out how to explain it, but I'm not staying here until you change the locks." Her whole body was trembling, and it wasn't only from the procedure she just had. Becky bent over at the waist and let out a small whimper. "Okay, not feeling so good."

"They put some pain meds in your IV, but those are going to start wearing off soon." He hugged her gently and led her into the house. "You need to lay down. I'll make you something to eat, and then I'll run to the store and get new locks. Okay?"

Becky was in no position to argue as she trudged toward the bedroom. "Come with me. I need to make sure there are no other surprises."

Bryan walked her in, and she made him check all the closets and the bathroom. Nothing seemed out of place. He pulled down the covers on the bed and motioned for Becky to get in.

He was back in a few minutes with a small plate of food and a bottle of Powerade. "I walked the whole house. The back door and sliding glass door were both locked. Everything looks fine. I'm sure there's a reasonable explanation behind the bears, but I'm okay with changing the locks if it makes you feel better."

She sat up quickly. "Well, I'm not staying with the locks we have now." She winced in pain. "I mean, I can't leave right this second, but I will eventually. You know, when I can actually move."

"I know, I know. Don't worry, I'm on it. I'll head over to the hardware store. Try to eat a little of your lunch. The doctor's office said you could take some Tylenol if you start feeling too bad. There's two on the plate."

Becky was starting to feel a little better now that she was lying down again. Weakly, she gave him a thumbs-up.

He stood next to the bed and rubbed his right temple. "You know, it wouldn't explain who left the bears, but you did go back into the house this morning to feed the cat. Do you think you forgot to lock the door?"

She closed her eyes for a moment as she considered it. "I locked it. I'm sure I did." She paused. "You know something? Last week when it was so nice out, I opened some of the windows to let some fresh air in the house. Are they all locked?"

He left and was back several minutes later. "I checked every single window. All locked. Do you want me to ask Mrs. Ritter to stay with you while I'm gone?"

Becky hesitated and then shook her head. "I'll be okay. Can you just bring me my cell phone so I can call Jules and Tonya and just double check that neither one of them had anything to do with this?"

He brought her the phone and kissed her on the forehead. "I'll be back soon."

As he walked out of the bedroom, she called out after him. "Lock the door when you leave, and please don't take too long."

She called Jules first. "I don't know what's happening, but now I know this isn't my imagination. Who would put those bears in my house?"

"Well, it wasn't me," Jules said. "I'd say it was a cute idea if I didn't think you'd try to smack me through the phone. There's no one else you can think of that might have left them? What about Ros?"

"The only person who has a key to the house is Mrs. Ritter. She said she didn't do it. I hardly think she'd lie about it."

"It is crazy. I mean, it must be someone who knew you had the retrieval today. What about Tonya?"

"She's my next call, but I can't imagine her doing something like this. And how'd she get in to leave them?"

Jules hesitated. "Bryan's parents? His brother?"

"I guess he told them the retrieval was today, but they don't have keys either."

Jules started to laugh. "Maybe you bought them and forgot? I know that sounds hard to believe, but what else could it be?"

Becky scowled. "That would be even harder to believe than someone breaking into the house to leave them there."

"But you said there's no sign anyone broke in. Maybe the accident is causing some weird memory lapse. The doctor did say that was a possibility, right?"

"I can't accept that I could forget not only buying the bears but putting them out on the couch like that. I mean, c'mon, you more than anyone know how superstitious I am about buying anything before I'm pregnant. Someone left them there, but it certainly wasn't me. Until the locks are changed or we figure out who left them, I'm more than a little creeped out."

"I don't blame you." Jules paused. "Well, I have some big news if you're interested."

"Oh, you know I am. Sorry, it's been all about me lately. I can blame the hormones or the car accident. Pick one. It's been a rough couple of weeks."

"I understand, trust me. I've been knee-deep in my DNA stuff. Since I got my results back from the first site, I've been trying to figure out how to make sense of it all. One of my clients did her DNA, and she helped me a little. I got a new match. It's a good one. Lucy16 is her ID, and she has a family tree attached." Jules's voice lifted. "Can you believe that? I mean, I'm related to someone named Lucy, and if she's related to me, then some of those people in her tree are related to me too. How cool is that?"

Becky put the phone on speaker and laid it next to her so she wouldn't have to hold it up to her ear. She closed her eyes while she listened.

"I sent her an email, but so far she hasn't responded. She could help me figure everything out. Her tree could lead me to one of my birth parents. She has to be related to one of them somehow."

"Wow, that's awesome. You'll figure it all out. I know you will."

"It's a total obsession, that's for sure. And I'm not stopping until I find her. Or him. But I really want to find her, you know? My birth father may not even know I exist. Um, surprise, it's a girl!"

After several moments of small talk, they said goodbye, and Becky dialed the number for the boutique next.

"Hey, it's me," Becky said when Tonya answered.

"Beck? Why are you calling here? Didn't you go for the egg retrieval? I thought you were supposed to be home resting by now."

Becky told her the story of coming home to find the bears on the couch. "I freaked out. Bryan just left to get new locks."

"Well, you're right, it wasn't me," Tonya said. "But it is totally bizarre. Who would do that? And how would they have gotten in to put them there?"

"Exactly my point. Bryan thought maybe you or Jules brought them over. I called her before you, and she didn't know anything about it either." Becky let out a small, uncomfortable laugh. "She thinks maybe I bought them and forgot."

Tonya was silent for a moment. "Well, there's got to be an explanation somewhere. I guess the doctor did say the accident could have some delayed symptoms. Was memory loss even a possibility? I mean, unless there's anyone else you can think of that would have—oh, gotta go, a customer just walked in. Feel better. Hopefully I'll see you tomorrow."

Becky tossed the phone on the bed and stared at it. She thought buying anything for the baby at this point was bad luck. There was no way she bought those bears.

Then Becky reached for her phone, dialed, and asked for Kim.

She answered breathlessly like the girls had found her in one of the exam rooms and she had raced back to the desk to pick up the phone. "Becky, is everything okay? Wasn't your retrieval today?"

"Yeah. I mean, I feel somewhat like I've been punched in the stomach for a bunch of different reasons. I know you told me that officially you aren't my nurse anymore, that you were done with me."

Kim laughed. "Let's not put it like that. Let's say you graduated and moved on."

"Okay, I graduated. Could I still ask you something?" Becky paused. "I don't know who else to ask right now."

"Shoot. I'm here for you, and there's probably nothing I haven't already heard. Unless you want to ask me how your eggs are doing in the lab. They don't tell me anything, and I don't understand much of what they do over there."

"No, it's not about my retrieval or what's going on at the lab." She hesitated. "I know I've been on a lot of hormones and drugs. Do any of them cause memory loss?"

"Well, it would depend on exactly what you're talking about," Kim said. "It's not a true symptom that I know of, but IVF is a very complicated process. It's possible to get caught up in it and become forgetful or lose things."

Becky thought of her misplaced keys. This didn't feel like the same thing. "Could I actually do something and then have no memory of doing it?"

"Here's what I can tell you, but I'm not a doctor. I think it's common to become forgetful while you have your focus on all your appointments, your shots, and trying to get pregnant. That's compounded by the fact that you've been working full-time while you're going through this. Did I also see in your chart that you had some sort of car accident?"

So, she had seen the notes.

Kim continued to explain. "True memory loss could be neurological. Forgetting your lunch on the counter when you leave for work? Well, that could just be a by-product of having too much on your mind. That wouldn't be at all unreasonable with what you're going through. Does that help?"

"I think so." Becky winced as she told the lie. Her stomach was starting to cramp, and this conversation wasn't bringing her much comfort.

"Right now, I would concentrate on recovering from the retrieval. If you still have questions, you should ask Dr. Levine during your next appointment. Maybe it's also worth checking back in with the doctor who treated you after the accident."

"Okay, thanks. I'm sure it's nothing. I can go relax now."

She disconnected the call. After popping the Tylenol in her mouth, she washed them down with the drink Bryan had given her. She was mentally and physically exhausted. As the pain eased, sleep claimed her so she could temporarily stop tormenting herself.

***

Five hours later, her eyes hesitantly opened. She looked around the bedroom in confusion. Gingerly, she eased out of bed and shuffled out of the room to look for Bryan.

Her husband, lying on the couch watching television, glanced up at her. "Hey, babe, you're up."

Her eyes scanned the room. The bears had disappeared, and she had no interest in knowing where he had put them.

"You okay?" he asked as he sat up.

"Eh. I've felt better. Is the lock changed?"

Bryan lifted himself up from the couch and took her hand to walk her to the front door.

As he opened the door to show her, she glanced down at the new lock. It didn't look like the one that used to be there, and it had numbers on it. "I don't understand what you did here."

"It's a combination lock." He smiled at her. "You never have to worry about losing your keys again." He demonstrated as he explained. "You push this button here at the top and then push the four-digit code. I used your birthday as the code. Once you enter the code, the light will turn green. Turn this knob, and it will unlock the door on the inside." He turned the knob and swung the door open. "Voila. You do the same thing and turn the knob in the other direction to lock it."

"Seems easy enough," she said as she nodded in approval. "I like the idea that it doesn't need a key."

"I know we don't use the back door much, but I changed that one too while I was at it. They're both the same code." He pulled Becky close. "I don't know what's going on, but we'll figure it out together. As long as you have me, you have nothing to be afraid of here. Should we give the code to Mrs. Ritter, just in case?"

Her face tightened. "I would feel better if only the two of us have the code for now. At least until we figure out what's going on."

Becky tried to sleep that night, but nothing she did made her comfortable. She glanced over at Bryan's sleeping form. Even with new locks on the doors, she still wasn't sure she felt safe. Without an explanation for the bears, she didn't even know if she had a valid reason to be afraid.

She finally fell asleep, but her sleep was restless. The events of the day played out in her dreams while she tossed and turned. A whimper escaped her lips.

She was being chased, running and running until she felt her chest might explode. Trying to catch her breath, she looked back. Behind her as far as she could see, there they were, one endless line after another. She opened her mouth, but the scream of terror stuck in her throat. She spun around and ran. An entire army of menacing blue and pink bears was chasing her.

CHAPTER TWENTY

Becky

A s the first hazy hints of sunshine washed over her, Becky gently stretched and assessed how she felt. The boutique would be a welcome distraction.

Moving at a slow pace, she untangled herself from the covers. She glanced over to the other side of the bed. Bryan's deep, rhythmic breathing suggested he was still asleep.

She grabbed her cell phone from the nightstand and padded barefoot to the kitchen. Shaking two Tylenol from the bottle into the palm of her hand, she pulled a red Powerade out of the refrigerator and slugged them down. Now that she was up and moving, she didn't feel as uncomfortable as yesterday, but extra insurance couldn't hurt.

"Oh, good you're up," Becky said when Tonya answered her call.

"More than up. I just got back from a seven-mile run. How do you feel?"

"Well, I can tell you I don't feel up to a seven-mile run. But I'm not up to that on my best day. I'm awake, which is more than I can say for Bryan."

"Oh, poor thing. Was the cup too much for him yesterday?"

Becky smiled as she slid into the kitchen chair. "He *was* pretty proud of himself."

Tonya groaned. "Well, Michelle started yesterday, and she's doing great. I'm telling you, we were lucky to find her so quickly to replace Anna. She's picking it all up fast. Obviously, she's not ready to close by herself, so if you're not up to coming in today, I can handle it."

Tonya had covered so much for her already. Becky felt a twinge of discomfort, but it was nothing she couldn't handle. "I'm not supposed to drive for twenty-four hours, but as long as I don't lift anything heavy, I'm sure I could sit at the store just as easily this afternoon as I can sit here, and I'll have Michelle to help me. I can come in around noon."

Tonya hesitated. "Okay, but only if you're sure. If you start feeling crappy and change your mind, it's not a problem. Just let me know."

Bryan stumbled into the kitchen, and Becky watched him as he pawed at the cabinet holding his coffee hostage.

"Bryan's up, so let me run. I'll talk to you later."

Her husband raked his fingers through his disheveled hair as his wide-mouthed yawn released an audible groan. "Who was that?" he asked as he got the coffee ready to brew.

Becky hesitated. "Tonya. I just called her to check in."

He spun around. "Tell me you're not going in today."

"I said if I felt up to it, I would go in this afternoon so that she didn't have to close. She has covered for me a lot, you know."

Bryan jabbed the start button on the coffee machine. "I get that. But do you think that's a good idea? I can work from home today and stay with you."

"You've missed a lot of work too. Honestly, I don't feel too terrible."

He fixed his gaze on the cup he had placed underneath the flow of steaming dark brown liquid. "You're very stubborn, you know."

"Well, what would—" Becky's phone vibrated on the table. "Maybe it's the lab." Her stomach lurched.

She answered and put it on speakerphone. "Hello?"

"Hi, I'm looking for Becky Morgan."

Becky glanced at Bryan and nodded. "This is Becky."

"Good morning. I'm calling from the embryology lab with your fertilization results. You had twelve eggs retrieved. Of those, only nine were mature, and then two of those fertilized abnormally. So, you have seven fertilized eggs, and we'll keep watching them to see how they develop by day three. Someone will call you with an update Sunday."

Becky bit on her bottom lip and slumped back in her chair.

"Hello? Are you still there?" the voice on the phone asked.

"Oh, yeah, sorry, I'm still here. Thanks for calling." Becky disconnected the call and frowned at Bryan.

"Okay, so we have seven fertilized eggs," Bryan said. "That's still a good number."

Becky gave a small shrug that expressed her disappointment. "I guess I was expecting more. Losing five. That hurts."

"Don't panic just yet. We don't need a dozen babies, right? He gave her a half-smile. "How would we handle that many?"

It was hard for Becky not to think back to those early days when they had been falling in love. They had laid in bed, his fingers intertwined with hers as they talked about their future. That age-old question had invariably come up. "How many kids do you want?" she had asked.

His response had been immediate. "A whole houseful."

She had laughed. "I can just see you with your hand in the air when they're looking for a soccer coach. All the little kids will flock to you like moths to a flame. Like me." She had kissed him. "How lucky will our kids be to have you for a dad?"

Now here she was. Hoping and praying that she might get pregnant so they could have one child. She had never even considered this would be so hard.

Bryan reached across the table and grabbed her hand.

"I know," Becky said, her tone full of resignation. "I just feel like the more we have, the better our chances. But I'm going to stay positive."

"How about I make you a good breakfast before I go to work? I hate to say it, but I can make some scrambled eggs. Probably not a great theme for today, huh?"

Becky snorted. "Maybe not, but I'm starving, so I'll take it."

He stared at her while she ate her breakfast. "Stop gawking." Becky took a big sip of water. "See, I'm hydrating."

"Uh, huh. I know you. You'll get to the store and forget you're supposed to be taking it easy."

"I won't, I swear. Besides, I'm not moving fast enough to forget." She got up from the table and ambled to the sink to leave her dishes. "Thanks for breakfast. A hot shower and I'll be good as new."

On her way to the bathroom, she leaned over and kissed him. "Go to work. I'll see you later."

As she allowed the hot water to rain down on her, her mind drifted back to the call with the lab. Seven fertilized eggs. She just hoped seven was enough to make at least one baby.

After turning off the water, she stuck her hand out and reached for her towel. She wrapped herself up in it and she pulled back the curtain. A scream escaped from deep within her throat as she reeled back against the shower wall. The mystery of the bears already had her on edge, and now Bryan appeared out of nowhere like a scene from a bad horror movie.

"Damn, Bryan!" She took a deep breath as her heart settled back into its normal rhythm.

"What? I just came to tell you I'm leaving. I'm going to hit the gym on the way in and shower there. On the kitchen counter is a cooler with everything you need for today. Take it with you." He brushed his lips against hers, still wet from the shower. "Call me if you need me."

The sound of the front door closing echoed into the bedroom as she dried herself off and threw on her robe. Startled, she whipped around as a flash of orange fur flew into the room and dove under the bed.

"What the hell, Sherlock?" Becky's gaze drifted toward the doorway of the bedroom. There were noises in the house that left goosebumps on her arms. Bryan had left. She had heard the door shut behind him. After the events of the day before, there was no way he wouldn't have locked it.

Becky leaned her back against the bedroom wall and slowly inched toward the open doorway. She peered around the edge. This wasn't her imagination. Someone was moving around in her kitchen. Maybe whoever left the bears was back.

She cast a panicked glance around the room looking for something, anything. There was nothing even close to a weapon at her disposal.

She swore under her breath as she remembered the call with the lab. Her phone was still sitting on the kitchen table.

Adrenaline had her heart thumping wildly. The distinct sound of shoes echoed on the hardwood floor. They were heading in her direction. She held her breath as her gaze skipped around the bedroom and she plotted where she could hide.

A voice called out. "Hey, Beck?"

Becky froze for a moment and then cautiously stepped out of the bedroom and peeked into the hall. She clutched her chest and exhaled deeply when she saw Jules coming toward her, coffee mug in hand.

"Hey, Bryan let me in as he was leaving." She looked past Becky into the bedroom. "I guess Sherlock wasn't a big fan of seeing me so early in the morning." Jules raised the mug in her hand. "Hope it's okay I made some coffee. I'm exhausted. All these late nights with family trees and censuses—" She studied the shell-shocked expression on Becky's face. "You okay? You look like you saw a ghost."

"What is *wrong* with you two? You scared the crap out of me."

Jules looked befuddled at her friend's reaction. She followed Becky back into the bedroom. "Sorry. I was worried after yesterday. I'm on my way to meet a client, but I wanted to check up on you. Any more scary stuffed animals?"

"Very funny. Bryan changed the locks, but I can't wait to get out of here to go to work."

Jules sat on the bed and sipped her coffee. "You're going to the boutique? You feel okay after the retrieval yesterday?"

"Yeah, although Bryan pretty much wanted to quarantine me in the house." Becky scowled as she rooted around in her closet. "I don't feel too bad. Tonya's covered so much for me. I feel like I need to give her a break. We hired a new girl to replace Anna, but she can't really handle being on her own yet."

"Wow. That was fast."

"Yeah, her name's Michelle. I wish I could take credit for finding her. She just happened to come in while Tonya and I were talking about placing an ad. Perfect timing."

"With all the drama about the bears yesterday, I forgot to ask. How was the retrieval? How many eggs did you get?"

Becky threw a dress over her head, pulled it down over her bloated middle, and stepped out of her closet. "Well, I had twelve eggs retrieved."

"Twelve? Beck, that's awesome."

"The key word there was *had*. Only seven fertilized."

"Well, seven is a lucky number. That must mean something, right?" Jules said, her voice lifting with optimism.

Becky held up her hands. "From your mouth to the fertility god's ears."

Jules glanced around the room. "Where are the mystery bears, by the way?"

"I don't know what Bryan did with them, and I don't care. You two wonder why every little noise has me jumping out of my skin." She jabbed her finger in the air and used it to make her point. "Those bears prove I was right. Those bears prove someone was in my house."

CHAPTER TWENTY-ONE

Becky

As Becky came in the back door of the boutique, she deposited the cooler Bryan had packed on her desk. She wandered out of the office and found Tonya.

Becky nodded in the new girl's direction. "How's she doing?"

"Great. I'm not sure how we got so lucky, but she's a keeper."

Michelle was a young girl in her early twenties, with stylish young taste that seemed perfect for the store. She wore her long dark brown hair straight as a pin and parted in the middle. Blue nail polish, on both her fingers and toes, made her seem much younger than Becky. First appearances had been deceiving. When she opened her mouth to speak, what came out was more mature than the age on her driver's license.

Michelle had finished with the customer and walked over to where Becky and Tonya were huddled. "Hi, ladies. Can anyone get in on this?"

"We're just talking about how great you are," Becky said.

"Well, thanks. I do love it here. That customer was so nice. She bought almost five-hundred bucks worth of stuff."

Tonya laughed. "She does like to spend. One of the regulars. We have lots of those." She turned her attention to Becky. "If you're good. I'm going to take off. All those new sundresses in the stockroom are ready to go out if you can handle that."

"Yeah, I'm fine. I hurt my back, so maybe if I need anything heavy lifted, Michelle can help me." The only one who knew about the IVF was Tonya. Becky wasn't comfortable telling anyone else just yet but figured a back injury was a good excuse to take it easy.

Michelle offered a smile to Becky. "Of course."

Becky disappeared into the back and found the rolling rack Tonya had left for her. While her mind wandered to the call from the lab, Becky transferred the dresses to an empty circular rack on the sales floor. As promised, she was trying to take it easy, but she wasn't sure she felt up to dealing with customers. She had on the most generously sized dress she owned, but her stomach felt huge. If anyone asked her if she was pregnant or when she was due, she'd probably break down and cry right there on the spot.

The Tylenol had her feeling okay, but she was starting to feel the lack of sleep from the night before. She glanced at her watch and let her eyes close for a moment. A long afternoon loomed ahead. She'd already had coffee, but maybe she could have another. At this point, they already had her eggs.

The sound of the bell above the front door jangled behind her as it was opened from the outside. She glanced around, but she could hear Michelle in the fitting room with a customer. So much for escaping into the back with some caffeine.

She mentally steeled herself as she turned around. "Hi, good aft—" Her smile froze uncomfortably on her face. Dread hit the pit of her stomach. It was Friday.

"Hey, Anna." The speed of Becky's heartbeat quickened. Anna's eyes drilled into her as they stood awkwardly face to face.

"Don't hey me. I'm here for my paycheck. Can we just get this over with?"

Always impeccably put together when she came to work, today Anna looked like she had just rolled out of bed. She was naturally fair and blond with light eyebrows and lashes that were always heavily made up so they didn't disappear on her face. She wasn't wearing a stitch of makeup which made her look pale and sickly. Her white-blond hair was pulled up in a ponytail, and she was wearing a stained T-shirt and a pair of ripped, faded jeans. Had Becky seen her walking down the street, it might have taken a moment to recognize her.

As Becky shuffled toward the office in the back of the store, Anna's footsteps sounded uncomfortably close behind her. Her eyes drifted toward the fitting room, but Michelle and the customer were still inside.

Sitting down at her desk, she winced slightly. Avoiding Anna's gaze, she reached into the desk drawer to her right and pulled out the company checkbook.

Anna scowled. "Oh, for fuck's sake, you haven't even written it yet?" She stood over Becky, hands on her hips, while she waited for her check.

She snapped her gum, and Becky flinched. Her stomach churned at the smell of bubblegum wafting over her.

"You know this is bullshit, right?" Anna asked. "I would never steal from here."

Becky's fingers stumbled over the numbers on her keyboard as she tried to enter Anna's hours. She knew her lack of response was making the tension in the small office worse, but there was nothing she could say to make it better.

"I considered everyone here family." Anna's voice was rising in volume. "Do you think I would steal from my family? Or anyone for that matter? Is that what you believe too?"

With relief, Becky noted the final amount the payroll program had computed for Anna's final check. She filled out the stub and corresponding check and tore it from the book. Her handwriting didn't look recognizable, but it was written and hopefully accurate.

Becky glanced up. Her neck felt hot, angry red splotches betraying just how uncomfortable this was making her. "Anna, I'm not entirely sure what happened. I know Tonya made a decision, and there's not much I can do about it."

Anna threw up her hands. "You're partners. How does she get to decide I'm a thief and you don't get a say and I don't get to defend myself? You hired me, but she gets to fire me?"

Becky spoke in a low, controlled voice. "Honestly, I thought you always did a great job. I trusted you, and you were like family to us." She paused. "I'm sorry. I don't know what to say."

Becky held up Anna's check, but she didn't reach for it. An awkward silence hung in the air of the small office. Becky knew Tonya would never reconsider, and yet she heard herself say the words. "I can try to talk to Tonya and see what she says. Maybe there's another explanation."

"Maybe? See, you still don't believe me." Anna's lips drew back in a snarl. "You didn't know how good you had it when I was here. You wanted to come in late, leave early, take the weekend off? Who was always there to pitch in? Me. You'll be sorry. You'll both be sorry. Someday you'll realize you were wrong about me, and it will be too late because I won't be accepting your apologies."

Anna snatched the check from Becky's hand, spun on her heel, and stormed out of the office.

Becky followed her. Her hand flew to her mouth as Anna pretended to trip accidentally. She lunged for a metal rack to right herself, making it clatter loudly on the marble floor as it fell. Handbags spilled in all directions.

Anna's eyes locked on Michelle who had rushed over at the sound of the crash. "Oh, honey, you'd better pick that up," she said, her voice dripping with contempt. "Good luck in this fucking place."

Anna shoved the glass door open and spun back around to face Becky. "You and Tonya. You both suck. Karma's a bitch; just remember that."

As Becky carefully stooped down to help Michelle with the mess, she was shaking. She hadn't lied. Anna had been like family. She knew she was struggling financially, but Becky would never have believed she'd steal from the store.

Tonya had no actual proof it was Anna. She was the logical explanation, but what if there was something else going on that they didn't know about? Becky hoped like hell Tonya didn't turn out to be wrong.

CHAPTER TWENTY-TWO

Felicia

Felicia rocked in her chair and stared outside. She liked to watch the birds as they flitted from tree to tree. Ellie had been in to say good morning and had gone to pick up her breakfast.

The door creaked. She glanced over as it swung open.

"Oh," she uttered in confusion. Recognition slid over her face, and her eyes lit up. "Becky? What a nice surprise." Becky rarely came for breakfast.

The corners of Felicia's mouth turned up. "Did you bring me any treats?"

"As a matter of fact, I brought you some cookies." Her daughter handed the bag to Felicia. "Chocolate chip."

Felicia immediately reached into the bag and removed a cookie. She took a bite. "Want one?"

"Nope, I'm all good. Don't let Ellie catch you eating cookies before breakfast. You'll get me in trouble."

Felicia frowned.

"Not in real trouble. Don't worry about it." Felicia was sitting in her rocker, and Becky sat down in the guest chair next to her. "So, how are you feeling today?"

Felicia crunched her cookie. She glanced around the room for something to drink. She was having a hard time swallowing the dry cookie. Felicia gestured toward the table by her bed.

"You need water?" There was a plastic pitcher with a cup on the table next to Felicia's bed. After pouring half a glass, Becky extended it to her. "Here. Drink."

Felicia lifted her head and took a sip. The cookie had made it hard to breathe, and as the water washed it down her throat, she felt some relief. She took a deep breath as her chest opened back up. Felicia handed Becky the cup, and she set it on the table.

"Not so good? Maybe wait until Ellie can bring you some milk or something. So, aside from the dry cookie, how are you doing?"

"Today seems to be a pretty good day. I didn't even need the card you put on my nightstand to remind me where I am. I'm glad you came to visit me."

"Well, if it's a good day, then I'm glad I came today too. The doctor says you should push yourself to try to remember things, so you don't forget them. It must be hard. It even happens to me sometimes, and it makes me crazy. It has to be very frustrating for you."

Felicia nodded. "Some days I can't remember I need to brush my teeth, but then I can remember something from thirty years ago as clear as day."

"Do you remember when we used to live in this town when I was a little girl?"

Felicia smiled as she reached into her long-term memory which held Becky's childhood intact. "Oh, yes." Felicia closed her eyes. She visualized what she was telling Becky. "You were so adorable. I used to dress you in pretty dresses with patent leather Mary Janes and socks with the frilly tops. You looked like you came right out of a catalog. People used to stop me in the supermarket to tell me how beautiful you were. I felt like the luckiest mommy in the world."

"I'm sure I was the luckiest daughter in the world. What else do you remember today? Do you remember Dad?"

Felicia was used to this game. Becky was always bringing up things to try to stretch her memory. The nurses had told her it would be helpful. "Use it or lose it," they said constantly.

"Of course I remember your father. He was a good man, and he loved you so much. When you were a baby, I'm not sure he expected how much he would fall in love with you right from the very beginning. He loved to take you to the park and push you in the swing. You would beg him to push you higher and higher. I'm not sure who enjoyed it more, you or him."

"I wish I remembered him pushing me in the swing. Maybe we can go out one day and go to that park. Would you like that? Do you remember where it was?"

Felicia thought for a moment. "It was near the house we used to live in. I remember pushing you in the stroller to go there. That's where you met Jules. Her mom took her in her stroller there too, and we would push you in the swings together. You two just loved playing together. Her mom comes to visit me here sometimes."

"It must have been sad for us to move away."

"It was." Felicia looked down at her hands and then over at Becky. "We had to move because your daddy got a new job. We moved a bunch of times because of Daddy's job, and I always felt bad taking you away from your friends. You were so sad to leave Jules, you made up an imaginary friend. I would hear you in your room talking to her."

A smile tugged at the corners of Becky's mouth. "Really? That's interesting. I don't remember that at all."

"Whenever I asked who you were talking to, you would tell me no one, so I let it be. Do you remember that time we took you on the rides at the fair, and Daddy got so sick on the spinning teacups?" Felicia smiled at the memory of her big strong husband holding his stomach when they got off and darting behind a carnival trailer to throw up.

Felicia watched as her daughter shrugged.

"I don't remember that at all. I wish I did."

"You wanted to go on it, and he would have done anything for you." Felicia cocked her head to the side. "I miss him so much. Do you miss him too, Becky?"

"I wish he was here right now."

"Oh, Becky, so do I." Felicia studied her daughter's face. "You look like you're working too hard. You should take some time off to relax. Life goes by too fast to spend so much time working." Ken had worked too hard, and then he was gone.

"There's lots going on, Mom. You know, with the baby. Remember? I should be pregnant soon."

"Oh, I can't wait for that. I love babies."

"I can't wait either. Soon, Mom, soon."

The door swung open, and Ellie entered the room carrying Felicia's breakfast. She stumbled and steadied the tray as the juice cup wobbled.

"Oh, Becky, you startled me. I didn't expect to see you this early. Do you both want to go down and have breakfast in the dining room? It's not a problem to send this back."

Felicia looked at her daughter, her eyes flickering with eager anticipation. "Can you eat with me?"

Becky then shifted her gaze from Ellie to Felicia. "I'm sorry, I can't. I have to be somewhere, and I just realized I'm gonna be late. Next time I come, we can eat in the dining room for lunch. I do love the tuna melt down there."

"Oh, okay, honey." Felicia's eyes glistened. "Will you come back and visit me soon?"

"Of course, I'll be back."

"Maybe you'll have that baby with you next time I see you."

"Not quite yet." Becky patted her belly. "But soon. The baby will be in here and growing any day now."

Ellie put the breakfast tray down on Felicia's table. "Miss Becky, do you have a quick minute before you go? I know Dr. Burke called you about wanting to adjust your mom's medication, right?"

She hesitated. "Oh, right. Yes, he did."

"I just need you to sign off on the paperwork. I have it at the desk if you could give me a minute."

Becky frowned slightly. "Um, okay. I have about a minute, and then I have to head out."

Ellie scurried out of the room and returned with a folder. She took the top sheet of paper out and laid it on top and handed it to Becky. "Oh, shoot, let me get a pen." She laughed. "Sorry, it's still early. I haven't even had my coffee yet."

She returned and handed a pen to Becky. "It should be everything the doctor discussed with you." She smiled. "It's good news. He thinks she's improving a bit."

Becky glanced at Felicia and then at the piece of paper. She paused and then carefully signed at the bottom. With the pen resting on top, she handed the paper and folder back to Ellie.

She directed her attention back to Felicia. "I'll be back soon, Mom. I need to go now so I'm not late for my appointment. But remember, next time we'll have lunch. Maybe I'll even take you out to a restaurant and then maybe to the park. We could even drive by the old house. Would you like that?"

Felicia's eyes were glued on her daughter, but she didn't answer.

Ellie leaned over and told Becky, "Too many decisions and questions for her to answer all at once."

"Oh." Becky fixed her gaze on Felicia. "Do you want to go out and eat lunch with me one day?"

Felicia's glance skipped between the two women. She felt dizzy. She opened her mouth, but no words came out.

"Mom? You're allowed to leave with me, Mom. I'm your daughter." Becky leaned over and kissed Felicia on the cheek. "I have to go, but I'll be back soon, don't worry."

Felicia sat rigid in her rocker as Becky left the room, her gaze unfocused as she stared out the window.

Ellie walked over and rubbed Felicia's shoulder. "You okay?"

Felicia turned her head, and her eyes searched Ellie's.

The nurse studied her and offered a reassuring smile. "You'll be okay if you leave with Becky for a little while. I know it can seem scary, but you'll be safe. Your daughter won't let anything happen to you. You trust Becky, right?"

Felicia hesitated, then nodded, the movement so slow it was almost imperceptible.

CHAPTER TWENTY-THREE

Becky

Becky brushed her bangs off her forehead and scrutinized her reflection in the mirror. The bruise was barely noticeable now. Michelle had helped her return the rental car so she could get hers back from the body shop. With no apparent reminders of the accident, she could just forget it had ever happened.

Opening the bathroom door, she winced as it creaked. As she peered out, she saw Bryan hadn't stirred.

She tiptoed across the bedroom to her closet. Rooting through her clothes, she scowled. She didn't know what she could wear that would accommodate her oversized stomach. Most women probably threw on sweatpants or leggings to get through this time in the IVF process, but she could just imagine Tonya's face if she showed up at the boutique wearing those.

She flipped through the clothes in her closets, sliding hangers down the rod, looking for anything that might work until she paused at a simple loose-fitting pin-tucked dress. It was a pretty pattern, light blue with white trim around the collar and hemline and a forgiving middle. She fingered the sleeve and noticed the tags were still attached. Examining them, she noted that the dress was her size. Though it wasn't from the boutique, it was from a department store she shopped at sometimes.

She stared at the dress as she willed herself to recall buying it. The answer didn't come. Even though it was hanging in her closet, she was sure she had never seen this dress before.

Behind that dress were three more, all loose-fitting but stylish. All from the same store. All had the price tags still attached. Staring at them in her closet, Becky realized they were exactly what she needed, and they would take her through the early stages of her pregnancy as well. And yet, stare as she might, there wasn't a single recollection of shopping for them, buying them, or hanging them in her closet.

With few other choices, she undid the small clip holding the tags in place on the blue dress and threw it over her head. It fit perfectly. As she slid her feet into a comfortable pair of flats, she heard her husband's sleepy voice behind her. "You look pretty."

She felt the anxiety lift off her. Now it made sense. Bryan didn't usually buy her clothes, knowing she mostly wore the boutique offerings, but he must have known she wouldn't have anything that fit. She had mentioned struggling to find clothes that fit right before the retrieval. He had paid attention. She turned around to find Bryan propped up on his elbow in bed, watching her get dressed.

"Well, look who's up," she said.

He smiled sheepishly.

"Hey, did you—" Before she could thank him for the dresses, the shrill ring of her cell phone interrupted her. She ran to answer it.

She glanced at the caller ID and yelled out for him. "Bryan! It's the lab."

He catapulted out of bed and joined her in the kitchen. He stood by her side as she took a deep breath and answered the call, putting it on speakerphone so he could hear too.

It was a nurse named Valerie. Becky felt terrible the poor girl was working on the weekend, but she wanted to hear the number.

Valerie rattled off from the notes in Becky's file. "You had seven fertilized eggs."

Had. That didn't sound like they all made it. Becky's stomach twisted, and she held her breath.

Val continued, "Today on day three, you have six embryos. The last one did not continue to develop. Dr. Levine has you noted for a day five transfer. So, we'll continue to watch to see how these develop over the next two days. Normally we would expect forty to fifty percent of embryos will make it to the blastocyst stage for transfer."

Becky caught her breath. So less than half of what she had now. "And then they grade them and take the best one for transfer?"

"That's right. They'll also watch any blasts that remain to see if they are high enough quality to be frozen. They'll give them until day six if necessary."

"But my transfer will definitely be on day five?"

"Yes, unless something changes dramatically, but right now they look good. Someone will call you tomorrow with your transfer time for Tuesday. You should have been given all the instructions the day of your retrieval, but if you need them, I can email them to you."

"Nope, we have them."

"Okay, good. We'll see you on Tuesday morning."

"Thanks for calling on a Sunday," Becky said. "We appreciate it."

As she disconnected the call, she realized they weren't over the finish line yet. Anything could happen, and there was still a chance the embryo might not implant in her uterus. But they were one step closer, and she would take it.

She stared vacantly at nothing as she tried to recall all the nuances of her conversation with the lab. She had no idea if six was a good number and wished she knew someone who had gone through this to ask.

Bryan clapped his hands in front of her. "Hey, Earth to Becky. You okay?"

Becky looked over at him. "Sorry, I guess I'm in my own little world."

"Well, let the daddy in, would ya? Six is good."

"I hope so. And even if half of them don't develop into blasts, that's still three or maybe four if we're lucky."

"We only need one," Bryan said. "Remember that. This'll be fine."

Becky took a deep breath. "You're right. We just need one." She pulled down the calendar from the side of the refrigerator and grabbed a red pen from the basket on the counter. In big block letters she wrote EMBRYO TRANSFER on Tuesday's date. With a glance at Bryan, she circled it before putting it back up, this time on the front of the refrigerator. "Tuesday. Big day for us."

Becky was relieved the call had come in the morning. She had agreed to go in and cover the store with Michelle for a few hours that afternoon. She shuddered to think how she would have managed if the call had come later and it was bad news.

"So, what's your plan today while I go to the store?" Becky asked.

"Some guys from the office asked about going to play racquetball at the club by the office this afternoon. We'll probably go and grab a quick beer or two afterward, but I should be home before you. Running all over the court will be a good way to work off all this embryo stress."

Becky smiled coyly and walked over to rub his shoulders. She kissed his neck, first on one side and then the other. "Oh, remember the days when we used to have much better ways to relieve stress on a Sunday afternoon?"

Bryan turned around swiftly, grabbed his wife, and pulled her down gently onto his lap. She squealed, and they both took a moment to recognize a moment from their old lives.

She gazed into Bryan's eyes. "We're going to be okay, honey. Once we have our baby, we'll forget all of this ever happened, and we'll go back to being us again. Well, us plus a baby." She kissed him tenderly on the lips, the fun moment turning serious. "I love you more than anything in the world. I can't wait for you to be a daddy."

"I love you more. Now, get off and go to work. You're crushing me." They both laughed because Becky was so much smaller than him.

"Just wait till I'm preggers and sitting on your lap." Becky twisted her wrist and glanced at her watch. "Shoot, I'm late. Gotta go."

As she pulled open the front door to leave, she glanced back at him. "How lucky am I to have you for a husband? I almost forgot to thank you for the dresses."

Bryan cocked his head and gave her a quizzical look. "What dresses?"

CHAPTER TWENTY-FOUR

Becky

Becky pulled into the driveway, but Bryan's side was empty. It was almost six and just starting to get dark. He had left to play racquetball hours ago.

The mystery of the dresses had nagged at her all day. If they weren't from Bryan and she didn't buy them, she had no idea where they had come from. She could just imagine telling her husband that someone had broken into the house, even after he had changed the locks, to leave clothes in her closet. There had to be an explanation. She just hadn't figured out what it could be.

Looking forward to a quiet night with Bryan, she decided not to mention it. He already thought her imagination was in overdrive, and she knew she was more stressed than usual. She only had two days until the transfer, and then she knew the anxiety would be even worse while they waited for the pregnancy test. Dr. Levine had told her she couldn't test for two weeks. That would be a brutal amount of time to wonder if the transfer had been successful.

As she walked into the bedroom to change, she paused and tilted her head. She smelled perfume. Her perfume. Usually reserved for date nights with Bryan, she hadn't worn it in weeks. She sniffed the air again, but now she wasn't sure the scent was really there. She glanced around the room. Everything looked the way she had left it. Her perfume bottle sat on her dresser in its usual spot. Rubbing her temples, she exhaled loudly. She didn't trust any of her senses anymore.

"Sherlock," she called out as she dug in the drawers for a pair of comfortable leggings. "Momma's home, where are you?" He usually came running when she called him, belly swaying, meowing in his chirpy little way. Nothing.

She pulled open the kitchen cabinet, grabbed a can of wet cat food, and popped the metal top as loudly as she could. She waited, watching the entrance to the kitchen, anticipating his appearance. The sound of possible food usually brought him scurrying, meowing in his soft way that said he was ready to eat. She frowned as she realized there was no movement, no sign of him. He might have hidden if there were strangers in the house, but he wouldn't hide from her.

Bryan must have accidentally locked him on the porch when he left. She unlocked the door, slid open the slider, and scoured the porch, glancing fervently into his favorite spots. They were all empty, and the screen door was closed.

Unlike most cats, Sherlock never even tried to get outside. Becky always figured his early days, scared and alone in the bushes outside the boutique, had scarred him from ever wanting to see what was in the outside world.

She circled back to the spare room and peered under the bed into one of his favorite hiding spots. As her eyes adjusted to the darkness, she could see the outlines of bins of wrapping paper and Christmas ornaments, but no pointed ears poking up between them or amber eyes looking back at her.

Frenzied, she went systematically from room to room, looking under her bed and under couches and in closets. She checked behind furniture and on top of the bookshelf where he occasionally went to hide. He couldn't just disappear. As her heart began to race, she looked in every nook and cranny of every room before coming to the sinking realization that her cat simply wasn't in the house. Nausea hit her stomach. Sherlock was gone.

She picked up the phone to call Bryan.

He didn't even say hello when he answered. "I know, I know. I'm late. I'm just pulling in the driveway now."

Becky hung up and walked toward the front door, opening it from one side as he stood on the other.

He greeted her with a roguish grin. "Greeted at the door, I love it. You must have missed me today." He took in the expression on her face, and his smile faded. "Aw, Beck, what's the matter?"

"Sherlock's gone." A whimper escaped her lips.

"Oh, come on, come here." He wrapped his arms around her petite frame and pulled her close. "He's not gone. You know that silly cat likes to play hide and seek. I'm sure he's here someplace."

As she pulled back, her bottom lip quivered. "He may hide from you, but he doesn't hide from me. I'm telling you, he's not here." Her eyes searched his for comfort, desperate with the hope that her husband could fix this for her.

"Okay, calm down. I'll help you look."

Bryan walked through the house much like Becky had done, dropping to the floor to look under beds and behind furniture. There was no sign of the cat.

"Maybe he slipped past you and then you closed the sliding door," Becky said. "Did you leave him locked outside when you left? Is it possible someone took him off the porch?"

"I'm almost positive he was sleeping on the couch when I went to play racquetball. Besides, you know that cat won't let anyone pick him up but you."

Out on the porch, Bryan tested each screen panel to make sure they were intact and weren't loose enough where the cat could have pushed his way out.

Becky shook her head. "He wouldn't have tried to push the screens out. You know that. The other day, the door blew open and he didn't even try to go out."

As she entered the house, her eyes welled up until she couldn't hold in her emotions any longer.

"Come here. We'll figure this out." Bryan hugged her again. He rubbed her back as his T-shirt dampened with her tears. "He got out somehow, but he wouldn't have gone far."

She pulled out of his embrace and fixed her gaze up at him. "Bryan, he's never been outside this house. How would he know how to find his way back? What if something scared him and he just kept running and hiding? He's never going to go to anyone outside, you know that."

At that moment, Becky regretted she hadn't gotten Sherlock a collar. Even if he had one, no one would be able to get close enough to read it. It wasn't like a dog running down the street that people would stop to help to return him to his rightful owner.

She slumped down on the couch with her hands covering her face.

Bryan sat down next to her. He put his arm around her shoulders and leaned toward her, his face next to hers. "You're sure he was here this morning, right?"

Becky nodded somberly.

"And I'm pretty sure he was here when I left. However he managed to get out, we'll find him." He rubbed her shoulder. "Let's go outside and look." Bryan glanced over at the picture window as he lifted himself from the couch. "I'll get a light."

He opened the kitchen drawer, rummaged through the accumulation of junk, and pulled out a flashlight. He switched it on. "C'mon, let's go find him."

They started in the backyard, checking in the bushes and under the BBQ, anywhere he might be curled into a ball in fright. They walked around the house to the front and Bryan shined his flashlight into the bushes and through the plants while Becky called his name.

"Here, why don't you take the flashlight and look. I'll go talk to Mrs. Ritter and see if she saw anything and at least tell her to keep an eye out for him."

Her hands trembling, Becky took the flashlight and nodded miserably.

Bryan headed over to the other side of the street and rang Mrs. Ritter's doorbell. Becky watched as the porch light came on, and the door opened.

A few minutes later, Bryan jogged back across the street, and Mrs. Ritter's porch light extinguished behind him. He approached Becky who was bending over by the neighbor's bushes on the other side of their house calling Sherlock's name.

"Anything?" he asked.

"Nope." Her voice quivered. "Bryan, he's just gone." She looked at him hopefully. "Did Mrs. Ritter see anything?"

He gently took the flashlight from her. "No, but she was out today playing cards with her friends. Don't worry. I'll make up some flyers, and we'll post them in the neighborhood. Mrs. Ritter said she would help put them up. I'm sure you have a recent picture of him on your phone. Send it to me, and I'll use that."

She looked up at him with wet eyes, her blotchy face a mask of mascara and sadness. "How could he just disappear, Bryan? How? It doesn't make any sense."

"I don't know, Beck. Somehow, he must have slipped out. Let's prop the door to the porch open tonight and put some food out there. I'm sure he'll find his way back in and be there in the morning."

Her face crumpled as she shook her head. "I feel like I'm never going to get him back."

CHAPTER TWENTY-FIVE

Becky

Becky shuffled wearily into the kitchen the next morning, her slippers scuffing the floor. Lifting her feet took too much effort. Usually, Sherlock got out of bed when she did and trotted off ahead of her for his breakfast. As she stared downward, he was noticeably absent. Her bottom lip trembled.

Bryan looked up from the table, his face serious, and his lips set in a straight line. As she studied his expression, it was obvious. He had no good news to share about Sherlock.

"Morning. I made you coffee."

She didn't respond. At the kitchen counter, she leaned both palms on the edge to hold her up. Sherlock's face stared back at her from the stack of flyers Bryan had printed. Tears bubbled up and started to fall, dotting the flyer on the top of the pile with wet splotches over the words, "Missing Cat."

Bryan came up behind her at the counter and wrapped his arms around her. "We'll find him, Beck. I already gave a stack to Mrs. Ritter this morning. She said she'd put them in mailboxes up and down the street. You drive out the front entrance on your way to work and put some up, and I'll go out the back and do the same.

Since you don't always have your phone on you at work, I put both our cell numbers, okay?"

Becky nodded in subdued agreement, but she felt like she was in a daze. She stood slumped over at the counter, her gaze fixed on the amber eyes staring out at her from the page. They stared back with a look of contentment. Sherlock's trust had been aimed at her. This wouldn't be the same face other people would see on the outside. Only she saw the side of him portrayed in the picture. Anyone else would see a scared, skittish cat with fearful eyes, ready to run if they got too close. That is, if they saw him at all.

Bryan pushed the hair back from her face and tucked it behind her ear. He caressed her cheek with a kiss and gently spun her around to face him. "I have a meeting this morning, so I have to get going so I have time to put these up. Don't forget. You put yours up out the front entrance." He leaned forward and grazed her forehead with his lips. "This will be okay. We'll find him, Beck."

When he had left with half the pile of flyers, she moved her feet in slow motion to the coffeemaker. She sipped the cup of coffee he made her, but misery left her with no appetite for breakfast. She placed her mug back on the counter and shoulders hunched, made her way over to the sliding glass door. Arms crossed in front of her and her forehead leaning on the glass, she scanned the length of the small porch. Bryan had filled Sherlock's bowl with food and left it next to a bowl of water. One of her half-dead potted plants had been used to prop open the screen door.

She swallowed hard past the lump in her throat. She couldn't imagine never seeing Sherlock again, never feeling the wetness of his soft nose nuzzling against her cheek at night while he purred. Wherever he was, he was alone. He had to be petrified.

She wandered into the bedroom, pulled open the curtains, and focused on the bushes searching for any glimpse of orange fur that might give away his hiding spot. There was nothing. As she closed the curtains, her gaze moved to the candle on her desk.

Jules had said she probably forgot lighting it. While she could admit that was a possibility, she would have never lit it on the expensive antique rolltop desk. Bryan had bought it for her when they got engaged, and it had cost a small fortune. There was no way. But then again, she had dresses in her closet she didn't remember buying.

She brought the glass jar to her nose and inhaled the fragrant smell of lilac. However it had been lit, she wasn't taking any more chances. She carried it to the kitchen, then swapped the candle for her coffee cup. As she chugged the lukewarm liquid, she hoped it would work quickly to wake her up and erase her sleepless night.

She managed to get ready for work and found herself drawn again to stare out the sliding glass door. Sherlock's spot in the corner, where his tail twitched while he watched the birds, was just an empty patch of tile. Choking back a sob, she stepped back and saw her reflection. Puffy eyes, her forehead creased with worry. She watched the tears slide down her cheeks and pause on her chin before leaving reminders on her shoes.

As much as she wanted to stay, sit there all day and watch for him, the store would be a welcome distraction. Silently, she said a prayer she'd come home and find him curled up sleeping in her chair. Swiping at her tears, she grabbed her purse and cell phone and hurried out the door.

She was halfway to work when her cell phone rang. Bryan.

"Hey. I put up about a dozen of the flyers out the back this morning. Did you have any problems hanging yours?"

Her heart raced as she turned her gaze to the passenger seat. Empty. She hadn't even taken the flyers, but she didn't know how to tell her husband she had forgotten to put them up.

"Nope," she said, her face hot as she told the lie. "I hung mine too."

"Okay, good. Hopefully, someone will see him. Even if Sherlock doesn't go to them, they can tell us where he's hiding, and you can grab him. Somebody at work mentioned putting out a trap, but I think he'd be too scared to go in it and who knows what else we might accidentally catch."

"Uh, huh." Becky pressed down on the gas pedal. Her phone beeped with another call. She ignored it as she scanned the road to find the next available exit to get off the highway and go back home.

She cursed herself for forgetting the flyers. No one wanted to find Sherlock more than her, and yet she hadn't remembered them. She recalled Kim's comment about forgetting things. She was overwhelmed with too much on her mind, but still, this wasn't forgetting a lunch. This was Sherlock, and he was missing.

Her thoughts were interrupted by Bryan's voice. "I have to run. Try not to worry, Beck. Hopefully, we'll hear something from someone today. If I get any calls, I'll let you know. Love you."

As she disconnected the call, she got off the exit. She circled around and got back on the highway heading in the other direction back toward the house.

She glanced at her phone and hit the speaker button to play voicemail. *Hi, this message is for Becky Morgan. This is the embryology lab. Your embryo transfer tomorrow is scheduled for 10:30 AM. Unfortunately, since yesterday, three of your embryos arrested, but the three that are left look good. They'll assess them tomorrow and transfer the best one. Don't forget you need a full bladder for the procedure. Please arrive thirty minutes before your scheduled appointment. We'll see you at 10 AM tomorrow, Tuesday.*

Three of her embryos had died. They had warned her it was possible, but damn. Was the universe just using her for target practice?

Tires squealing, she whipped into the driveway. Leaving everything in the car, she raced up to the front door, punched in the code, then burst inside. She froze and her throat tightened. Wafting into the living room was the sweet smell of lilacs comingled with the acrid smell of smoke.

CHAPTER TWENTY-SIX

Jules

"Slow down," Jules said. "What happened?" Becky sounded frantic, and Jules couldn't understand what she was saying. Becky took a deep, stuttered breath. "I don't even know where to start. I'm pretty sure I'm losing my mind."

"You are not losing your mind," Jules said in a matter-of-fact tone as if the idea was ludicrous. "Start at the beginning."

"I came home from work last night, and Sherlock was gone."

"Gone where? He doesn't go out."

"Exactly. And yet, he's just gone. Bryan made up flyers, and I was supposed to hang them on my way into work this morning."

"Okay, so maybe someone will see him and call you. Don't worry. That cat worships you. He must have gotten out somehow, but he'll come back."

"I left for work, and I forgot the flyers. I turned around and went back to get them—" Becky's voice cracked, and she paused as if to steady her voice so she could continue. "Remember that candle I told you about that had been lit on my desk? Well, I moved it to the kitchen. But I didn't light it. I swear I didn't."

Jules heard the terror in her friend's voice. Fearfully, in a soft voice, she asked, "Beck, what happened?"

Becky choked back a sob. "It was lit. When I went back to get the flyers, it was burning. It caught the paper towels and the cabinet on fire. If I hadn't gone back—if Bryan hadn't insisted we have a fire extinguisher—" She let the thoughts go unfinished.

Jules gasped, and shock brought her hand up to cover her mouth. "Oh my god, Beck. That's really scary. At least you're okay. The smoke detector wasn't going off?"

Becky didn't answer for a moment. "Now that you mention it, the smoke detector wasn't going off. I'm sure that's my fault too for not changing out the batteries. Aren't you supposed to do that when the clock changes? Oh, god, Jules, how do I even explain this to Bryan when I don't even understand it myself?"

"You're okay, and that's all that will matter to Bryan. The rest can be fixed. There must be an explanation. Were you distracted by anything? I mean, maybe you lit it but forgot?"

"I don't think so. But with Sherlock missing, maybe I wasn't paying attention. But why would I—do you think it's possible I had one of those silent strokes? Like my mom? They always tell me my blood pressure is okay, but who knows."

"Beck, you are not having a stroke."

"Then what?" There was a small whimper. "I print reports for Tonya that I swear I leave on her desk and she tells me they're not there. When she finds them, they're never where I thought I put them. I would swear she's trying to make me think I'm going crazy, but it's happening at home too. I smell cigarettes and my perfume that I haven't worn in forever. I'm constantly losing things. I can't find the necklace you gave me last Christmas, and I *just* had it."

"You probably just forgot where you put it. I'm sure it will turn up."

"Yesterday, I found dresses in my closet that I have no recollection whatsoever of buying." Becky's voice shook. "I'm starting to freak out a little bit here."

"Well, that's not proof of anything. I find stuff all the time like that. One good sale and I'm filling my closet. Sometimes I buy something I like and go to hang it up and find out I already have it. You have a lot on your mind with all those shots, not to mention Anna getting fired and trying to run the boutique."

"There's more. The lab called. We lost three embryos. Which they told us was possible. I guess I should have been prepared. We still have three, and they look good. My transfer is scheduled for tomorrow morning."

"Well, okay, I know it's disappointing to lose some, but you're still going to have one of those embryos transferred tomorrow. That's just science and odds. That has nothing to do with you losing your mind."

"I guess. It just all feels overwhelming—"

"I mean, really, it's no wonder you're distracted," Jules said. "Just put all that nonsense out of your mind and concentrate on your transfer tomorrow. Once you have that tiny embryo inside you, none of this will matter."

Becky sniffled. "See, this is why I call you. Thanks for putting it all into perspective. Anything on the DNA hunt?"

"I'm working on it, but no news to report yet. I had to send Lucy yet another email. The one person who might be able to help me seems determined to ignore me."

"Okay, keep me posted. I guess I better call Tonya and get myself to work. She's probably wondering where I am. And I guess I need to figure what the hell I'm going to tell Bryan."

CHAPTER TWENTY-SEVEN

Becky

Becky sent Bryan a text when she got to work. She couldn't talk to him on the phone right now, she would lose it completely. She had no idea how she would even begin to explain the fire so that he didn't think she was crazy. *Lab called. We lost 3 embryos yesterday. 3 left look good. Transfer tomorrow at 10:30 AM. We need to be there at 10. Talk later.*

Becky leaned back in her chair and rubbed her eyes. The idea that she had lit that candle and left the house made her blood run cold. She grappled with the uneasiness building in her chest.

And then there was Sherlock. She had finally hung the flyers on her way in, but there was no reasonable explanation for how he had just disappeared. She felt gutted as if someone had used a pocketknife to cut out her heart to toss it on the desk in front of her.

She dropped her chin to her chest and closed her eyes. As she opened them, the black and white checkered pattern of one of the dresses she didn't remember buying stared back at her. Becky rubbed the back of her neck and tried to dismiss the idea that maybe she really was going crazy.

She leaned back in her chair and gazed up at the ceiling. Finally, she brought her attention back to her computer screen, put her hands on the keyboard, and typed in the address for their credit card company. She pressed her lips together as the home page came up on the screen. Her mind drifted to the little book of passwords next to her computer at home. After typing in her log-in information, she focused on the screen as her account loaded.

She scanned the current statement: Bryan's work lunches, gas, grocery store charges, her lunch with Jules. As she scanned through the plethora of charges, she drew in a deep breath.

There, listed indisputably on their bill, was a charge for Duffy's Department Store for $267.93. As she stared at the screen, she exhaled in a series of short breaths. When she asked Bryan, he didn't seem to know anything about the dresses, so he hadn't bought them. She didn't even need to mentally calculate the price tags on them to know this was the charge that proved, despite no recollection whatsoever, she was the one who had bought those dresses. And then a sobering thought hit her. Maybe she bought the bears too.

Not knowing exactly where they had been purchased, she scrutinized the bill again for any charge that might potentially fit. She studied the charges on the statement one by one, trying to account for each item on their bill.

Her cell phone buzzed next to her, pulling her attention from the computer. She glanced down at the caller ID but didn't recognize the number. Her pulse quickened. Maybe it was someone about the cat.

"Becky?" the voice asked when she answered. "Becky, this is Brenda from Dr. Levine's office."

She had expected to hear someone asking about Sherlock. The voice sounded familiar, and Becky's forehead creased in confusion. "I'm sorry, who did you say this was?"

"It's Brenda from Dr. Levine's office. Sorry, I'm new. We've been having phone issues today, so sorry if I've confused you." The voice paused. "Unfortunately, I need to cancel your appointment tomorrow."

Every muscle in Becky's body went rigid. "I don't—I don't understand." Her heart suddenly started doing backflips in her chest. If she didn't have an appointment tomorrow, they wouldn't be able to transfer the embryo. Maybe this girl had her confused with someone else. Or maybe they had decided to let her embryo grow an extra day and were moving her appointment to Wednesday.

"They called me this morning with my appointment for tomorrow," Becky said. "I'm having my embryo transfer at 10:30. Are they moving my appointment time?" Maybe they were just moving it. She begged silently for the new girl to say she had made a mistake.

"This is Becky Morgan, right?" Brenda asked. "No, they're not moving it. It's canceled. I have the notes from your file right here. Your embryos arrested so there's nothing to transfer tomorrow, which is why I need to cancel."

"Wait, what?" Bile inched up into her throat. This woman was just confused. "No, no. They left me a message this morning. Three of my embryos did arrest *yesterday,* but I have three left. She told me they looked good. She scheduled the appointment for 10:30 tomorrow morning."

"Uh, huh. I see that in your file. Three arrested yesterday, and the other three arrested this morning." Brenda paused. "These things happen sometimes. Usually, it's some sort of genetic issue. Even if you had transferred them, they probably wouldn't have survived."

Becky felt like she was listening through a wind tunnel, trying to snatch hold of the words to make sense of what they meant. She gasped for air. "So, what you are saying to me is I have no embryos at all? None? I had three good ones when she called this morning!"

Becky felt like she was falling, spiraling down into a dark hole. "How could they all die? How? How could that happen?"

"I'm not sure," Brenda said, her clipped tone indicating she was getting irritated. "They just told me to call and cancel your appointment. That's all I know."

Becky struggled to speak. "Okay, I need to talk to Dr. Levine. I need to talk to him *right now*."

Brenda hesitated. "I'm sorry. He's out of town. Family emergency."

Becky's face contorted. She couldn't possibly have heard that right. "Then how the hell was he going to do my procedure tomorrow?" If she had eaten anything for breakfast, it would be sitting in a pile on the floor right now.

"He has someone very competent covering his procedures. Dr. Levine didn't expect to be out of town, but he had a death in his family. He does usually schedule a follow-up appointment so you can go through this cycle and talk about how you want to move forward. Would you like me to set that up for you? I have May tenth at 10 am. Does that work?"

Anger brought Becky out of her chair. "That's over two weeks away!"

"I know. That's all I have. I can let you know if there's a cancellation."

Becky's mind was racing. She felt like she was standing in quicksand. Moving forward seemed impossible. She let out a loud, frustrated groan. "Fine," she said through gritted teeth.

"Okay, so I have you scheduled for a follow-up appointment," Brenda said matter-of-factly. "May tenth at—"

Becky disconnected the call. It was over. There was no need to say goodbye.

As the chill of disbelief coursed through her, she stood frozen. Her legs finally refused to hold her any longer, and she wilted to the floor. She felt her phone slip from her hand and only vaguely heard the sound as it hit the floor. All those shots for nothing. Her pulverized dream of having a baby, of Bryan being a father, emerged from her throat in a series of guttural wails that echoed off the office walls. Torrents of tears threatened to drown her with her own sadness.

The sound of Tonya's heels clattered toward her until they stopped. She put her arm around Becky's neck and leaned into her. "Beck, breathe. Tell me what happened. Is Bryan okay? Who was that on the phone?"

"It's over." Becky moaned like a wounded animal. The words came out in spurts. "No baby—no embryos—appointment canceled—start all over—"

From above her, she heard Tonya's voice filled with panic as she spewed out the words, "You need to come to the boutique as soon as possible. Hurry!"

CHAPTER TWENTY-EIGHT

Bryan

Bryan tucked a blanket around Becky and pushed her hair off her face. She had finally fallen asleep, but even as she slept, sadness was etched on her face.

The frantic call from Tonya had taken him right back to the way he felt the night of the accident. He could hear Becky sobbing, moaning in the background. He had just packed up his desk and flown out the door.

After squealing into the employee parking lot, he parked at the curb. Then he'd yanked open the back door, scanning the area for an explanation for Tonya's call. His wife was on the floor, her body curled up in the fetal position next to her desk.

Confused, he rushed over and knelt beside her. "Beck, are you okay?"

She looked up at him, her face splotchy and stained with tears. She opened her mouth, but only a soft, strangled noise escaped. Her body slumped back down.

Bryan's gaze flew to Tonya. "Tonya, what the hell happened?"

Tonya leaned in and lowered her voice. "Best I could understand, it had something to do with her transfer tomorrow. I think they called to cancel it."

Bryan frowned and shook his head. "I don't understand. She sent me a text this morning. We still had three embryos, and they made the appointment for the transfer tomorrow morning."

"She told me the same thing when she came in. Apparently, after they made the appointment, the three embryos didn't make it."

"Oh," he said, his voice barely above a whisper. "So, none of them made it?" He ran his fingers through his hair and gripped the side of his head as he tried to process this. His eyes glistened as the source of his wife's anguish became clear.

He knelt next to her, but she didn't turn her head, didn't face him. Her face was buried in the crook of her arm as she stared vacantly at the dirty floor.

"Beck, I know this is devastating. It is for me too. I love you. I love you more than anything. We'll get through this." He went to gather her in his arms, but her body stiffened. "C'mon, babe, let me take you home."

He put his arm underneath her so she could lean on him as he lifted her off the floor, but her form went limp. Even without her cooperation, her size was no battle for him. He held her up against him in a standing position.

Tonya moved awkwardly in the small space. "Here, let me help." She picked up Becky's cell phone from the floor, stuck it in her purse, and put the strap over Bryan's free arm.

"I'm so sorry," Tonya said in a soft voice as she opened the back door.

Bryan held his wife up so she could walk to the car. It would have been easier just to carry her. As he folded her into the front seat, he glimpsed Tonya still standing in the open doorway.

"Thank you," he mouthed to her.

He tried to talk to Becky while he drove, but she said nothing. It was as if her grief had swallowed her ability to speak. She had withdrawn into a shell she had placed around herself, and it was clear no one, not even him, was allowed in.

She trudged on her own into the house before Bryan had even made his way out of the car.

She turned toward him as he walked through the door, swollen eyes set in a pale face stained with tears and makeup. "Any news on Sherlock?" she asked, her voice soft and hesitant as if she didn't really expect there to be good news. "Did anyone call from the flyer?"

Bryan choked out the words, and they broke his heart to have to say them. "No. No calls."

She walked over to the sliding glass door, unlocked it, and slid it open. She glanced outside and then slid the door closed. "I probably didn't deserve to have a baby. I couldn't even keep my cat safe."

"Don't say that. He'll be back, and one has nothing to do with the other. Come here." He reached his arms out toward her.

Becky didn't move. She glanced at the scorched cabinet covered in the foam she had sprayed to extinguish the flames. "Oh, and there was a fire." Her voice was flat and emotionless.

Bryan dipped his head. "I noticed that." She had tried to clean it up, but the fire extinguisher still sat leaned up against the table, and one of the cabinets would need to be replaced. This wasn't the time to ask what had happened. "As long as you're okay, that's all that matters." Bryan walked toward her. If she wouldn't come to him, he would go to her.

He tried to hug her, but she broke free and wandered aimlessly through the house as if she had no idea what she was supposed to do or where she could go to escape her pain.

She finally collapsed on the couch, staring blindly at her hands. Occasionally tears would trickle from her eyes and down her cheeks until they dripped from her chin into her lap. He watched as she sat, her eyes glazed as if she had succumbed to a trance. He watched as her chest rose and fell. She blinked, and her body was there. But the rest of her? He had no idea where she had gone, but she wasn't there with him.

His fists balled up by his sides, he fought back the urge to take his frustration out against the wall. Bryan was hardwired to fix things. He hadn't a clue how to make this better for her. He sat on the chair in the living room, slumped over with his head in his hands.

Finally, he spoke, his voice breaking through the stagnant silence. "You must be hungry. I can make you something."

"I can't eat." Her voice was barely above a whisper, and her face twisted as if she had been punched in the gut and the pain hadn't subsided.

She stood and stumbled wearily into the bedroom and fell onto the bed. She tugged a blanket over her and laid her head down. He sat down next to her and watched as the tears rolled sideways down her cheeks and soaked her pillow. Her eyes heavy, she looked up at him. "I'm sure it was my fault. It had to be my eggs or maybe something I didn't do right with the hormones."

"It is not your fault." His voice softened. "This process isn't foolproof. No one gets a guarantee."

"Maybe I shouldn't have had coffee, and I was too stressed about everything." She was blubbering. "I got into the accident and had that CT scan. Maybe that was bad for my eggs, and now because of me, you don't get to be a father. It's all my fault. I'm so sorry I let you down. Bryan, I'm so sorry." She cried until her nose was so stuffy she could no longer breathe through it, and she resorted to gulping air through her mouth.

He rubbed her shoulder. "You did nothing wrong. We'll figure out where we go from here, but don't you for one second think this is your fault."

She laid there staring blankly at the wall as she placed her cheek back down on the dampened pillowcase. Her eyes fluttered as Bryan stroked her hair. Within a few minutes, her emotions had worn her into submission and sleep allowed her a brief respite from her sadness.

He kissed her cheek as she lay sleeping, her tears staining his lips. He slid off the bed quietly and shut the bedroom door gently behind him. He found his phone and collapsed onto the couch to call Tonya.

She answered his call on the first ring and didn't even say hello. She let out a deep breath as if she had been holding it since they had walked out the back door hours earlier. "How is she?"

"It's not good. I wish I had better news. It's like she's in her own little world about this and she won't let me in at all. She feels like she's to blame, that maybe she did something wrong."

"Oh, Bryan, I'm so sorry. She's wanted this for so long, and I know she felt like she was so close. It's got to be hard to know she has to start all over again. And I'm sure all those hormones flowing through her system aren't making this any easier. To be honest, she's been acting a little off at work lately. Don't take any of this personally."

Bryan let out his frustration in one deep breath. "I know. I'm trying. It just breaks my heart to see her like this and know there's nothing I can do to fix how she feels. I'm not sure if she'll be in tomorrow or not. Are you good at the store if she's not up to it?"

"Of course. Michelle has turned out to be a godsend. She's looking for more hours, so we'll be fine. I just want Becky to feel better, so don't worry about the store at all."

Bryan hung up and sat on the couch, staring into space much the way Becky had done earlier. He couldn't believe the excitement of the last week had now left them in such emotional torment. Would it have been worse if they had done the transfer and then the embryo didn't implant successfully? Both were equally crushing, he decided. The result was the same. There would be no baby.

Yes, this was heartbreaking, but he had faith they would find their way back to try again. Right now, he needed to hold on to that belief with both hands.

He looked down at the time on his phone. It wasn't that late, but he didn't have the strength to call and tell his parents or his brother yet. The bad news would have to wait. He forced himself to his feet, turned out all the lights, and quietly crawled into bed next to his sleeping wife.

CHAPTER TWENTY-NINE

Becky

Becky was awake, but everything seemed fuzzy. She tried to swallow, to run her tongue over her teeth, but they felt coated with a dry grit. Her eyes wouldn't open completely, her swollen lids refusing to cooperate. The tears and the call from the doctor's office all came rushing back to her. So much for waking up from this nightmare.

She propped herself up on her elbow and peered out through the narrow slits. Like looking through a windowpane smeared with dirt, she could make out Bryan staring at her.

"Do you want me to get you an ice pack?" he asked. "See if you can bring the swelling down a little so you can see?"

"Don't bother." She let her eyes close, and mercifully, the darkness returned. She laid her head back down, but she could still hear Bryan's voice.

"I can bring you coffee. I already made it."

She didn't even open her eyes. "No thanks. Can you call Tonya and tell her I'm not coming in to work?"

"Sure. I can stay home today with you."

"You don't need to stay home."

"Beck …" He hesitated. "Do you want me to call Jules?"

"I don't want to talk to anyone." Jules had left several messages. Becky hadn't called her back because she couldn't bear to have to tell her the news. Part of her was even irrationally resentful of that stupid family tree she had wanted to do. Maybe it had still been bad luck even though she hadn't done it. Or maybe Anna really had cursed her with bad karma. She wanted to find somewhere to place the blame because right now the burden felt like a weighted vest she couldn't take off.

"I'll have Dave help me so I can get your car back home from the boutique."

It wasn't like she needed her car. She wasn't leaving the bed. It would take effort she didn't have to explain that to him, so she simply muttered, "Okay."

Bryan sat down on the bed next to her. "Babe, I don't want to leave you like this."

"There's nothing you can do to change it. Just go to work."

Bryan exhaled and ran his fingers through his hair. "Okay, if you're sure you'll be okay, maybe the distraction will be good. Keep my mind off everything."

Becky flinched, and her eyes were like small slits in her face as she shot him a withering stare. "How nice for you." She rolled over on her side. "I'm going back to sleep."

"Beck …" His voice drifted off as if he didn't know how to respond. She could feel him hovering over her, hesitating, barely breathing. Finally, he kissed her gently on the top of her head, and then she heard the barely audible click of the door closing behind him.

***

Becky rolled over as sunlight streamed into the bedroom and roused her from the comforting cocoon of oblivious sleep. Disoriented, her hand reached for the other side of the bed and patted Bryan's side. Empty. Glowing red numbers on the alarm clock told her it was ten-forty. They should be at the doctor's office right now, having their embryo transferred. She had dared to hope she'd sleep through that reminder.

She got up and stumbled to her desk. After unplugging the power cord from her laptop, she brought it back into the bed.

She propped her pillow up against the headboard and leaned on it. With the laptop across her thighs, she logged in. She searched "embryos arrest day four" and waited for the results. It wasn't that common, but it could happen. She wasn't the only one. One poor woman had gone for her transfer appointment only to have the doctor tell her after they prepped her for the procedure that they were all gone. That would have been an even worse kind of hell.

She scanned the results, leaned back, and closed her eyes. It wasn't like it mattered anymore. Nothing she could do would bring them back. She had accepted that the first three didn't make it. They had warned her. But the other three were real. They were one day away from being nestled inside her, growing. In her mind, those were her babies just waiting for nature to let them become what they were destined to be.

She shut the laptop and tossed it next to her on the bed, then closed her eyes, turned on her side, and went back to sleep.

As she stirred for the third time, or maybe the fourth, she glanced out the window. The view of the sky, an orange and purple haze painted on the horizon, told her the sun was going down. This day, the day she had marked worthlessly as important on the calendar, would finally be over.

CHAPTER THIRTY

Jules

Jules inserted her key into the front door and pushed it open. From above her on the second floor, her mother's voice echoed down the wooden staircase to the entryway. "Julianne, that you?"

"Yeah, Ma," she said as she closed the door behind her and then made her way up the stairs.

"You're back sooner than I expected." The older woman closed the paperback book she had been reading and tossed it on the coffee table.

"Yeah, I know." Jules threw her bag on the kitchen table. "Can you believe my appointment didn't even show?"

Jules always met new clients in a public place instead of her home office. Her parents had expressed concern when she decided to set up the studio in her house. They didn't like strangers coming in and out. Most of her clients were lovely, and she had no problem with them coming to her home. But until she met them, she always went with better safe than sorry.

Her mother's softly wrinkled face frowned in confusion. "Really? That's odd. Wasn't this the woman who absolutely had to have you shoot her baby shower?"

"That's what I thought. I went to the address she gave me. It was an office building, not a coffee shop. I even listened to her message again in the car to make sure I'd written it down right. Drove up and down the street. Thought maybe she had just given me the wrong number. There was no coffee shop anywhere that I could find. So I came home."

"Did you try calling her?"

"Yeah, I tried calling her, but it just rang and rang. No answer, no voicemail. No nothing. She'll need to find a new photographer for her shower." A tinge of aggravation had crept into her voice. "I mean, really, that was a long drive for nothing. The whole thing was kind of rude."

Jules tried to reel in her frustration. Her crankiness was aimed at the woman who sent her on the wild goose hunt, not her mom. The search for her birth parents had already left an undercurrent of uncertainty when they were together. It hurt. They had always gotten along, so to know the awkwardness was because of her was painful. She didn't want it to seem like her search was changing anything between them. That would prove her mother's worry was valid.

Jules had ordered a new bed, and while she loved the setup of her place, most delivery men outwardly groaned when they eyed both sets of narrow stairs. Jules always tipped them well to compensate for the hassle. The money she had left for this purpose still sat folded up on the kitchen table.

"It doesn't look like they've been here with the new bed."

Jules's mom shook her head and glanced at her watch. "No, but they still have a couple of hours left in the window they gave you." She fluffed her short silver hair and struggled to get off of the couch. "This couch always swallows me up, I swear."

Jules extended her hand and her mother gladly accepted the assistance. Once she was upright and steady on both feet, her mom trotted off to the kitchen. She called back over her shoulder. "Can I make you something for lunch before I go?"

A smile tugged at Jules's lips. Her mom was amazing, and she adored her. How could she even be looking for her birth mother when she knew it was hurting her?

"No, thanks, Mom. I got something on my way back. But help yourself if you want something."

"Thanks, sweetie. I made coffee when I got here. Since you're back, I think I'll go meet up with your father."

"Oh. You're leaving already?" Her mom had pulled in just before Jules left. They hadn't had much time together.

"Well, your dad wanted to go look for a new dishwasher today. I think ours is on its last legs. The last thing I want to do is go back to washing dishes by hand."

Jules didn't cook much, so there was never much in the way of dirty dishes at her house. Maybe if she had somebody to eat with, it would be different. Cooking for one seemed unnecessary and a reminder that she was single and alone.

"Well, thanks for coming over. I didn't want to reschedule the delivery, and it seemed like that appointment would have led to a good job. That woman just called last night. It seems weird she could have forgotten in that short amount of time, especially when she made it seem so important."

Jules's mom patted her daughter on the arm. "Oh, well, what can you do? Besides, it's her loss. She won't find a photographer as good as you."

They hugged goodbye, and Jules held her mother just a beat longer than usual before kissing her soft cheek. The door creaked on the first level as her mom made it to the bottom, and Jules heard the deadbolt turn as she used her key to lock the door.

She grabbed a Diet Coke from the refrigerator and popped the top. The fizz sprayed the bottom of her nose as she took a long sip. She swiped at the dampness with the back of her hand while she tried to shake the aggravation of the missed appointment. Such a waste of time. She pulled out a chair at the kitchen table and plopped down.

She noticed her mom hadn't said a word about her DNA search. Her parents had always been there for her, and they'd been part of all the big decisions in her life. This one felt like something they didn't want to know anything about.

She retrieved her laptop from her tote bag. After checking her email, she scowled. Still nothing from the mystery match. Damn. She had no way of figuring out who Lucy16 was if she didn't respond to Jules's messages. It was frustrating. Her mystery relative just seemed to be ignoring her.

She glanced at her DNA matches. There was nothing new. Jules clicked on the matches she had in common with the mystery relative. So far, she hadn't been able to find the link between this woman's tree and any of the other shared matches.

Since the first results had yielded nothing she could use yet, she had been waiting for one of the other two companies to deliver her matches. Day after day, she had checked and found nothing. Today, as she checked one of the other sites, there it was. Her results were ready. Holding her breath, she clicked on the tab with her DNA matches.

Eyes narrowing, she scanned the page, finally focusing on the names at the top of the list—her closest matches. She exhaled in stuttered breaths and blinked hard. "Well, I'll be damned."

She had hit genetic paydirt.

CHAPTER THIRTY-ONE

Bryan

Bryan stared at the kitchen clock, obsessed with watching the minutes tick. She had to be home soon. Pulling open the oven door, he checked on dinner. The baked ziti and meatballs were starting to bubble, the aroma of marinara sauce and Italian spices filling the kitchen—her favorite.

It had taken a few days, but Becky had finally consented to go back to work. She was going through the motions, but the wall she had put up was still firmly in place. Right now, he felt like a stranger looking in at his life. He wanted his wife back.

He needed someone to talk to that could help him try to understand. "Hey, Mom," he said when she answered.

"Hey, buddy, how're you doing? How's Becky?"

Bryan had given them the news that the embryo transfer wasn't happening, but the call had been brief. The anticipation of the transfer date to the pits of despair had occurred at warp speed.

He rubbed his eyes with his fingers while he spoke. "I don't know, Mom. I think my wife disappeared the day the embryos did."

"The wife you love is still in there," his mom said with conviction. "Right now, the grief is so thick; she can't see through it. Just be patient."

"But I'm hurting too!" His frustration was evident in his voice. "Why aren't we leaning on each other? When did I become the enemy?"

"I know you're sad too, Bryan. But for women, that biological urge to have a child can be overwhelming. Men and women grieve differently. Give her time. You're *not* the enemy, honey."

"It sure feels like I am. It's like she just *wants* to be miserable. Don't we eventually have to try to go back to our old life? I mean, seriously, Mom, it feels like that may never happen."

"I know it feels like that now. She'll find her way back to you. What about the cat?"

Bryan shook his head as he answered. "Nothing. That's another thing. How does Sherlock just disappear into thin air?"

Bryan's mother exhaled loudly. "It certainly doesn't seem fair. Poor girl."

"Maybe I should—" He paused, and in the momentary silence, a metallic click came from the front door. "Mom, she's home. I gotta go. Thanks for listening."

"Your dad and I love you. Hang in there."

Bryan headed into the living room to greet Becky. Her face was emotionless.

"Hey," he said in a soft voice. "I made dinner. I just have to melt a little cheese on top."

She shook her head. "I'm not hungry."

"Nope. Not gonna happen, Beck. You have to eat." He offered her a tentative smile. "You love my ziti and meatballs." He took her by the arm and led her to the kitchen table. "Sit."

He grabbed the bag of shredded mozzarella from the fridge and glanced over his shoulder to make sure she didn't escape. A quick look down to pour a generous amount of cheese on top, and he turned his attention back on Becky.

She sat slumped in her chair, elbows on the table, her head resting in her hands.

"Just needs a couple of minutes and we'll be ready," he said.

Once he presented dinner, her fork dragged the pasta around, leaving artistic streaks of marinara sauce on the white ceramic plate. The usual enthusiasm with which she attacked her favorite pasta dish was absent.

"So," he said, his tone casual as he speared ziti on his fork, "how was work?"

She stared down at her food. "Fine."

"I'm sure Tonya's happy to have you back."

A tenuous shrug. "I guess."

The nerves under his skin tingled with frustration. He didn't know how to break through, but he wasn't giving up. "Have you talked to Jules? Any idea how the DNA hunt is going?"

"Haven't talked to her. Don't know."

He lifted an eyebrow. Becky told her best friend everything. Apparently, she wasn't letting Jules help her either. He watched as his wife moved the food in a circular pattern on her plate. "Beck," he said, his voice soft. "At least eat a little."

She took a small hesitant bite as if the food might poison her.

Becky hadn't wanted to talk about the IVF at all, but that wasn't helping.

"Have you talked to Dr. Levine?" he asked.

She brought her gaze up from her plate and met his eyes. "Nope. I'm not sure he's even supposed to be calling me."

Bryan frowned. "What? Beck, call *him*."

"He had a family emergency. They said he was out of town. If I want to ask him anything, I can do it on the tenth."

A puzzled look crossed Bryan's face. "What does that mean? May tenth?"

"When they canceled my transfer, she set up a follow-up appointment on May tenth. I Googled some stuff. Apparently, that's our WTF appointment. As in what the fuck happened to our embryos." Her tone was bitter.

He studied his wife, hurt that she hadn't told him any of this. "Why didn't you tell me they set that up?"

"Because I'm not sure I'm going." Her eyes became wet. "I don't know if I can go through this again. And I don't know if I can go through it with that office."

"Beck—" Bryan's voice softened.

"I trusted them with our dream to have a baby, and no one even had the decency to call and say they were sorry." Becky pursed her lips. "I guess I have to wait two weeks for that."

"Why don't you call Kim? You liked her. Maybe she can help tell you what happened."

Becky shook her head. "She doesn't know the first thing about what happens in the lab, and I've realized I'm just another patient to them. They don't—" She paused. "I looked online. That woman on the phone was right. These things do happen sometimes. It just sucks that it happened to us."

She wiped away tears. "Besides, does it even matter why it happened? Maybe it was my eggs. Maybe it was your sperm. Maybe it was just fate telling us we weren't meant to have a baby." She pushed her plate away. "I really can't eat anymore. I need to go change."

Bryan stared at her back as he watched her leave. Of course it mattered *why* it happened. If they could figure that out, maybe they could fix it for next time. Had she been serious when she said she wasn't up to a next time? What about what *he* wanted?

He cleaned up the kitchen after the dinner she had barely touched. They couldn't go on this way. Her refusal to let him in so he could help her had to stop. He'd hold her until she stopped fighting him and accepted they were on the same side.

As he entered the dimly lit bedroom, he made out her shape huddled under the covers. Without a word to him, she had gone to bed. He tilted his head, and in the stillness, her soft, even breathing told him she was asleep.

Through the small opening in the curtains, he noted the last rays of sunlight falling behind the trees. It wasn't even dark out yet.

There had never been a time in their relationship he didn't feel they were deeply connected, but now she only seemed to care about how she felt, how much she was suffering. She had wanted to do the IVF. Now that it hadn't worked, she got to decide they were done? She got to decide whether they got answers about why it didn't work? There were two of them in this relationship.

At the moment, it didn't feel that way.

CHAPTER THIRTY-TWO

Becky

Mornings were a special kind of hell. Sleep let her forget but waking up brought Becky's reality crashing back over her. As she shuffled into the kitchen, Bryan grabbed his coffee and chugged it. It was almost as if he'd be within his rights to leave for work if his mug were empty.

She passed by him and made her way over to the sliding glass door and slid it open. Day after day, the scene on the porch was the same, like a vacant ghost town deserted of any evidence of life. Even her plants had finally withered up from neglect, leaving their brown dried up leaves in a haphazard circle of death around them. She forcefully slid the door closed. Bryan flinched as the uncomfortable thud of metal on metal cut through the silence in the kitchen.

She stomped toward the table where he was sitting, collapsing into one of the chairs with a defeated groan. She needed her husband to tell her this would all be okay. Instead, he said nothing.

She glared at him and scowled. "He could still come back, you know. I'm not giving up on him."

Finally, Bryan spoke, but the words weren't what she expected to hear, what she *needed* for him to say. "Listen, Beck, I was thinking, if you want to get another cat, you know it's okay with me. We can go to the shelter and look to see if they have any kittens."

The words stung as if he'd slapped her and told her Sherlock was dead in a ditch somewhere. "I should forget he existed and move on? Replace him? Just because you hated him?"

He pressed his lips together and hesitated before he responded. "That's not fair, Becky. I didn't hate your cat, but the disinterest was mutual. I knew you loved him, and that was good enough for me. I'm not saying I hope he doesn't come back, but if he doesn't, all I'm saying is when you're ready—"

She looked at the floor and then brought her gaze back up to meet his, her eyes cold and unflinching. "Maybe you'll be ready to give up on me soon too. Find a new wife. One that can give you a baby."

No sooner were the words out of her mouth, she wanted to snatch them back. The words of self-pity she'd been thinking had escaped like a round of arrows aimed at Bryan. She had crossed a line.

His face froze in a grimace, and then he erupted. "I just want whatever it's gonna take to make you feel better. I couldn't give you the baby you wanted, and I don't know where your damn cat is hiding. I'm just grasping at straws here. Forgive me for trying to help my wife find her way back to any sort of happiness."

The legs of his chair scraped angrily against the floor as he forced his chair back from the table and stood up. He whipped his coffee mug at the sink, the sound of ceramic smashing into pieces as it collided with the stainless steel.

He lunged for his briefcase. "I'm going to work." He set his jaw as he snatched up his phone from the table. "Yeah, I know. That makes me a horrible person too."

The harsh sound of the front door slamming rang loudly in her ears. Becky sat rigid at the kitchen table and tried to catch her breath. Bryan wasn't the enemy, but she wanted to strike out for the injustice of what had happened. Her poor husband hadn't done anything wrong. He was just the closest target, and she had lashed out at him. At that moment, she despised the weakness and anger that now lived inside her. She hated how she was hurting him.

Even though she knew she should have chased after him and apologized, she felt paralyzed. She didn't know if she could express regret for feeling he could have what he wanted with someone else. It was true. She had failed him as a wife.

Rocking back and forth in her chair, Becky's emotions swirled around her like a tornado picking up speed. The baby they wouldn't have, Sherlock frightened and hungry wondering why she wasn't saving him, the deep-seated fear that she and Bryan might not survive this.

Her sobs crested over her like white-capped waves in a storm. She couldn't breathe. It felt like she was drowning.

CHAPTER THIRTY-THREE

Becky

Becky peeled the post-it off the counter. Bryan had left it right next to the coffee maker where he knew she'd see it. A piece of yellow sticky paper to explain why she woke up and her husband was already gone. *Went to gym.* No heart. No smiley face. No term of endearment. He didn't even sign it—just a note with three words.

He hadn't even woken her up when he left. She wasn't sure she blamed him.

Their fight yesterday morning had been awful. They had both awkwardly dismissed it when they came home from work, but it was clear they were wounding each other in new ways daily. It was her fault, she knew that.

The deep depression she felt over the failed IVF was an emotional straitjacket she couldn't get out of no matter how much she twisted and turned. She hadn't told anyone the news. Not Jules. Not her mother. Becky knew she had to face reality, but the pain was still so raw. Saying the words out loud would make them real.

She slugged down the remnants of her coffee and placed the cup in the sink. The container with Sherlock's food still sat on the top of the refrigerator. They hadn't moved his bowl from the porch, but it had finally been discovered by a trail of ants. Was he—she couldn't even consider that something might have happened to him.

No one understood her attachment to him. Bryan tolerated him, but she'd been harsh when she accused him of hating Sherlock. That hadn't been fair. The idea that he was outside somewhere, scared to death and wondering what had happened ... If there were anything left in her heart to crush, this would have crumbled it like dust.

Mrs. Ritter's basket still sat on the kitchen counter, the banana muffins long gone. Becky scooped up the basket by the handle and headed across the street.

As Becky pushed the button for the bell, she heard the chime inside the house announcing her. After a moment, the sound of quick footsteps grew louder as they approached the door and it swung open.

"Oh, Becky, dear, come in." The older woman had a watering can in her hand. "I'm just watering the flowers on the back deck. Come on, follow me back. Everything's starting to bloom, and it's all just so pretty."

She followed Mrs. Ritter through the tidy house and out the back door. She was right. The backyard had exploded in color like nature had flung a painter's palette of bright, vibrant hues over everything. Becky soaked it in, but the cheerful blooms did nothing to improve her mood.

Mrs. Ritter glanced over at Becky as she put the muffin basket on the patio table. "How are you these days?" she asked as she bent over to water hot pink inpatients in a colorful ceramic pot.

"Not too good." Tears welled up in Becky's eyes and slid down her cheeks.

The waterworks caught Mrs. Ritter by surprise. "Oh, you poor thing, sit down." She pointed toward one of the patio chairs. Becky obliged and sunk sadly into the cushion.

Mrs. Ritter put the watering can down and sat across from her. "What's wrong, honey?"

Becky sniffled. "What isn't wrong?"

"You haven't found your cat yet, I presume?"

"No, and Sherlock is just the tip of the horrible iceberg. I feel like I'm going crazy and taking it out on everyone around me." The time had come to let the words out. She swallowed hard. "The IVF—well, it didn't work. We didn't even get to the appointment where they were going to transfer the embryo. The embryos didn't make it." Becky looked down at her hands, wondering if the lump if her throat would let her continue. "None of them made it."

Mrs. Ritter flinched, but she sat silent.

Becky looked up at her, her eyes betraying the deep sense of loss that had broken her spirit. "I know Bryan is hurting too, and I know he wants to comfort me, but I don't seem to know how to let him do that. I just feel like a big failure, and now I feel like we're falling apart."

Mrs. Ritter met her eyes with concern etched on her face. "So, what do you think you will do next?"

Becky shifted in her seat. "What do you mean? You mean, will we do IVF again?"

"Well, dear, first I think you and Bryan need to reconnect. You may have lost your way, but I have faith you can find your way back. You both just need to put the focus back on the love you share. Then together you can deal with this loss and decide if you want to try again."

Becky's voice trembled. "I'm scared to death to do IVF again, but I'm more scared for us *not* to be parents. I don't know if I can go my whole life without kids, and you know Bryan would be just the best dad ever. How could I do that to him? I know he loves me, but am I enough? Could I ever be enough if we couldn't have kids?"

The older woman offered a reassuring smile. "You need to have faith that things will work out for you and Bryan. You love each other."

"I tried to have faith in the IVF, but that didn't get me anywhere."

"Your story isn't finished, dear. I know it's not." Mrs. Ritter hesitated. "The world has a funny way of making it all work out the way it's supposed to. Sometimes, in an instant, everything changes. Don't give up just yet, honey."

Becky shrugged off her cardigan. The sun grew warmer as it rose in the sky, and the conversation was making her sweat. "I'm glad I came over this morning. You've given me a lot to think about." She stood and hugged Mrs. Ritter. She was glad she had decided to confide in her. This kind of conversation didn't seem possible with her mom anymore. "I'm so happy we moved into the house across the street from you."

The older woman stepped back and smiled warmly at Becky. "I am too. What would I do without you kids?"

Becky glanced at her watch. "Oh, wow, it's later than I thought. I need to get going."

"One more thing, dear. I wouldn't give up on Sherlock just yet. I have a feeling he'll find his way back too. Maybe I'll get some food and put it around here to see if he's lost on my side of the street."

"I hope you're right. I could really use my little buddy to cheer me up."

CHAPTER THIRTY-FOUR

Jules

Something was wrong. Jules just knew it. Her messages to Becky had gone unreturned. They both got busy, but something in her gut told her this was more than just the usual chaos. Becky had been dreading the two-week wait after the embryo transfer, but not calling back for days wasn't like her. Jules said a silent prayer it had gone well.

She pulled her car into the lot and parked and then dialed Becky's number. When she heard the beep yet again, she let out a frustrated groan before leaving a message. *Okay, I'm starting to get a little nervous about you. I'm meeting clients at The Mayfair on Palm and Magnolia. Can you sneak away to meet me for lunch at the deli across the street? I should be done by noon.* Jules paused. *I miss you. Hope everything is okay.*

The young couple Jules was meeting was waiting by the gazebo. "This light coming through the trees is going to be incredible for your photos," Jules said as she made her way down the brick path leading to the couple.

Becky had once asked her if it bothered her to shoot weddings. Jules took in Doreen and Chris, the young couple beaming in front of her. If anything, they gave her hope that people could find true love.

She went through the shot list for the wedding day with them. Photos before the ceremony. Family pictures after. She'd do the staged photos everyone expected, but at times, she'd fade into the background to capture the moments that usually went unseen by the bride and groom.

"Will you be doing all the traditional stuff? Cutting of the cake?" Jules glanced up from her list.

Doreen laughed. "We want to do the cutting of the cake. Chris has already been warned that my gown cost a fortune, so I'd better not be wearing any frosting after the groom feeds the bride."

Chris took her hand in his and looked at Jules. "Happy wife, happy life. Isn't that what they say?" He leaned over and kissed his bride-to-be.

"So I've heard," Jules said. "What about the bouquet toss and garter?"

The couple exchanged a glance.

"We want all the traditional stuff, though my grandmother will be at the wedding, so Chris won't be taking off my garter with his teeth. Well, not at the wedding anyway ..." Doreen offered a mischievous smile. "I have tons of single friends. The bouquet toss is a definite."

Jules nodded and scribbled herself a note as she recalled Becky and Bryan's wedding.

Becky had made her way to the stage and coerced the microphone away from the lead singer of the band. "Jules Dalton?" she called out, her voice demanding as her eyes scanned through the guests in the room. No official announcement. She hadn't even bothered to line up the single women at the wedding. As Jules looked up, her best friend's bouquet had come flying at her like a fragrant torpedo.

So far, it hadn't helped Jules's cause to get down the aisle herself, but she kept the flowers bound in ribbon as a dried-up beacon of hope. Her time would come. Someday there would be a man who wanted to stand at an altar for her. He'd wait, his eyes lit up with anticipation, as she made her way to him in a spectacular white gown. She might have had that with Tim, but she had messed it up. She hadn't heard anything after the night at the restaurant. It was clear he had moved on.

When she had all the information she needed and had taken some test shots, she hugged the bride and groom goodbye. "Your day will be beautiful, and I'll make sure you have the pictures to remember every minute of it."

"So much planning for one day. I've been on a diet for months just to get into my dress." Doreen looked over at Jules. "You must have been a beautiful bride."

Jules shrugged and pointed at her ring finger. "Not married. And unfortunately, very single."

A crimson flush appeared on Doreen's face. "Oh, I'm sorry. I didn't mean ..." She turned toward her groom-to-be. "Hon, you must know someone we can set up with Jules. Do you have any friends good enough for her? I mean, we need someone nice and handsome and—"

Jules held up her hand. "It's fine. I had a chance to get to the altar once, but it just wasn't meant to be." She offered a wistful smile. "Now I realize I probably should have held on to that one a little tighter." She hugged Doreen again. "But next weekend is about the two of you, and I can't wait. I'll see you on Saturday morning, and we'll start capturing your special day with some beautiful pictures."

Jules turned and headed back down the path, angling her face toward the sunshine. It was a beautiful day, not too hot, and the sun felt delicious on her skin. She glanced at her car in the parking lot, then headed toward the road. No use moving her car when the deli was just across the street. She'd be right on time to meet Becky, and if she didn't show, Jules could at least get something for lunch to take home.

She reached into her purse and rustled through its contents for her phone. Relief flooded over her as she read Becky's text message that she was on her way. That nagging feeling still sat in the pit of her stomach. A little lunch to catch up and maybe she'd be reassured that her worry was unfounded.

As she stepped off the curb, she heard Doreen call out from behind her.

"Hey, Jules. One last thing."

Jules turned sharply and staggered onto the lawn, her ankle turning as her heel embedded itself in the soft grass. She groaned and glanced down at her brand-new sandal. "Ow." She looked back and saw Doreen's expression change in an instant, her eyes round and horrified as her hand flew to her mouth.

Jules's forehead creased in confusion. Doreen had just been happy and excited. She couldn't imagine what could have happened since she had left the couple only a few moments earlier. Jules followed Doreen's gaze as it went past her and up the road from where she was standing.

Jules hadn't noticed the car heading right for her.

CHAPTER THIRTY-FIVE

Becky

Guilt gnawed at Becky about the unreturned calls. Jules was her person. No demands. No expectations. She would just listen and try to help her feel better. There was too much pressure trying to talk to Bryan about how she felt. He just wanted her to be her old self, and Becky didn't have the faintest idea how to do that.

As she drove closer to the restaurant, her lips curved up into a smile at her perfect timing. In the distance, she could see that Jules was finished with her clients and getting ready to head across the street to the deli. As much as Becky didn't want to have to talk about the failed IVF, she let out a sigh of relief that the burden of telling her best friend would soon be lifted. She could already hear her friend's soft, comforting voice. "I'm here for whatever you need. That's what best friends are for."

Becky heard the car behind her accelerate, gunning it as it sped up and veered illegally around her. "What the hell?" This wasn't even an exceptionally busy road. In another moment, the driver would have had an open lane to go around her. As the car sped past, she didn't even have time to catch a glimpse of the person behind the wheel.

Becky's gaze fixed on her friend. Jules was looking down at her phone, no doubt reading Becky's text confirming she was on her way. In an instant, the horrific realization of what was about to happen hit her. Jules hadn't noticed anything was wrong. The car seemed to be aimed directly at her as she got ready to cross the street.

As the scene in front of her unfolded in slow motion, a blood-curdling howl rose from deep within Becky's throat, filling the inside of the car. "Oh my god, no!"

Time stood still. Becky gaped, mentally bracing herself for what seemed inevitable. Jules looked up and glanced behind her. She stumbled back onto the grass and out of the car's path. The air escaped Becky's lungs in a loud whoosh. She watched as the car tapped its brakes several feet from where Jules now stood and then screeched away.

Becky pulled her car to the curb right where the other vehicle had paused. Trembling, she slammed the gearshift into park and threw open the door. A young couple was already surrounding Jules, and Becky nudged her way in.

"What the hell were they thinking?" Becky grabbed Jules's arm. "Are you okay?"

Jules rubbed her ankle. "So, apparently, it took me almost getting wiped out by a car for you to return my calls."

Her friend's tone indicated she was joking, but relief flooded over Becky that she was okay. The rapid beating of her heart slowly returned to normal.

"I'm so sorry," Becky said. "I was coming for lunch. You have the text to prove it. Although, I thought I was going to watch you get mowed down. Jules, that was horrible."

The woman beside Jules nodded, her face still a mask of shock. "Right? It looked like that car was *trying* to hit her."

Jules pulled her shoe out of the grass and wiped at the dirt. "Probably some stupid kid texting and not paying attention. I'm fine, really. But damn, these are brand new Manolos." She slid her shoe back on her foot and pointed at the deli across the street as if nothing had happened. "Come on, let's eat. I'm starving."

Becky shook her head in disbelief at her friend's cavalier attitude. She gestured at her car at the curb. "Get in. I'm driving you there this time."

They drove in silence until Becky pulled the car into a parking spot at the deli and turned off the engine. Jules glanced over, her expression serious as they both got out. As Becky clicked the button on her keychain to lock the car doors, she broke the awkward silence. "Michelle said she would cover the boutique so I could come to meet you. I told her I would bring her back lunch, so don't let me forget."

"So the new girl's working out? That's great." Jules hesitated and then added, "And what about you? I know you, Becky Morgan, almost better than I know myself. Something's not right."

Becky stared down at the asphalt in the parking lot. The words that fell out of her mouth were soft and wobbly as if saying them out loud was strangling her insides.

"There isn't going to be a baby. I told you I had three embryos when they called to schedule my appointment for Tuesday morning. Monday afternoon they called back and canceled it." She looked up and met Jules's gaze. "Told me that the embryos didn't make it. None of them. Not even one."

"Oh, Beck. I'm so sorry." Jules wrapped her arms around her in a fierce, protective hug. Becky closed her eyes. She didn't want Jules to let her go. The pain she had endured had isolated her, and instead of leaning on Jules and Bryan, she had shut out the people she loved most.

Finally pulling back, Becky wiped at her tears with the back of her hand. "These things happen sometimes, or so I was told." She sniffled. "I knew there was a chance it wouldn't work, but I didn't want to accept it. I fully expected I would be pregnant, and I almost can't even wrap my brain around the fact that I won't even get the chance to wonder if the transfer was successful."

Becky bowed her head to hide her tear-stained face as an older couple walked by them to their car. This wasn't exactly the place she had expected to have this conversation.

Her best friend dismissed them with a wave of her hand. "Don't worry about them. You're allowed to cry any damn place you please."

Becky allowed herself a small smile. "I do feel better that I've told you. I figured you might send out a search party if I didn't come meet you today."

Jules grabbed Becky's hands and stared into her eyes. "I'm your best friend. When you're happy, I'm happy. And when your heart's broken, my heart is broken too. We'll figure this out."

Becky nodded somberly.

"C'mon, let's get you something to eat. You'll feel better, and if you're up to it, I have some pretty spectacular news."

CHAPTER THIRTY-SIX

Jules

After picking up their lunches at the end of the counter, Jules gestured toward a table in a private corner out of the steady stream of customers. She wanted Becky to feel comfortable to be able to talk to her about what was going on in her life.

"I'm sorry I worried you," Becky said as she popped the top on her Diet Coke. "I used to get depressed every month when I wasn't pregnant. But this—this took me down. I couldn't even get out of bed for a couple of days."

Jules scowled. "I wish you would have called me. You know I would have come over."

Becky shrugged. "Bryan wanted to call you, but I told him not to. I haven't even told my mom yet. I just wasn't up to talking to anyone. Even my husband."

"How is he taking it?"

"I think he just wants us to go back to normal. Back to the way we were. But I feel different. I'm sad, and I'm frustrated, and I just feel... I just feel like a failure." Becky took a sip of her soda and stared at her sandwich.

Jules reached across the table. "Don't be so hard on yourself. This wasn't your fault. I'm sure Bryan doesn't feel like it was either."

Becky cast her eyes down into her lap. "I don't know what's happening to us." She paused as she brought her gaze up. "I mean, I know it's my fault. We had a huge fight the other day."

Jules raised an eyebrow. "Really? You two never fight."

"Well, the hormones didn't help when we first started IVF. I was so cranky I could barely stand myself. But those fights were nothing compared to this one. I know he just wants to help me. I just don't seem to know how to let him. Between the transfer being canceled and Sherlock missing—" Becky let out a weary sigh. "I'm a mess. *We're* a mess."

Jules let out a breath and pressed her lips together. No wonder Becky had cracked. Between the fight with Bryan, her missing cat, and the canceled transfer, she had to have felt like the things most important to her were slipping through her fingers.

Jules scrutinized her friend's face. "That's a lot to handle all at once for anyone. I can't believe there's still been no sign of Sherlock."

Becky shrugged and bit her bottom lip. "I know. I can't even talk about him without crying. At least all the weird stuff that had me thinking I was losing my mind has stopped."

"You were never losing your mind. I told you that." Jules picked up her sandwich, examined it, and then took a bite.

Becky nodded hesitantly as if she still wasn't sure that was true. "All I can say for sure is nothing has unexpectedly moved, I haven't tried to burn down the house again, and there's nothing in my closet I don't remember buying since my transfer was canceled. I also stopped taking all the fertility drugs. Maybe it was related, even though the doctor's office said it wasn't."

"Well, I told you it was all the stress from everything you had going on. You just need to take some time to regroup. You and

Bryan need to reconnect and get back on the same side, that's all. That man adores you, and I don't see that changing. Maybe with a break, y'all can figure out what happened and try again."

Becky picked at her chips. "Maybe." She gave her head a shake, looked across the table at Jules and offered a small smile. "Enough about me. You said you had some news. If I recall correctly, you used the word spectacular—" She paused and let out a loud groan. "Oh, no. Did you find your birth mother? Was I so wrapped up in my own problems that I didn't call you back? Oh, Jules, I am so—"

"No, no. You're good." She wagged her finger at Becky. "I would have just come over and busted down your door if that had happened."

Becky exhaled. "Well, that's a relief. I mean, not that you didn't find her. Just that I didn't miss your big moment. Okay, tell me what you found."

"You're sure?"

Becky leaned in over the table. "Of course I'm sure. I don't understand much about how it all works, but I know how much you want to find her, and I want that for you."

Jules took a deep breath. It wasn't just that she wanted to find her birth mother. She *needed* to find her. The news she had was spectacular for her search, but she just wished it didn't have to come on the heels of Becky's disappointment.

Jules glanced around the restaurant and then leaned in toward Becky. "You don't know how much I appreciate that. When you know where you come from, it's hard to understand the point-of-view of someone who knows absolutely nothing about where they started. People who have no idea how it feels—they dismiss it as nothing because my adopted parents were so great. One has nothing to do with the other."

"I understand. You'll find her. I know you will. So, tell me this spectacular news."

"Well, I told you about Lucy16, right? She could be a first cousin once removed, but she could also be a half-great-aunt or a half-first cousin."

Becky tilted her head, and her forehead creased as if she seemed to be trying to understand. Jules took in the befuddled look on her friend's face.

"This will make sense, I promise. Anyway, I've emailed this Lucy repeatedly and nothing. She won't respond, but I can see she's online every day. Her ID is Lucy16, and I can't figure out who she is with just that. Without her last name, I can't even Facebook stalk her. I mean, at least I have the decency to use my real name as my ID and make it easy for people." She leaned in. "And then my results came in on the other site. And guess who's there? It's like Lucy tested in both places just to torture me."

Becky frowned. "I wonder why she just doesn't want to answer you. I mean, you are related."

"Well, I wondered if maybe she has something to hide, you know? Especially since she tested at both sites like me." Jules took a sip of her sweet tea. "I looked at her family tree, and something's not right. Her ethnicity doesn't seem to match what's on her tree, and I'm starting to think that maybe her tree isn't her biological tree. None of our shared matches show any names on her tree. So, I started thinking, maybe she's adopted too."

"Oh, wow," Becky said. "Can you imagine if she was adopted too? That'd be a crazy coincidence. You must be frustrated to be so close—"

"Oh, yes, I was. I was pretty aggravated with Lucy and her tree until a few days ago." Jules grinned like the Cheshire cat.

Becky's eyes grew wide. "She answered your email? Is she adopted too?"

Jules shook her head. "Nope, still nothing. Sadly, I'm not sure she wants to be related to me." A satisfied expression crossed her face. "But on the second site, Lucy isn't my top match."

"No?" Becky leaned in with anticipation. "And—who is?"

A wide smile covered Jules's face. "Oh, it's a doozy. Like winning the genealogy lottery. 890 glorious shared cMs of DNA. A first cousin. You know what that means?"

Becky cringed. "Um. I should know this, right? Let me think."

"I'll help you out." Jules's eyes lit up. "If she's my first cousin, that means we share grandparents. If we have the same grandparents, that means that one of her parents and one of my birth parents are siblings."

Becky's hands flew up to cover her mouth, and then she lowered them. "Oh, I get it now. That *is* spectacular news. Now what do you do?"

"Luckily, this match had the decency to use her name, so I found her on Facebook and sent her a message there too. That doesn't always go so well because if you're not Facebook friends, it goes into this 'other' folder that most people don't even know they have. But I have to try, right?"

Becky nodded with earnest. "Of course you do."

"She's fairly young, so she definitely doesn't match any of the other possibilities. I'm almost positive she has to be a first cousin."

Becky offered her friend a genuine smile. "Jules, I have a good feeling about this."

Jules hoped Becky was right. "Who knows. She probably thinks I'm a total scam. She hasn't responded, so I'm starting to get a little nervous."

"So, if this cousin finally answers you, she'd have to know who your birth mother is, right?" Becky hesitated and tilted her head. "Wait, it could also be your birth father, right?"

"Well, I'm not positive, but I've done a little detective work. I'm actually getting pretty good at this." Jules folded her arms and placed them on the table in front of her. "I was able to figure out who my match's parents are. Remember, one of her parents is a sibling to one of my birth parents. It appears that her father is an only child, so he had no siblings. Her mother had two sisters but no brothers. If neither one of her parents had a brother, then this can't be a match to my birth father. That means one of her mother's sisters is my birth mother." She leaned back in her chair and tapped the table. "Ta-da!"

Clarity crossed Becky's face.

"My new match and Lucy aren't matches to each other. That should mean that my first cousin is on my mother's side, and Lucy must be from my birth father's side."

"I know you really wanted to find her first," Becky said. "You're close. Really close."

"I mean, maybe she never told anyone about me, but I'd have to think if your sister were pregnant, you would know, right?" Jules hesitated. "I guess I was a little disappointed at first. I thought I'd open up my matches, and there she'd be because she's been looking for me all this time."

"Maybe she doesn't realize she can use DNA to find you. I thought all those tests showed was your ethnicity. I didn't even realize you got matches to people you're related to until you told me."

"You could be right. Maybe she didn't know she could find me this way." Jules rubbed her hands together and emitted an evil laugh. "But I've got a first cousin, and she can't be far behind."

"I hate to say this, but I didn't really think you'd be able to use DNA to figure it out, but damn, I do believe you're going to find her." Becky studied her friend's face. "Are you nervous or excited?"

Jules lifted one shoulder in a half-hearted shrug. The idea of being this close to finding her birth mother had left her with a swirl of emotions. "A little of both, I guess. I already feel like she rejected me once. If she doesn't want anything to do with me, I don't know how I'll feel. Devastated probably. Who knows, maybe she was just young and wanted me to have a better life. Maybe she'll be overjoyed when the stork drops her adult daughter on her front porch."

"She'd be lucky to have you in her life and I'm lucky to have you as my friend. I really needed this today." Becky grabbed the bag with Michelle's lunch. "I should get back to work. Let me take you to your car. There's no way I'm letting you cross the road again."

Jules laughed as she stood and grabbed her purse. "Don't be silly. I'm fine. Nothing happened, but I'll take the ride."

As she pulled in next to Jules's car, Becky glanced over at her. "I hope you hear from your first cousin soon. Keep me posted. I won't disappear again. I promise."

"You know I will." Jules met Becky's eyes with a stern stare. "And if you need me, you call me. I mean it."

Becky summoned a deep breath. "I will. I've still got to tell my mother there's not going to be a baby. I hope I only have to tell her once."

CHAPTER THIRTY-SEVEN

Becky

The smell of freshly cut grass filled the air as Becky struggled to empty her mom's mailbox. The mailman had just shoved the mail in, day after day, until it was wedged in there, a brick of junk mail, sale papers, and catalogs.

With the pile of mail in the crook of her arm, she reluctantly headed up the front stairs to the porch. Becky let out a deep, prolonged sigh as she pushed open the door and scanned the living room. It always made her heart hurt to come here. The house still looked like her mom had just run to the grocery store and would be back any minute.

She made her way into her mom's small kitchen. Cottage-cute she had called the place when her mom decided to buy it. Small but charming with its wide front porch and fenced in backyard. She was supposed to grow old here instead of in a room at a memory care assisted living facility.

Becky squeezed her eyes shut for a minute and then sorted most of the mail into the trash can. She couldn't imagine selling this little house but keeping it made no sense. It wasn't like her mom would be coming back to live here.

She physically ached to be here without her mom. Becky wandered into the living room and ran her hand through the layer of dust on the wooden top of the piano. This piano had given her mother so much happiness, and it now sat untouched like a silent reminder of how much she had lost. She hit a few keys, the off-pitch notes ringing out through the stillness and quiet of the house. She'd always wished she could play like her mother, but she didn't have a musical bone in her body. Becky rubbed her hands together. The dust flew off, drifting through the air toward the floor.

The nurses at Tranquility were always telling her she could help her mom's memory with cues and reminders. Ellie had asked if there were old photo albums, and Becky had made plans to get them and bring them to her mom. With everything that happened, she had pushed that promise to the back of her mind. Her mom wouldn't realize how long she had taken to get them, but Becky knew.

On the bottom shelf of the armoire that held the flat-screen TV, she found the albums. Luckily, they weren't covered with much dust. She pulled them out one by one and laid them on the coffee table. Sitting cross-legged on the floor, she pulled the first one into her lap. Her parents' vacation pictures. A small smile played across her face when she saw the size of the margarita her mom was holding. Becky put the album aside and pulled down the next one.

Baby pictures. Lots and lots of baby pictures of Becky. She flipped through the album, a pensive look growing on her face. She had seen most of these before, but the photos of her with her dad made her wistful. He had seemed strong and invincible in her eyes. It still seemed unfair that his heart had given out and taken him away so young.

As she turned the pages, a single photo stuck in the spine of the album fell loose. She flipped it over—nothing written on the back. She studied the faces in the picture. Her mother wore a pained expression on her face that suggested she wished she was anywhere but where the photo was taken. Or maybe it was because she was huge. Her mom was pregnant, and her dad had his arm protectively around her.

On the other side of her dad was an older couple. Becky's eyes widened. The family resemblance was undeniable. There was no way this wasn't her dad's father. For a moment, she recalled what Jules always said to her about never seeing anyone that looked like her. With this one picture, Becky now understood.

What had happened after this photo that they all stopped speaking to each other? She'd probably never know. She stuck the picture back in the album and put it on top of the one with the vacation pictures.

The next album was before her time, and she got goosebumps as she ran her fingers over her parents' wedding picture. They had looked so happy, so in love. She and Bryan had that kind of love. As she swallowed past the lump in her throat, she needed to believe this was still true.

She picked up the short stack of albums she had gone through and left the others sitting on the coffee table. These would be enough for now.

Anxiety coursed through her as she thought of cleaning out the house to sell it. She remembered the crate of records she had planned to look for while she was here. She let her eyes close for a moment. Her heart had been through enough for one day.

She took the photo albums and stacked them on the kitchen table.

As she grabbed the mail from the desk, she thought about the picture she had found of her dad's parents, her grandparents. She'd stumbled on their will in the desk drawer as she was looking for her mom's insurance information. She wondered again about her dad's life insurance policy and the money he had left her. Was it really life insurance or money from his parents?

She slipped into the desk chair and leaned over while she slid open the drawer. The files were all labeled, and she flipped through them. The one labeled life insurance had information about Felicia's policy but nothing about her dad's or any information about a claim.

It had been silly to think there would still be something in her mom's file. Becky caught her breath, startled to realize she'd been without her dad for more than fifteen years. Every so often, at the grocery store or at the mall, she'd catch a whiff of his sandalwood cologne. If she closed her eyes, she'd go back in time, and she could almost feel his arms wrapped around her as a little girl.

Part of her believed her father had seen her heartbreak when he died. He'd felt her fear that she would be alone and nudged Bryan down that sidewalk toward her when they met. She could imagine her dad shaking his head at her now that she didn't appreciate the good man he had found for her. Bryan was like her dad in so many ways. She couldn't let them drift apart until there was no way to put them back together again.

As she was about to shut the drawer, she noticed one last file tucked in the back, a metal bar separating it from the rest. This one had no label. Becky stuck her hand all the way into the back, gripped the top of the manila folder, and pulled it out.

After placing it on the desk, she skimmed the contents as confusion creased her face. Several typed pages stapled together seemed to detail someone's movements. She flipped back to the first page. There was a name at the top of the letterhead with the letters "P.I." after it. Whoever had written this had been following someone he referred to throughout as "the subject." Who was the subject, and why did her parents need to know that at 10:05 AM the subject had left his residence?

She studied the date on the first page. This report had been typed up the summer before her freshman year of high school. It crossed her mind that this had also been the year her grandparents had died. She remembered when her father had announced they wouldn't be going to either of their funerals.

Behind the report, there were several maps in the file, specific areas designated with a yellow highlighter. She flipped past the maps to a large white envelope with the word "photos" handwritten in black ink. The person who had ripped it open to get to the photos inside had not returned them to the envelope. It was empty.

There was a credit card receipt, but time had faded the ink until the details were no longer legible. One item remained. Yellowed and curling at the edges, it appeared to be a newspaper article. She unfolded it carefully and read the headline. Leaning back in her chair, she rubbed her temples as she tried to make sense of it.

Why did her mom have an article about a shooting at a convenience store?

CHAPTER THIRTY-EIGHT

Becky

Becky held the photo albums in the crook of her arm as she approached the nurses' station outside her mother's room. The folder she had taken from her mom's desk drawer had remained in the car. She wanted to take it home, spread the contents on the kitchen table, and ask Bryan to help her decipher it. It would have to wait. Somehow it felt like she and her husband had a bigger mystery to solve, like how to put their marriage back together.

Ellie was out this week for her daughter's ankle surgery. Her replacement, a middle-aged woman with an unruly head of salt and pepper hair and a dour expression, stood behind the desk. Becky gave her a hesitant smile. "I'm just here to see my mom. Felicia Williams, room 236."

The woman's emotionless stare made Becky uncomfortable. Maybe she thought Becky was one of those daughters who didn't visit nearly enough. True, she hadn't been in all week, but this was unusual. After the week she had—

She scolded herself for caring what this woman thought of her. There was no need to justify herself. Becky shifted her weight from side to side as she stood there. She didn't know why she was waiting. She didn't need this woman's permission to see her mom.

Finally, the nurse responded as she scrutinized Becky. "She's not in her room. They said they were going outside. Apparently, she can't get enough of the courtyard today."

Her mom loved to go outside, but there were places she didn't have the freedom to wander off by herself. Maybe one of the nurses had taken pity on her that Ellie's replacement was nothing like Ellie. "That's fine. I'll just wait in her room."

Becky felt the woman's stony stare continue to drill into the back of her head as she strode toward room 236. The door to her mom's room was open, and as Becky entered to wait, she heard voices in the hall.

Ros was clearly with her mom as her muffled voice drifted toward the doorway. "If it ever comes to it, I'll tell her. Becky will understand. How could she—"

"Understand what?" Becky asked as the two women came through the doorway.

Roslyn's eyes widened, and a flush splashed across her cheeks. "Oh, Becky, you startled me." She turned toward Becky's mother, standing right behind her. "Felicia, Becky's here."

"I just got here," Becky said. "That miserable nurse told me someone had gone for a walk with my mom. I'm glad it was you. So, what will I understand?"

Ros stopped to hug her and spoke softly into her ear. "It's nothing important. Your mother is just thinking ahead, and she's afraid Tranquility is eating up your inheritance."

Becky scowled. "Well, that's just silly. I want my mother to have the best care possible, no matter how much it costs."

Ros pulled back and nodded. "I know, but you know your mother worries about you. So, I haven't seen you since—" She glanced over at Felicia who had fallen into her rocking chair and was fanning herself. "Since the accident," she said quietly. "You look okay."

"From that, yeah."

Ros glanced at Felicia and then back at Becky. "Uh, oh."

"Yup. I have some stuff I have to tell her."

Ros leaned in and whispered in Becky's ear. "Well, she's a little off today, so don't be too concerned. She's been saying some stuff that doesn't make much sense."

The warning filled Becky with dread. If her mom was having a bad day, maybe she shouldn't tell her about the baby. If she told her and she didn't remember, she'd have to tell the whole story again on her next visit.

She bent over to hug her mom, her face glistening with sweat from being outside. Becky cleared her throat and tried to steady her voice. "Hi, Mom. I wanted to spend a little time with you today. How was your walk?"

Felicia looked up, her expression confused as if she had already forgotten her daughter was there. "Becky?" Her glance skipped from Becky to Ros and back to Becky. "I have to tell you something."

Becky glanced over at Roslyn. Her mom could want to tell her something from five minutes ago, or it could be from thirty years ago. It was hard to know sometimes what she was thinking.

Ros tried to catch her friend's gaze. "Felicia?"

Felicia rocked and turned her gaze to Becky. "Would you get me some water?"

"Sure, Mom." Becky got up and poured water into a glass from the pitcher on the table.

Felicia's glance went from her daughter to Ros as Becky handed her the cup. She nodded as she took a sip and then let out a deep breath. "That feels so much better. It's already so hot outside."

Becky pulled a chair over and sat in front of her mother. "Yeah, it is, Mom. Summer's coming soon."

Becky fanned herself, but the weather wasn't what was making her sweat. "I have to tell you something too, Mom." She hesitated. She just had to make herself get the words out. "The IVF didn't work, so there isn't going to be a baby in nine months. I don't know what we're going to do or if we're going to try again." Roslyn was like family, so Becky didn't mind if she heard the news. "Bryan and I have some tough decisions to make."

Roslyn stood and hugged Becky again. "I'm so sorry, honey. I know how much you wanted this to happen."

Felicia's expression clouded over with confusion. "You told me there's going to be a baby."

Becky rubbed her temples. "I know, Mom. I thought I'd be pregnant. I don't know what happened except that apparently these things do happen, and it doesn't work." It didn't seem necessary to tell her all the embryos had died. Her voice cracked, and she blinked hard to keep the tears at bay.

"You told me yesterday there was going to be a baby," Felicia said, her tone adamant as if she could bully her daughter into agreeing.

Becky was trembling. She turned to Ros, her eyes pleading for help.

Roslyn went over and held Felicia's hand to try to comfort her. "It's okay, Felicia. Becky thought it was going to work, but unfortunately, it didn't, so now they'll have to figure out if they want to try again. You're just confusing the days, which is okay. Becky has been busy with work and the IVF, so she hasn't been to visit in a little bit."

Felicia yanked her hand away. "I know what day it is!" She scowled as she watched Roslyn and Becky exchange a look. "I'm not confused. Stop making it seem like I don't know what I'm talking about. You told me there would be a baby, and then you said you had to get your weapons and report for the war."

Becky felt her shoulders droop, and she hung her head for a moment. She'd talk to Ellie when she came back about her mom's medication. Maybe it needed to be adjusted again.

Becky slumped into the extra chair next to Ros. There was no point in arguing with her about it. Becky would fret over this for days, and most likely her mom wouldn't even remember they'd had this conversation after she left.

Ros offered her a sympathetic nod and a small smile. It was hard for both of them on days like this.

Anxiety ramped up Becky's heartbeat. "I stopped by the house and got your photo albums. I'm going to leave them here in case you want to look at old pictures. I have to get to work, but we can go through them the next time I visit if you want." She placed the stack of albums on the small table by the television.

She blinked back tears as she leaned over and kissed her mom on the cheek. "I'll be back soon, I promise."

She looked over at Roslyn and asked if she was staying for a while. Roslyn nodded, and Becky mouthed "thank you" before slipping out the door. She was so grateful that Ros was still a best friend to her mother, even after all these years. It helped to have someone else who remembered how her mom used to be and understood how different she was now.

As she left to head to the boutique, the woman behind the desk frowned at her. Becky scowled in return. The pain of what she had lost left her struggling to breathe. The last thing she needed today was this ill-tempered woman's attitude.

CHAPTER THIRTY-NINE

Becky

Someone was calling her. Becky fought to open her eyes, but her lids felt weighted down. As she peered out through narrowed slits, she heard her name again.

"Becky, are you okay?" Tonya asked, concern evident in her tone.

Attempting to focus, Becky took in her situation—cardboard underneath her, boxes stacked up, metal shelving and racks piled into one corner. Over Tonya's head, the fluorescent lights of the stockroom shined down on her.

She tried to sit up but was having a hard time making her way out of the fog.

"Were you sleeping? How long have you been in here?" Tonya offered her a hand.

Even at the height of her IVF treatment, Becky had never fallen asleep at the store. She stood, wobbled unsteadily on her feet, and collapsed back down on top of the boxes.

"I don't—I don't know what happened." Becky rubbed her temples as she tried to remember. "I went to see my mom. When I got here, I went to get coffee for Michelle and me. I remember doing payroll, and then I was going to leave to go pick up the flip flop order." She glanced up at Tonya to explain. "The delivery guy for the sandal designer was sick."

Tonya pushed Becky's hair off her face, but it didn't stay and fell forward again. "Michelle told me you left to pick up the sandal order. I got here a couple of hours ago and wondered where you went since your car wasn't here." Tonya's gaze swept the stockroom. "Did you leave the boxes in your car?"

Confusion creased Becky's forehead. She sat for a moment staring at the floor as she tried to remember. "I didn't—I didn't go," she said, hesitation in her voice. Becky glanced at her watch, and her pulse accelerated. The last thing she remembered was writing paychecks hours ago. It was now after 2:00 PM. She shot Tonya an urgent stare. "Wait, did you say my car isn't here?"

Becky stumbled out of the stockroom into the office. She pulled desperately on the door handle to the back parking lot. Her car sat in its usual spot next to Tonya's.

She spun around, and her eyes bore into her partner.

Tonya held up her hands and shrugged. "It wasn't here when I got here at noon. That's all I know. I've been on the sales floor helping Michelle move racks around."

Becky slumped in her chair and put her head in her hands. She wanted to cry, an ugly cry that would release all the sadness, confusion, and frustration that had built up inside her.

Tonya crouched down beside her friend. "Beck, you're okay. You've been through a lot lately. Have you been sleeping at night? Maybe it just all caught up with you."

She remembered the frustration of the meeting with her mother earlier. It had left her emotionally exhausted. "Okay, so let's say I was so tired, I fell asleep." Her voice shook. "But if I never went out, where was my car when you got here?"

Tonya studied her for a moment as if she was considering her response. "Maybe I was wrong. Maybe I just assumed you went out because Michelle told me you did, and I didn't see you when I got here."

Becky gave her a long contemplative look while she swiped at her tears. "Really?"

"Really. I'll send Michelle to pick up the sandals now, so don't worry about that. Do you feel okay, or do you want to go home? I can handle it if you want to leave."

Becky took a deep breath. "No, I can pull myself together."

"Okay, take as long as you need. You can come out and help when you're ready. Okay?"

Becky gave her a half-hearted nod. "Okay. Thanks."

She squeezed her eyes shut as she sat at her desk. Her thoughts wandered to Bryan. Their relationship was one thing she could fix. He had always been her support system, and she needed him now more than ever.

When Michelle returned with their order, Becky helped her unpack everything from her car. Tonya must have covered for her bizarre nap in the stockroom because Michelle didn't mention anything about having to go pick up the order.

"Oh," Michelle said abruptly as they stacked the boxes in the stockroom. "There was a guy here earlier looking for you. Right after you went out."

Becky's chest tightened. Michelle thought she had gone out. "A guy?" she asked, her hand starting to tremble as she grabbed a shoebox. "One of the suppliers, maybe?"

Michelle gave a small shrug. "Don't think so. He came in and asked for you by name. I checked to see if you were still in the office, but you had already left. He said he'd come back another time."

Becky exhaled softly. So, Michelle just assumed she'd left because she wasn't in the office. She wrinkled her nose. "I wonder who it was."

A sly smile crossed Michelle's face. "I'm not sure, but he was pretty cute."

Becky held up her left hand and pointed to her wedding ring. "I guess I'll see if he comes back." Becky had bigger things to worry about. She gave Michelle a half-hearted smile. "But you're welcome to him."

When she searched her memory for what had happened earlier, the only recollection she had was a feeling of overwhelming exhaustion. As she tried to keep herself busy, her mind continually drifted to look for an explanation. There wasn't one that made sense.

She just needed to get through the day, and then she would go home and make things right with Bryan. They had enough to fix. Telling him about her bizarre nap in the stockroom seemed unnecessary.

Later that afternoon, the bell jingled over the front door. As she glanced up, a young mother struggled to hold the door to push the stroller in ahead of her. The baby, chewing on some sort of toy, stared straight ahead at Becky. Their eyes locked as the baby held out the toy, dripping with drool, in her direction.

Becky froze, her feet unable to move, her eyes refusing to look away. As the baby focused on her and let out an enthusiastic giggle, Becky's legs weakened as if she might crumple right there in the middle of the store.

Then Tonya's hand was on her arm. "Go," she said, her tone terse. "I've got this."

Becky scurried to the safety of the office where she collapsed into her chair. She put her head down on the desk, a puddle underneath her face where her misery fell like a faucet with a broken knob.

One look at the sweet angelic face staring at her and her grief had overwhelmed her. The mother must have wondered what was wrong. Most people gushed over babies. Becky had looked at hers and fled.

As she stared down at the desk, the sound of Tonya's heels clicking on the floor grew louder until it stopped beside her.

Tonya stroked Becky's hair as her face was buried in her arms folded on her desk. "Hey, you okay?"

"Nope. Not even a little bit," Becky said, her voice muffled against the wet crook of her arm. "Am I ever going to get over this?"

"You've been through so much already, but I know you. This isn't over. With a little bit of time, you'll be back up swinging. You'll get your baby. I have no doubt."

Becky lifted her head, and Tonya winced as she took in her makeup-stained face. "Oh, that's not good." She walked over to her desk and got Becky a tissue. "You've had a rough day. It's almost time for you to go home anyway. Why don't you see if you can pull yourself together enough to drive home."

Becky nodded while trying to wipe the makeup from her face. "I'll see if I can fix this in the bathroom, then I'll head out. Thanks." She eased out of her chair and got to her feet.

Tonya studied her. "You'll be okay?"

Becky's shoulders drooped as a heavy sigh escaped her lips. "Yeah. I'll be in tomorrow. Don't worry."

As she headed home, the reality of everything that had happened that day wrapped around her until she felt like she couldn't breathe. Maybe she had fallen asleep at the store as a way to shut it all out for a bit.

She might even be able to accept that misery had worn her down. But if her car hadn't been there when Tonya got to work—she couldn't even finish the thought. The idea that she had gone out made her stomach twist.

Any memory of leaving the store was missing.

CHAPTER FORTY

Bryan

Bryan had tried to make it through the day at the office. Every time he shut his eyes he saw the whole scene unfold again in his mind. He'd finally told Dave and Alex he was taking off a little early. They didn't say anything, but he saw it in their eyes. Pity. He hated that.

Autopilot. That must be how he made the ride home. He didn't remember getting in the car at the office, didn't remember one minute of the drive.

He staggered out of the car into the driveway. Fumbled with the damn code on the front door, his oversized fingers uncooperative as he tried to input the date of her birthday. He jabbed at the buttons again ... 1104. Finally, the light turned green.

Slamming the door behind him, he felt a certain satisfaction at the sound it made. Like an angry punctuation mark.

He locked it behind him and scanned the living room. It looked the same. He would have expected it to look different. Like a bomb had exploded. Why should their home look like everything was normal when his insides had been ransacked?

Stumbling, he made his way into the kitchen, tossed his stuff on the table. He grabbed the handle and yanked open the refrigerator door. Pulled out the carton of orange juice and chugged right from the package as if somehow Becky could see and feel his defiance. He shook his head in disgust at how irrelevant this act really was. He squeezed his eyes shut and gritted his teeth.

He took his anger out on the refrigerator door, his excessive force shaking the entire appliance. Sherlock's food, still in the container on top, wobbled unsteadily before finally teetering over the edge. It hit the floor with a resounding thud, the momentum of the fall allowing the top to break free. Dry cat food scattered.

He glanced down at the mess strewn on the white tile. It didn't matter. The cat was gone. He didn't need his food, and Bryan wasn't planning to make a single move to clean it up. She cared more about that cat missing than anything that had happened between them. That had never been more obvious than this afternoon. Maybe he needed to post flyers that his wife had disappeared.

He pulled out the kitchen chair and used his foot to kick at the legs. With the chair sitting cockeyed to the table, he fell into the seat, then leaned back and stared at the ceiling. *Why, Becky? Why would you do this?* No matter how many times he asked himself the question that day, his brain couldn't wrap itself around any answer that made sense.

Examine what he saw at lunchtime from all angles. That's what the logical side of him demanded. Maybe what he thought he glimpsed wasn't accurate. Then he remembered his friends. They'd been standing right there with him and had come to the same conclusion. It was written all over their faces.

He slammed his fist into the table. A moment later, he picked it up and rubbed the heel of his hand. His eyes grew damp, and he knew it wasn't because he'd hurt himself.

This required something stronger than orange juice. He shoved the chair back, and in two long strides, he was at the bottom of the pantry, rummaging through the bottles of alcohol. "It's a Jack and Coke day," he said out loud. "Hold the Coke."

With the bottle in his left hand, he scoured the kitchen cabinet. He grabbed the shot glass with his right hand. Tried to ignore the writing on it. Mexico. Their honeymoon. How it had all looked so different then.

His eyes drifted to the scorched cabinet. His wife had never even attempted to explain how that had happened. It seemed she didn't share anything with him anymore.

He collapsed back into the chair, unscrewing the cap on the bottle as he sat. He tipped it at the shot glass and squinted as he overpoured. It was growing dim in the kitchen. He hadn't bothered to turn on a single light in the house.

He tossed the shot back and winced as the liquid traveled down his throat. The painful burning felt oddly comforting. Proof he could still feel something. He wondered how many of these he would need until he felt nothing. He poured another. He threw it back and slammed the shot glass on the table.

Sure, things hadn't been great between them since the IVF failed, but he couldn't believe Becky had done this. She knew his routines, knew he'd be there.

He didn't know what he was going to say when she finally got home. A piece of him hoped she'd have a reasonable explanation and he could forget today had ever happened. He scoffed. There wouldn't be an explanation. There couldn't be.

He was numb, but he didn't know if he could credit the alcohol just yet. He slumped over the table, his head in his hands. In the silence, he heard the metallic click of the front door being unlocked.

She was home.

CHAPTER FORTY-ONE

Becky

Becky's hand gripped the doorknob, but she hesitated. Her chest felt tight like fear held her insides in its grasp. She was holding onto her sanity by the tips of her fingers.

She took a deep breath to steady herself and forced herself to turn the knob. The determination she had felt that morning to make things right with Bryan returned, but the house was dark as she entered. His car had been in the driveway, but her husband didn't seem to be home.

It was dusk outside. Only the faint glow of what was left of daylight streamed through the front window and gave her any light to see inside. As her eyes adjusted, she caught her breath. She wasn't alone.

As she squinted, she could make out her husband's silhouette sitting at the kitchen table, his back to the door she had just come through. She froze as her chest tightened. It was as if the lack of light let her see Bryan free of the haze that had clouded her vision lately. Suddenly, there in the shadows, she saw him through different eyes.

This figure in the dark didn't resemble the man she loved at all. Slumped over as if he had given up, his blond head leaned forward resting on his fists. Even in the darkness, she saw her fearless, confident husband seemed broken. She tried to swallow down the lump in her throat. She had done this to him.

Hesitantly, she softly called out his name. "Bryan?"

The figure in the darkness didn't move, didn't acknowledge he had heard her. His stillness was starting to scare her.

She raised her voice slightly. "Bryan? Are you okay? Why are you sitting in the dark?"

She shrugged her bag onto the living room couch and fumbled to turn on the end table lamp for light. For clarity. Maybe the darkness and shadows were deceiving her. As the lamp came on, soft light spilled into the kitchen. She expected her husband would turn to greet her, but he didn't move.

Guilt stabbed at her. Bryan had been suffering too, but she had been too selfish, too preoccupied with her own unhappiness to notice. The time had come to let her loss go and comfort her husband.

Making her way around the table, something crunched underneath her feet. She glanced around the kitchen trying to make out what was on the floor. Sherlock's food?

She approached him, but Bryan still didn't move, didn't react to her presence until she leaned over to hug him. At her touch, he jerked away.

In all their years together, she had never seen him like this. This was something different. Something angry. She observed his fists, tightly clenched as if he was trying to control bottled-up rage. She had waited too long to make this right.

"Bryan? Please talk to me," she pleaded. "I want us to go back to being us again. I love you. I'm sorry about everything."

Her husband stared straight ahead. A blank, vacant stare had taken over the face that had once looked at her with such adoration. His eyes were flat and emotionless, his expression frozen.

He was still in his work clothes, the tie loosened around his neck, his phone and keys on the kitchen table next to him. It appeared he had walked in and just collapsed in this chair. But then, her eyes caught something she had missed in the dark: a bottle of whiskey probably left over from the last party. He had a shot glass too, a willing participant in helping him take his mind off something he wanted to forget.

She stood awkwardly, waiting for him to answer or do something. He had pulled away from her hug, but now his lack of a response was beginning to elicit panic in her.

"Why won't you answer me?" Her voice rose an octave. "Bryan, you're scaring me."

Bryan blinked several times as if trying to reassert his emotional control. His eyes locked on hers and then darted away, looking anywhere but at her. Slow and deliberate, he bowed his head toward the table and finally spoke. "Where were you at lunchtime today?"

Her heart jumped up into her throat. Her mind was spinning trying to figure out if he knew something, or had simply wanted to have lunch and talk through their problems. There had been no missed call from him, and they rarely met up during the workday even in the best of circumstances. This had to be about more than just sharing a meal in the middle of the day. Much more.

"Did you want to have lunch today?" she asked, trying to sound casual, sure he could hear the wild pounding of her heart.

He glanced up at her, and she desperately tried to read the emotions on his face. What she saw filled her with fear. His strong jaw was firmly set. The clear, blue eyes which usually conveyed happiness looked cold. They held a mixture of disappointment and sadness, wet and red as if they were on the verge of releasing tears.

He stared down at the table and brushed at some imaginary crumbs. "No, Becky, I didn't want to have lunch." He repeated his question slowly and deliberately as if he already knew the answer but wanted the words to come from her lips. "What I want to know is where you were at lunchtime today."

His eyes seemed to silently beg hers to give him an answer. How long had he sat here doing shots? He didn't seem so drunk he didn't know what he was asking.

"Were you at the store? Did you go out for lunch? You run an errand? I mean, I know where I was. I'm asking where you were." The question was pointed and direct, the rising inflection in his voice demanding an answer.

Did he know? What explanation could she give him that would make sense? "Lunchtime? Let me think. I was—I didn't—"

She was stumbling, not knowing how to answer his question. She couldn't explain where she was at lunchtime because she wasn't sure herself. If her car had been missing, maybe she had gone out, but she had no clue where.

What she would have given to go back before they had veered so horribly off course. Back to a time when things made sense between them. She wanted the tension, stretched taut between them, to break and provide some relief so they could figure this out together.

But no. That was not going to happen.

For one uncomfortable moment after another, the air hung empty.

Finally, he pounded his fist against the table. The resounding thud echoed throughout the kitchen, further punctuating his demand for an answer.

Becky's eyes widened. Startled, she reeled backward.

Bryan shook his head back and forth in despair. "Why can't you answer the question, Becky? Why?"

He didn't blink as he stared at her and waited for an answer. She knew, at that moment the future of their relationship might depend on what she said next.

She wasn't sure she could tell him what had happened and expect he would believe her. "The only answer I can give you is that I was at the store at lunchtime, but it's—it's complicated. Things are happening, things that I don't understand."

He shook his head, an incredulous expression on his face. His eyes were filled with contempt as they bore into hers.

"You were there today. Don't even try to lie to me. Becky, I saw you."

CHAPTER FORTY-TWO

Becky

"You saw me? Where? When? I don't understand." Panic knotted her stomach. Fear stretched Becky's voice high and taut. "Bryan, you're scaring me."

In the silence of the room, the out of control thumping of her heart seemed to echo off the walls. The moments ticked by uncomfortably. Beads of sweat formed on her hairline as she waited for his voice to break through and give her anxiety some relief.

And then finally he spoke, his voice cutting through the stagnant air. "I saw you, Becky." His bottom lip quivered. "How did we get here? I feel like I don't even know you anymore. Do you have any idea how much that breaks my heart?"

She reached down and tilted his head toward her. She forced him to look up at her so she could see his face. "Bryan, you're scaring me. Please, tell me what you're talking about."

He stared right through her. "I came out of the office at lunchtime with Dave and Alex to walk to the sandwich shop on the corner of Summit and Broad. You were parked across the street. You got out of your car." His eyes connected with hers as if he was reciting a story she already knew. He held her gaze for a moment before looking away.

He paused as if he needed to collect himself. He inhaled deeply and released it in several long, stuttered breaths. "Imagine how I felt standing there watching my wife kiss another man and then walk off with him hand in hand. There's no innocent explanation for what I saw." He stared back at Becky's face as if he was looking for a tell or a flash of any emotion that might betray her.

As his penetrating gaze probed her face, the contents of her stomach curdled like bad milk. Becky shook her head vehemently.

"Becky, stop. I know you saw me. I didn't want to believe it, but I could tell Dave and Alex saw it too. I could see in their faces what they were thinking." His eyes swam in tears. "Why would you do that, Becky? Are we done, finished?" He swiped at his tears with the back of his hand.

She would never deliberately do anything to cause him pain. Like a slideshow, all the odd things she had done lately but couldn't remember flashed through her mind. Cheat on him? No matter where her grief had taken her, she couldn't imagine doing that. As she reached for him, his body went rigid, and he turned away from her.

"It's a weird coincidence that's all," she said, her tone insistent as she tried to convince him. "Maybe your eyes were playing tricks on you. I didn't tell you, but I came home one day and smelled my perfume. I knew I hadn't sprayed it. Our senses can play tricks on us. Maybe it was the way the light was hitting this other girl that made you *think* she looked like me."

He studied her, his gaze scanning her entire body. "Is that what you were wearing today?"

"What? Yeah." She glanced down at the dress she was wearing. "I mean, I didn't change after I left the store if that's what you mean."

He skewered her with his eyes. "You were wearing the same thing when I saw you."

He rammed the chair back from the table. Her mouth fell open as he pushed past her.

She followed him into their bedroom. In the doorway, she froze in disbelief. He had pulled a gym bag out of the closet and was packing his clothes in it. She rushed in and tried to grab the clothes out of his hand. "Bryan, stop it!"

He jerked away from her and shoved the stack of shirts in the bag.

"What are you doing?" she asked, her voice breaking. "You can't really believe I would do that to you. Bryan, please stop packing!"

He glanced over at her, his eyes still wet. "If anyone had ever told me we would be in this place, I would have thought they were crazy. But I know what I saw, and you know as well as I do, we haven't been in such a great place since the IVF didn't work."

Desperation raced through her. There had to be something she could say to convince him, and maybe herself, that he was wrong. Her last-ditch attempt meant offering some form of the truth. She wasn't sure he would believe her.

"I can't tell you for sure where I was at lunchtime because I fell asleep at the store. I was in the stockroom. Tonya found me, and I don't even remember going in there. The last thing I remember was doing payroll, and then it was three hours later. I know I wasn't anywhere cheating on you."

He narrowed his eyes as he stared at her, contemplating her story. "I'm not sure what to believe anymore."

Her eyes pleaded as panic set in. "Bryan, please. You know I love you."

He zipped up the bag and threw the strap over his shoulder. "I need to go stay with my brother for a few days to clear my head.

Maybe you should try to clear your head too. If you're falling asleep at work, something's not right."

"I know. There's so much I haven't told you, and I'm sorry. I should have trusted you. I've been feeling for a while that something's not right."

Bryan flinched. "You didn't—you didn't trust me?" A pained expression crossed his face. He squeezed his eyes shut tight.

"I'm sorry. You're right. I should have told—"

Bryan opened his eyes. "You might want to think about going for a follow-up visit to the neurologist, just to be sure everything's okay. Maybe there are some repercussions from the accident. Maybe it's too hard to accept what's happened. Maybe somehow you blame me for the IVF not working." His voice cracked. "All I know is something is going on with you, something you didn't want to share with me. I have no idea where my wife went." He hesitated. "I need to be by myself for a bit. Think this all through."

As he tried to leave, Becky grabbed at his arm. "We can figure this out. I know I've been selfish after everything that happened, but I promise things will be better."

He turned back to face her. "I wish we never did IVF. We still wouldn't have a baby, but maybe I would still have my wife."

He didn't slam the door as he left, but the finality of it closing behind him echoed through the house as if he had. He was gone. Becky struggled to catch her breath. It didn't seem real that he had left, but she looked around and couldn't ignore the evidence: a hanger on the floor, the drawers on Bryan's side of the dresser left open at odd angles, a pair of his socks still sitting on the bed.

She crumpled to the floor. Fear rippled through her. Bryan had been so sure of what he thought he had seen. He couldn't be right, but she wasn't sure about anything anymore. Was she losing her mind?

The pressure had built to an unbearable level. The floodgates opened, and she wasn't sure the tears would ever stop. Finally, as she laid on the floor, exhaustion and sleep took over and allowed her a temporary escape from the life she no longer recognized.

CHAPTER FORTY-THREE

Becky

In the middle of the night, Becky woke and peeled herself off the floor. She collapsed onto the bed without even bothering to get under the covers. Bryan's side was empty. Turning over, she faced the other direction. No Sherlock either in his usual spot by her pillow. Loneliness clawed at her insides.

Running a little late. Guilt ate at her as she sent the text the next morning. Tonya was supposed to have the day off, and Becky had committed she would make it in when she had left as a shattered mess the day before.

Tonya had to be reaching the end of her patience with all of Becky's problems. Right now, she couldn't face anyone, much less the customers at the boutique. Her eyes were bloodshot and swollen from crying herself to sleep. She needed some time to recover. She needed Jules to help her figure this all out.

After three rings, she heard her friend's sleepy voice. "Hey."

Becky pictured Jules lying in bed on the phone with her eyes closed. "Hey. Can I come over? I need to talk to you."

Jules suddenly sounded wide awake. "Beck, what's happening? You okay?"

"No, I'm not." Becky was whimpering, trying not to cry. "My life is a mess. I need someone to talk to that might be able to help me sort it all out."

"I'm getting up. I'll see you soon."

Crying had left her eyes puffy and swollen, and lack of sleep had completed the grotesque mask of misery she wore. She scowled at her reflection in the mirror and then realized miserably that it didn't make a difference. If she had lost Bryan, nothing else mattered. Well, except for her friendship with Jules, which she needed now more than ever.

As Jules opened her front door, she winced. "Oh ... bless your heart."

"That bad?"

"I know I shouldn't say this, but you look terrible."

Becky scrunched up her face. "Thanks."

"Come on up. I made coffee."

As Jules wrapped her hand around the mug of steaming liquid, she leaned forward in her chair. "Okay, shoot."

Becky blinked hard to try to hold back the tears. "I still can't seem to get over the IVF not working." She glanced at the table, then back up. "I've been awful to be around. And now I don't even know if I have Bryan anymore."

"Bryan knows it's not your fault. You said yourself that these things happen. It didn't have anything to do with you."

"It's not about the baby." Becky hesitated. The words sounded ridiculous as she said them out loud. "Bryan thinks I'm cheating on him."

Jules laughed and then scowled as her friend let out a small moan. "Oh, sorry. You're serious? How could he possibly think that? I know you said you had a fight, but why would he think you were cheating on him?"

A deep sigh escaped Becky's lips. "I can't seem to shake the feeling that I've failed him. I know he wants to try IVF again, but I'm scared to death. If it doesn't work—" Her voice shook. "What if I'm what keeps Bryan from being a dad?"

Jules reached across the table for Becky's hand. "Bryan loves you. He's not going to leave you because you're scared to try again. Just let yourself recover. I know you. You were meant to be a mom just as much as he was meant to be a dad. This will work out somehow, someway."

"Instead of leaning on each other, we've just—we just seem to be drifting apart. I want to let him in..." Becky paused and raked her fingers through her long hair. "Bryan thinks he saw me kissing another man by his office yesterday at lunchtime."

Jules put her coffee cup down on the table. "What? That's ridiculous. First off, I can't even imagine you two fighting. But, okay, let's say you were cheating on him, which, by the way, I know you're not. Why in the world would you be near his office? That would be the last place you would be."

Becky sat silent for a second. She brought her finger to her lips. "Right? It wouldn't make sense that I would do that."

Confusion crossed Jules's face. "Wait, are you saying it was you?"

"No. I mean, I don't know. I don't know anything anymore. I fell asleep at the store yesterday. Three hours I can't account for, and Tonya said my car was gone when she got there. Bryan said he saw me in my car ..." She hesitated as she dipped her head and rubbed her temples. She held up her hands as if she considered it might be possible. "So maybe—maybe I did go out."

Becky felt fresh tears threatening and reached for a napkin. "So many weird things have happened that I don't trust my memory about anything anymore. Bryan told me to go back to the doctor and get my head checked out. The doctor did say I could have delayed symptoms after the accident, and he mentioned memory loss and reckless behavior. You don't get much more reckless than kissing another man outside your husband's office, and for damn sure I don't remember doing it."

"Oh, come on. That makes no sense, Beck. Let's say you did go out and forgot all about it. Why would you want to cheat on Bryan, and who would you even be cheating on him with? Come on, you work in a women's boutique. Where would you have even found this guy?"

Becky raised her shoulders in a bewildered shrug as her thoughts drifted to the man who had come looking for her. "I don't have any answers. I just know that I can't lose Bryan. I know I got you out of bed. I appreciate you meeting me. I needed someone to talk through this with me."

"Stop. Of course I'm here." Jules reached for Becky's hand across the table. "There's nothing I wouldn't do for you."

A pang of guilt went through her after her friend's declaration. Becky thought about the family tree Jules had wanted to do and how she had pushed back. Maybe she'd been wrong not to agree to do it in support, but a gift for a baby that wasn't coming would have been a cruel reminder.

Becky took a sip of her coffee, now getting cold. "And there's still no sign of Sherlock. So, I lost my cat, our baby, and my husband. Nice work, huh? I'm nothing if not efficient."

"Oh, damn. I'm so sorry. I thought for sure the cat would be back by now."

Becky shook her head. "He's just disappeared into thin air. Or..." She couldn't finish the sentence. "No one has called from the flyers, and we've been leaving food out." She gave a weak smile. "Even Mrs. Ritter set up a Sherlock buffet at her house. But there's been nothing."

"Well, cats are pretty resourceful. I wouldn't give up just yet. There are always stories on the news about cats who turn up years later and in different states."

"I hope it's not years. You know how scared he is about everything. He must be petrified and—" Becky fanned herself with her hand. "Okay. I need to stop thinking about it or I don't know how I'll be able to fix myself enough to go to work after this. Tell me about the DNA hunt. How's it going?"

Jules hesitated.

"It's okay," Becky said. "You can tell me. I want to know, and I need some good news."

"Well, I finally got an email from Lucy. I guess she figured out I'd bug her until she answered."

"What did she say? Were you right? Is she adopted?"

"Not exactly. Apparently, she did the first test for fun. When her matches came in, she didn't understand them. She matched people she didn't know at all, and she had no matches to her father's side of the family. She was sure the test was wrong, so she did the second test for confirmation. The results were the same. The man she thought was her father—well, he wasn't."

Becky's eyes widened. "Oh, that's horrible."

"I know. I feel awful for her. She said that she's having a hard time with it which is why she didn't respond at first. If we're related on her biological father's side, she's in the same boat as me. She knows nothing."

"What about the other match, the first cousin? Did she answer you?"

"Well, if you're really sure you're up to hearing about it ..."

Becky crossed her arms in front of her on the table and leaned toward Jules. "I'm your best friend. I want this for you as much as you want it. I'm up to hearing about it."

Jules held up her right hand, her thumb and index finger an inch apart. "Well, I'm this close. I saw last night that the first cousin logged into her account. She must have gotten my message." A wide, electric grin spread across her face. "Get ready, Momma! I'm coming for ya!"

CHAPTER FORTY-FOUR

Felicia

Maybe Becky would come to visit her today. Felicia tried to remember her last visit. There was a baby. There wasn't a baby. She didn't know what to think, but she hoped there was a baby. She wanted to be a grandmother.

Her eyes wandered over to the small table in the room. The photo albums sat in a pile as a reminder that Becky had promised to go through them with her. She had gone to Felicia's house and gotten them.

Her daughter had told her she would need to sell her little house. Tranquility was her home now. A worried expression marred her gently lined face. There were things there she didn't want anyone to see. Things she didn't want Becky to find. Maybe it didn't even matter anymore. Deep down, she knew it probably did.

She opened the first album to pictures of her wedding day. Felicia ran her index finger over the picture as if touching Ken's face would bring him back to life. The flicker of a smile passed her lips.

When she and Ken got married, they had bought their first house. It was three bedrooms with a sunny kitchen and fruit trees in the back. A white fence bordered their front yard, green grass lush and full.

Ros and her family lived next door. She had come over with her two boys to introduce herself. "Do you have kids?" she asked.

Felicia shook her head. "Not yet. We just got married."

Ros beamed. "Well, congratulations, newlyweds."

And from that moment on, Felicia had a best friend. She knew Ros would do anything for her. She had proven that repeatedly. Felicia often realized how different her life would have been if they had never met.

The women's husbands became friends as well, and there were dinners out with the four of them and group vacations. Felicia wondered if there were pictures of their trip to Cozumel in one of the photo albums. Felicia had come home and sworn she would never drink tequila again.

And then finally it was Felicia's turn to be a mother when Becky was born. She quit her job to stay at home with her. She couldn't imagine not cherishing every single minute. They had crossed paths with Jules and her mom at the park one afternoon. The two girls were almost the same age, and they became inseparable.

It had been devastating when they had to move, but she knew they had no choice. Ken got a new job. Becky was in second grade, so she would go to a new school in a new town, in a new state. It broke her heart when her daughter cried for her best friend.

She and Roslyn kept in touch with phone calls and letters. Occasionally Felicia would sneak back for a visit, but it was never the same as being neighbors. When it came time to leave, her heart always longed to stay.

After Ken died, Roslyn and the family had come to the funeral. "It's time to come home," Roslyn had told her. "You need to be around people who love you."

They could have come back a few years earlier, but with Ken's job, they had decided to stay put and try to give Becky some consistency in high school. She had never really made good friends, almost as if she was afraid to get too close and then have to leave. They both needed support. It was time to go back.

She opened the next book and smiled. Becky's baby pictures. She flipped through the pages, the memories stacked on top of each other like looking through a kaleidoscope.

There was a loose picture stuck in the spine of the album. She pulled it out and held the photo in her hand. As she stared at it, a frown formed on her face. She remembered this day well, recalled the disagreement with Ken before they had gone to his parents' house. Felicia despised everything about them. They acted as if their money allowed them to dictate what was and wasn't acceptable. Felicia never understood how her warm, wonderful husband had come from these people who thought they were better than everyone else.

Felicia didn't like them, and she didn't like having to pretend with them. Ken had convinced her it would be easier. For his sake, she had relented.

When Becky came along, Ken's parents were disappointed she was a girl. "Maybe the next one will be a boy," they said as if Becky didn't matter. Driving home from that visit, Felicia had been furious. "See? Why do you cater to them? Who do your parents think they are?"

She tried to keep the peace for Ken's sake. Ignored their inquisitions. Kept their visits infrequent and brief. When they moved, she had been relieved to leave their regular visits behind, the only silver lining to relocating. They'd been back only once to visit.

Felicia shuddered when her mind drifted to how they had found out the truth. She remembered the call they had gotten, Ken's dad screaming at him over the phone. The relationship with Ken's parents had been irretrievably broken, but Felicia thought it had been broken way before then. It bothered her husband because he always said they had no one else, but Felicia didn't care that they had cut off all contact. As far as she was concerned, those rigid people didn't deserve her family. In a way, Felicia was grateful they had found out. Whatever happened to them, they deserved. As long as her family was safe, that was all that mattered.

After years of not speaking to them, Felicia had been shocked when the family lawyer tracked them down. A knock on their front door and there he was on their porch. He had found them like it was nothing. The very idea scared Felicia to death.

Apparently, cancer didn't care how much money they had. They had died within months of each other, the lawyer told them. With no one else, they had left their money to Ken. And then he died and left his inheritance to Felicia and Becky.

Becky was using their money to have a baby. Karma worked in mysterious ways sometimes.

She just hoped karma wouldn't work against her too.

CHAPTER FORTY-FIVE

Jules

Jules stared at the name on the piece of paper in front of her. Barbara Bennett. She had wondered for so long about the mother who carried her for nine months and then gave her up. Being adopted as an infant, she had no rights, not even the right to know the name of the woman who had given her life. Now, through the magic of DNA, she finally had it. Written on this piece of paper, in her own handwriting, was her birth mother's name.

She had logged in to her computer that morning to find a response to her message from her first cousin.

Well, hello! I received your message and am quite intrigued as to our connection and how we could be cousins. This is all very interesting as I did the DNA test to find out my ethnicity and had no idea all the information I would receive about relatives. This is fascinating! Let me talk to my mom and see if we can figure this out! Sasha

Jules hadn't wanted to appear too eager. She remembered how her client, Marion had warned her that getting involved in a family mystery sometimes caused people to shut down. She typed a more generic response and hit send.

Finally, several nerve-racking hours later, she hit refresh and there it was. She blinked several times to make sure she wasn't imagining it.

Jules, would you be okay if my mom, Bonnie, called you? If so, let me know your phone number, and I will pass it along. Sasha

Jules fumbled with the computer keys as she tried to type her number. She didn't even care anymore how eager she looked.

When her phone rang, Jules could feel her heart thudding wildly.

The voice on the other end was warm and delightful. "Honey," she said, "I've been thinking about you ever since Sasha told me she matched you with that DNA stuff. I don't understand it all, but she says you two are first cousins. I'll bet the farm you're gonna tell me you're adopted."

Jules laughed nervously. "You can keep the farm. I am."

"I figured. It's the only thing that makes sense. I'm the middle sister. I have a younger sister, Enid, and my older sister is Barb. May I ask how old you are?"

"I'll be thirty-two in December."

There was a pause as Bonnie seemed to be putting the pieces together. "Hmm. Obviously, I don't know for sure, but my younger sister would have been fourteen and Barb was twenty-two. I would have been eighteen at the time and just going to college. Seems to me that might have been when Barb told my parents she got a new job. She moved away for about six months. Then, just like that, she said the job wasn't for her, and she came back."

Jules's breath stalled. Was she hearing about her mother's pregnancy?

Bonnie continued. "She did get married a few years later and had a son named Jonas. The marriage didn't last more than a few years, but Jonas is great. He's a cop like his dad. After the divorce,

Barb went back to her maiden name which was Bennett, but Jonas kept his dad's name which was Kirkland."

Holy shit. I have a half-brother. Jules scribbled furiously. She wrote her mother's name down on a piece of paper followed by her half-brother's name. Her eyes widened as she stared at the names. These were real people, and they were related to her. This woman was her aunt. Jules's chest heaved in and out, and she drew in a deep, silent breath as she tried to gain some composure.

"If you're okay with it, I'll call my sister and tell her how you matched with Sasha. See what she says. It's probably not my place to speak on her behalf about something that's her business."

Bonnie had no clue about all the hours Jules had spent staring at her computer looking for the answers she seemed to have. "You have no idea how much this means to me." Jules hoped she sounded as sincere as she felt.

"It's my pleasure. Give me a little bit to get to my sister, and we'll see where this takes us, okay?"

"Okay, thanks again." Jules disconnected the call. She leaned back in her desk chair and stared up at the ceiling. Her mind was racing in a million directions.

She tapped out a text to Becky. *I found her and you'll never believe what else I found!! Call me!*

Jules tried to keep herself busy, but nerves had her stomach doing flips. Fear had bubbled up, and she tried to push it down, but questions invaded her mind. What if her birth mother didn't want to talk to her? Would Bonnie or Sasha call her and break that news to her? What if they didn't know how to tell her and never called back at all?

She went on Facebook and looked up her mother's name. Too many profiles with the same name. She had no idea what she looked like, so she was stuck as she scrolled through them looking for anyone who looked familiar. She found no one that looked like her. Her birth mother probably didn't even have a Facebook profile.

Then she typed her half-brother's name in the search box. It found a match. She clicked on the name, and his profile appeared on her screen. Her breath stalled as she stared at her computer.

Same nose, same chin. Her eyes welled up with tears. This had to be her half-brother. She clicked around in his profile, but he had it set to private. Damn. She had dared to hope there would be some pictures of him with his mom for her to study.

Her phone buzzed with a text, and she practically jumped out of her skin. It wasn't Becky. The message was from Sasha.

My mom is talking to Aunt Barb!

CHAPTER FORTY-SIX

Becky

ecky recalled what Bryan said about checking back in with the neurologist. When she searched "head injuries" on her computer, she found all the symptoms Dr. Summers had told her about. Issues with smell. Memory loss. But there, between all the hits, had been numerous articles about personality change. It was the only explanation.

She had left a message for Dr. Summers's office. She needed to get in today to see him so she could prove to Bryan she was serious about figuring this out.

She pulled in next to Tonya's car in the back parking lot and glanced at the clock on the dash. Becky was scheduled to open, but Tonya always had a hard time staying away. One day off and she couldn't wait to be back.

Becky pulled on the back door and it opened. She tossed the keys in her purse and threw her bag on her desk. Several steps out of the office, she backtracked to read the note on her desk. It was from Michelle. *That guy came in again looking for you after you left yesterday. He wouldn't leave his name. Said don't worry about it, he'd figure it out himself.*

Becky crumpled up the note and then hesitated. She uncrumpled the paper and used her fingers to try to smooth it flat on her desk. Her mind was spinning as she stared at it. Who was this guy who kept coming in looking for her? Could he somehow be related to what Bryan had seen? She took in a deep breath and shook her head as she convinced herself she was making more out of this than was necessary. This man stopping by was probably the husband of a customer she had helped or a supplier who wanted to sell them something. It was probably nothing. She threw the note back in the trash, tossed her purse in her bottom drawer, and wandered out of the office.

"Morning," she called out as she made her way over to the counter where Tonya was standing staring at her cell phone. Tonya turned her gaze in Becky's direction and offered a curt nod.

The smell of fresh oranges wafted in the air as she crossed the floor. "Is this the new orange essential oil?"

"Mmm-hmm." Tonya turned her attention back to her phone.

Becky offered a small smile. "Smells amazing."

Tonya didn't respond. She didn't even look up. Had something happened on her day off to put her in a bad mood? Maybe she was becoming frustrated with all of Becky's problems. She wasn't even sure she blamed her. But really, she hadn't been that late yesterday after she left Jules's house. The store had been fine with Michelle when she got there.

Becky hadn't even called to tell her what had happened with Bryan. Part of her worried that Tonya would recall the missing hours and decide that her car had been missing at exactly the time Bryan claimed to have seen her.

Despite the sunny fragrance that filled the store, the air around where they stood seemed chilly and tense. An uncomfortable silence hung in the air.

"So ... if you have the front covered, I'll go work on paperwork," Becky said, her tone and her expression betraying the awkwardness she felt. "I was out on the floor most of yesterday when I got here, so I could use the time to get caught up on invoices."

Tonya gave Becky a long contemplative look. "Fine."

Becky's shoulders sagged as Tonya's dismissal left her deflated. As she headed back to the office, her stomach churned. In her gut, she couldn't help but feel something else was about to go wrong.

As she lowered herself into her seat, she caught the muffled ring of her cell phone. She cocked her head trying to locate the sound until she remembered her purse was in the drawer. She grabbed it and answered just in time.

"Don't hang up," she said breathlessly.

"Becky Morgan?" the voice on the other end asked.

She let out a frustrated groan when the nurse from Dr. Summers's office told her he was fully booked that day and most of the week. She had begged, probably sounded a bit crazy.

"It's really urgent that I see him. I was in a car accident. He told me to come back in if anything happened. So much has happened. Please."

"Is this a medical emergency?" the nurse asked. "Maybe you should go to the ER?"

The emergency was that her marriage was in a death spiral, and Dr. Summers might be the only one who could help reverse it. Becky let out a weary sigh at the idea that this nurse might stand between her and an appointment. "It's not ER worthy, but I do need to see Dr. Summers as soon as possible. Please, can you help me?"

Finally, the nurse relented and told her she could squeeze her in the following morning. "Please, be on time. I'm double booking him, and I don't want to throw the day off completely."

Relief flooded over her. "I'll be on time, don't worry. Thank you!"

She felt a twinge of dread at telling Tonya she'd be out for a bit tomorrow. But this was urgent. She had to go and try to find answers, and Dr. Summers might be the only one who had them.

The rhythmic sound of heels clicking on the tile as they approached the office gave Becky a heads-up that Tonya was coming. She appeared in the doorway and leaned momentarily on the door frame. Her face was set in a hard stare as she approached Becky's desk.

Becky shifted her gaze away from the computer and up at Tonya. "Hey, what's up?"

Tonya rocked on her heels and then stood rigid. "Becky, money was missing last night. I went through the receipts from last night, and most of the cash was missing."

Becky's forehead creased in confusion as she surveyed the severe expression on Tonya's face. "Michelle locked up, but I closed out the register myself before I left. Is it possible my math was wrong?" She paused. "I've had a lot on my mind lately." That was an understatement.

Tonya stood over Becky and placed her cell phone on the desk. She drummed her fingers on Becky's desk, her manicured nails clicking in an aggravated rhythm. "Becky, stop. Your math wouldn't make money disappear."

"Are you saying you think I stole from the register?" Becky asked, her tone incredulous. "That doesn't make any sense."

"There's a lot of things going on here lately that don't make sense. Frankly, I'm worried about you."

Tonya had always been direct, but Becky was stunned with the insinuation that she had something to do with money missing.

"I thought maybe it was the hormones, and I tried to be patient," Tonya said. "But you're not even taking those anymore, and yes,

I'm sorry about everything that happened with the IVF. I know that wasn't easy. I also know it wasn't cheap."

With the mere mention of her failed IVF, a heavy lump formed in Becky's throat. She wasn't going to cry—no way.

"Becky, money is missing. This can't continue. This boutique is our livelihood. You know it's pretty much my whole life." Tonya hesitated and picked up her phone from the desk. "We've been friends for a long time, but I also need to protect the store."

"Protect it? From me?" Becky could barely choke the words out.

"Trust me, I never thought we'd be having this conversation either, but you've been distracted and acting odd for weeks now."

Becky tried to steady her voice but knew the red splotches on her neck betrayed how she really felt. "I'm worried about myself too. I have an appointment with the neurologist tomorrow. I want to check in to make sure I don't have any lasting effects from the accident. I know I can't blame anything on the hormones since I'm not even taking those anymore. But I'd never steal from the store. We're partners."

She studied Tonya's face to see if her plea had convinced her. It hadn't. Her mouth was still set in a hard line.

"Whatever's going on with you, you need to fix it. Otherwise, we're going to need to have a serious conversation about our future as partners." Tonya spun on her heels, and in several long strides she was gone.

Becky sat in disbelief of the conversation that had just happened. Resting her elbows on the desk, she used both hands to hold up her head. She closed her eyes and drew air deeply into her lungs. Tonya's accusation made no sense. Becky would have no reason to steal from the store. There had to be a logical explanation neither of them had considered.

She wandered out of the office, but Tonya was with a customer. The bell jangled above the door and a group of young girls made their way inside. Becky stole a glance at Tonya, but it seemed the conversation was over. She went to see how she could help the girls as she tried to ignore the despair gnawing at her insides.

The day dragged by without any unnecessary conversation with Tonya. They both spent the day helping customers but stayed out of each other's way. Finally, Becky glanced at her watch and felt relief wash over her. She wasn't scheduled to close, so she had made it through this uncomfortable day. Wincing, she realized Tonya probably wouldn't have let her close the register by herself anyway.

She scurried past Tonya on her way to the office and muttered goodbye under her breath. She wanted to go home even though there was nothing there for her. There didn't seem to be much for her at the boutique either. Her happy place was no longer happy.

She grabbed her purse and reached in to steal a look at her cell phone. There was a text from Jules. *I found her and you're not going to believe what else I found!! Call me!* Becky glanced at the time the text had been received and let out a weary sigh. Jules had sent it hours ago. Guilt weighed heavily on Becky that she hadn't responded to such a huge announcement.

Her best friend had dropped everything for her yesterday when she needed her, and now that she had answers, Becky had left her hanging. She scolded herself for being a terrible friend. Her life was in shambles, and her friendship with Jules appeared to be the only important part of her life still intact. She needed to keep it that way.

As she sat in her car, Becky closed her eyes and blinked back tears. She had escaped the store for the day, but tomorrow would bring her situation right back to where she was leaving it today. Nothing had been resolved.

As she pulled onto the main road, she saw Tonya through the front window. Her bottom lip quivered. She felt like an outsider at her own store.

She put her phone on hands-free and dialed Jules's number. After four rings, she got voicemail. *You've reached Jules and Southern Charm Photography. Leave me a message after the beep.*

"Hey, it's me. Sorry it took so long, but the store was a bit crazy today. It sounds like you have big news. I can't wait to hear about it! I'm leaving the store now. Call me back when you can."

Jules had really done it. She'd used her DNA to find her birth mother. Becky thought about the text she had sent and wondered what else she had found.

CHAPTER FORTY-SEVEN

Jules

Sasha had sent her message earlier in the day, and with no return call from anyone, Jules was coming to a sinking realization. This might not be the happy reunion she hoped to have. Maybe Barb had told her sister to mind her own business, and that was that. To be this close and not have answers—the very thought made her nauseous. She hadn't even heard back from Becky which made her check the settings on her phone to make sure it was working. She turned the ringer up as high as it would go.

She went into her studio and passed the hours going through shots of a corporate event she had taken a few days ago. The distraction was a welcome relief until she finally glanced down at the time on her computer. It was late, and she had heard nothing. The adrenaline of the earlier call had dissipated. Her body felt limp. She almost wished Sasha hadn't sent that text. Now she knew Bonnie and Barb had spoken, but the outcome was just a big black void.

The loud ring of her phone startled her, but it wasn't Becky or Bonnie. It was a number she didn't recognize. Her heart thumped in her ears as she answered the phone.

She couldn't even speak at first, so the caller spoke first.

"Jules?" It was a man's voice.

She prayed this wasn't about a photography job. She didn't think she could put two coherent sentences together at this point.

She cleared her throat and hoped her voice would work. "Yes, this is Jules."

"Well, hey there, Jules. This is Jonas, and I hear you're my sister."

Her mouth fell open. She had expected she might hear back from the aunt or the cousin who would tell her how the conversation had gone with her birth mother. She hadn't anticipated a call from her half-brother.

"Well, I guess technically I'm your half-sister unless you know something I don't know."

The voice on the other end erupted in loud, booming laughter. "Once you get to know me, you'll figure out pretty damn quick that I don't do anything halfway. As far as I'm concerned, you're my sister, and that's all there is to it."

The next two hours flew as they talked on the phone. Jules smiled when she realized the laugh on the other end of the line matched hers. They had the same sense of humor. He had grown up near her and lived only twenty minutes away. She told him about her photography business and her love of capturing life through her camera. He confirmed what Bonnie had told her about his parents being divorced but told Jules he was still very close to both of them.

"So, I hear you're a cop," Jules said.

"That I am." He laughed. "Can you imagine how hot that uniform gets in this wretched Florida humidity? I work in Creekside."

"Seriously? That's crazy. My best friend lives in Creekside."

"Just one more of those coincidences that can't really be a coincidence, right? Hopefully I've never had to meet your friend during working hours."

"Doubtful. She and her husband are pretty strait-laced. I'll bet you have some pretty interesting stories, though."

"There's never a dull moment, that's for sure."

There was a short pause on the line. It soon became clear why she had not heard anything earlier.

"So, Jules, you caused quite the flurry of family phone calls today. When my mom told me to come over for dinner tonight, I had no idea I was getting a sister for dessert. But don't get me wrong, I think it's great. I was an only child. I always wanted siblings."

Jules laughed. "Me too."

Suddenly Jonas's tone turned serious. He explained that his mom was still quite nervous about a reunion.

"It has nothing to do with you," he said. "It just reminds her of a rough time in her life. She told no one about you, not my grandparents, not even me, so you can imagine the shock she felt when her sister called and told her you were looking for her. I could tell how painful it was for her to tell me, but she said she wanted to make sure I heard the truth from her."

Jules felt dizzy as her mouth went dry. Did he just say Barb didn't want to meet her?

Jonas continued. "She was ashamed, not of you necessarily, but of the whole situation. She had an affair with her boss. He was, of course, married. It's an old story, but she ended up pregnant. Naturally, he didn't want anything to do with fessing up to his wife and my mom—our mom, I guess I should say—was young, only twenty-two. She made up this story to her parents about moving away while he put her up temporarily in an apartment and supported her financially. She told me that when they placed the baby in her arms, she wanted to change her mind and keep you."

"Really? She wanted to keep me?" With that one piece of information, Jules felt a weight fall off her shoulders. Her birth mother hadn't wanted to give her up.

"She did, but she wanted to do the right thing," Jonas said. "So, she put you up for adoption so a couple who was married could give you a better life than she ever could. But when she told me the story of how they had taken you from her and how she went home to her family without you, she broke down. She has carried around that heartbreak and guilt for a very long time."

Jules closed her eyes and listened intently to Jonas tell the story of how she had come to be. The relief she had felt only moments ago started to fade. What she heard was that her father hadn't wanted any part of her, and now her mother wasn't sure if she wanted to meet her. Both facts grabbed her insides and twisted them tight. While she tried to process it all in her head, she didn't respond.

Jonas's voice broke the silence on the line. "You still there?"

Jules opened her eyes and bit her bottom lip. "When I started this search, I guess I thought my birth mom would be the one telling me my story. So many times I imagined what it would be like when I found her. I hoped she'd be thrilled. It's what kept me searching, but she doesn't seem very happy to be found."

Jonas paused as he seemed to reflect on what he wanted to say next. "She just needs to let this sink in. It's weird because there were times she seemed to have this underlying sense of sadness about her. I asked her once, and she told me that sometimes things happen in life that change you. She would never tell me what she meant by that, but now I think she meant giving you up. When we talked about it today, she admitted she thought about you all the time over the years. She hoped you were growing up in a good home with loving parents, but Mother's Day and your birthday were sort of days that kicked her butt."

Jules murmured assent as if she understood, but inside she was screaming. If Barb was so sad about giving her up, it seemed unfathomable to Jules that she wouldn't want to meet her daughter. She didn't know if she could handle being rejected by her birth mother. Again. She thought about that day at the coffee shop when Marion had told her how her sister wanted nothing more than to find the son she had given up. Jules had imagined she'd find the same reaction. It made her feel dizzy to find out Barb even needed to think about it.

Jonas seemed to understand that she needed more clarification. "You have to understand. Back then, they told her when she gave you up that she would never see you again. They drilled into her that you would be someone else's daughter. You know, it's funny that you mentioned your love of photography. Mom paints sometimes. She calls it her therapy."

It had been just that kind of information Jules had always wanted to know. It appeared DNA did play a part in where her interests had come from.

Jonas continued. "She thought she would go to her grave without ever knowing what happened to you. Of course, that's before all this cutting-edge DNA and some kick-ass detective work by you. She feels incredibly guilty for giving you up, and she's just scared out of her mind that you hate her for it. She'll come around. I know she will. In the meantime, this brother wants to meet you. Do you drink coffee?"

They made plans to meet up the next morning for breakfast at a coffee shop, and as Jules hung up the phone, an entire range of emotions swirled through her. She didn't know Jonas yet, but she already felt like she could trust him.

If he told her it would be okay, she had to have faith that this would all work out. After all, he knew his mother better than anyone. The fact that she immediately wanted to tell him the truth had to mean something. If nothing else, her search had yielded her answers, not to mention a sibling.

After talking for a couple of hours on the phone, Jules felt excited, exhausted, exhilarated, and couldn't wait for it to be morning. She noticed a message from Becky on her phone, but it was late. There would be plenty to share after coffee with her brother the next day.

As Jules brushed her teeth and got ready for bed, she couldn't stop thinking about how surreal the day had been. Yesterday she knew nothing. For so long she had wanted to know where she started, and now she did.

As she crawled into bed, a sense of contentment fell over her. She was somebody's sister. She had never been able to say that.

CHAPTER FORTY-EIGHT

Becky

During the drive home, when Becky passed the spot of the accident, her mind drifted back to that night. The tree still bore the scar. It seemed possible she might too.

She had written off the accident as nothing. Maybe it was everything.

Becky stared at her phone and scowled. Jules hadn't called her back, and she desperately wanted to talk to Bryan. He'd find the whole idea that she'd steal from the store ridiculous. She desperately needed his voice of reason to talk her through it and settle the sick feeling in her stomach.

Her eyes welled up as a new round of tears threatened to fall. He just had to come back. She didn't know how to be without him.

When he left that awful night, he'd said he needed a few days. It had only been two, but it felt like forever. They had never gone two days without speaking. Not since the day she met him.

Tomorrow. She would call him after her appointment with Dr. Summers. Maybe she'd be able to tell Bryan that none of this was her fault. Every hope she had was pinned on Dr. Summers telling her he could fix this. She wanted her life back.

As she pulled into the driveway, Bryan's car was noticeably absent.

After she entered the code, she pushed open the door. She remembered how insistent she had been that the locks be changed. Bryan hadn't agreed that someone had been in their house, but he had done it. He had done it to give her peace of mind.

He had promised they would figure it out together. And now, here she was, using the new lock to get into a dark, empty house. There had been so much more to figure out since that day, and they hadn't done any of it together. That was her fault, and it had taken him leaving for her to realize it.

Coming home into darkness just made her feel worse. But even as she flipped on the light, it did nothing to change the way the house felt. Their home had always been filled with happiness and love. Without Bryan, it just felt ... empty.

As she slipped off her shoes and tossed her purse on the chair, her body went limp. No Sherlock running to greet her, throwing himself down in front of her for a belly rub. No Bryan cooking dinner in the kitchen. Tonya seemed convinced she was stealing from her own store, and her best friend had left her a pretty important message that she hadn't responded to until hours later. This didn't even feel like her life anymore.

Sherlock's food was still scattered across the kitchen tile, a reminder of the fight with Bryan. She grabbed the broom from the closet. As she fought back tears, she swept the cat food into a dustpan and into the trash and picked up the container it had spilled from. Becky opened the door off the kitchen that led to the laundry room and the back door. In the small space between the dryer and the wall, she stuck the container out of sight. She didn't need the constant reminder he was gone.

With the cat food cleaned up, she had no idea what to do next. She wandered without purpose through the house. Her feet frozen in the doorway, she stared into the spare room. What she saw was boxes, Bryan's *Star Wars* posters on the wall, suitcases waiting for them to take a trip.

But if she closed her eyes, she saw the nursery. Pastel colors with zoo animals stenciled on the walls. A white crib with a green and yellow bumper and gingham sheets. The rocker in the corner where she had imagined she would hold their baby while the rest of the world slept. She brought her fingers to her lips. She could almost feel soft hair against them while she breathed in the intoxicating smell of their newborn. Her chin quivered as she opened her eyes. Everything this room wasn't hurt her heart.

She made her way down to their bedroom. The covers were in a heap on the bed, one of the pillows tossed on the floor as she had tried to find some way to get comfortable without her husband the night before. Making the bed had seemed unnecessary when she left that morning.

She stripped off her work clothes and left them lying on the floor. She pulled her oversized fluffy pink robe off the hook in the bathroom and wrapped herself up in it.

Barefoot, she padded into the kitchen. Out of habit, she flipped on the porch light and glanced out the sliding glass door. She didn't really expect to see anything. It seemed as hopeless as the rest of her life right now. Sherlock wasn't coming back. Her mind had to accept that her skittish cat was probably no match for the outside world.

At the refrigerator, she pulled it open and stared inside, but her eyes saw nothing. What she saw instead was Bryan chopping garlic, assembling tacos, flipping pancakes onto her plate for breakfast on a Sunday morning. She could hear him singing off-key, music blaring, while he cooked. She could smell his marinara sauce bubbling in a pot on the stove. She laid her palm against her cheek. She could almost feel his soft T-shirt against her face as she leaned into him, his solid body against hers.

She needed relief from the angst that was making her whole body uncomfortable as if her skin didn't fit anymore. Leaning into the shower, she turned the knobs, testing the water under her hand until it was just hot enough. Slipping out of her robe, she stepped in. An audible gasp escaped her as the warm water pelted her skin.

She wanted to erase this day. Forget the way she felt when Tonya had looked at her with that accusatory stare. Extinguish the memory of Sherlock's soft body curled up and the way it felt when his body vibrated against hers. She needed to dull the ache she felt inside that Bryan wouldn't come walking through the door.

As the jets of water washed over her, her misery erupted in a convulsive gasp. Once released, her body shook uncontrollably. Sadness crested over her in waves again and again as the water and her tears swirled down the drain together. Dizzy and unsteady on her feet, she leaned against the shower wall to hold herself up.

Finally, she just succumbed. Her body failed her, sinking in a heap to the floor of the shower. The water rained down on her until it was cold and uncomfortable.

Her legs quivered underneath her as she stood. She turned the water handle to the off position and grabbed a towel from the rack next to the shower. She stepped out and stumbled into the bedroom.

As she pulled on pajamas, she let her gaze drift to Bryan's side of the bed. Her shoulders drooped as she let out a deep sigh. She needed to go to sleep and forget this day had ever happened.

She didn't even care that her hair was wet as she staggered back into the bathroom to find a hairband to put it up. She rummaged through the catch-all basket on the vanity and then the drawer and found nothing. She shook her head in disbelief. Finally, she reached into the far back corner of the drawer and emerged with a rubber band. She'd make do.

With her focus on collapsing into bed, she collected all her wet hair in one hand. As she stretched the rubber band with the other to wrap it around the wet mess atop her head, it ricocheted off her hand. Becky's throat tightened as she stifled a sob of frustration.

"Really?" she whimpered out loud. Still holding her wet ponytail, she let go.

She dropped to the floor to look for it, the hardwood unrelenting on her knees. The rubber band had to have gone somewhere. As her eyes scanned the baseboard, something under the bed caught her eye.

As she reached for it, she felt the familiar plastic handle even before she pulled out the bag. Her forehead creased with confusion. The bag wasn't hers. She couldn't imagine Bryan would have bought her something from her store and hidden it under their bed. As she dragged it out, she could tell it was too heavy to be clothing.

With a feeling of dread, she pulled open the bag and peered inside. It fell from her hands as if it had turned into molten lava and burned the skin off her fingers. Her heart skipped frantically with panic.

"No!" The room spun. Becky sucked in gulps of air as she tried to breathe before finally putting her head in her hands.

Inside the bag was all the missing jewelry from the store, the jewelry Anna had gotten fired for stealing.

CHAPTER FORTY-NINE

Jules

As Jules approached the front of the coffee shop, she was still trying to wrap her head around the fact that she was on her way to have coffee with her brother. She reminded herself to breathe.

When she was roughly twenty feet from the entrance, her pulse quickened. A man was waiting outside, his head bowed down looking at his phone.

As if on cue, the handsome man glanced up, and a grin filled his face. "I'm sure you're Jules," he said with conviction. "I would know you anywhere."

He embraced her in a hug, and she was sure he could feel the rapid thumping of her heart against his chest. As he stepped back, she tried to look him over without being too obvious she was staring at him. He was tall, at least six-foot, and well-built with his brown hair buzzed in a crew cut. He looked every bit the stereotypical police officer, but as Jules studied him further, she was amazed to see in person what she had noticed in his Facebook picture. There, on his face, was the male version of her nose and square-shaped chin.

Comfortable with him from the moment they sat down, Jules was awestruck. They took their coffee the same way and laughed when they both asked the waitress for low-fat milk at the same time.

"I'm digging the boots," Jonas said as he stirred his coffee.

Jules held up her foot to show off her black and red cowboy boots. "I can't wait to wear these for Georgia football. Woof!"

His mouth formed a circle and froze.

Jules's eyes widened in mock horror. "Oh, don't tell me we're going to have rivalry issues come football season. That would crush me."

"You went to the University of Georgia?"

She nodded. "My best friend thought I was crazy when I told her I just had to go to college in the south. Well, first she didn't understand that I had to go north to be in the south. I have this whole Scarlet O'Hara fantasy."

Jonas stared at her across the table and shook his head in disbelief. "Wow, this is crazy. I'm not sure if you know this, but you were born in Georgia. My mother—your mother—she went to UGA too."

Jules's mouth dropped open. "Stop it. Seriously? I was adopted in Florida. I wasn't born here too?"

"From what my mom told me, the birth father wanted the adoption in a neighboring state. I guess maybe he thought it would be harder to track. Interesting that my mom moved to this part of Florida a few years later. Most of the family is here now."

Her eyes grew misty and she fanned herself with her hand. "You know, they say a true southern belle is from where they were born. I can actually say I'm a Georgia native now. I *knew* I didn't feel right as a Florida girl. I've always thought I had some southern bred into me, felt drawn to go to school there. Wow."

"No kidding. It does say something about nature versus nurture, right? I mean, it can't just be a coincidence."

"I know I started this, but I'm still pretty much in shock that I'm sitting here. I'm so grateful to Sasha for doing that DNA test. You're the only biological relative I've ever met. Who knows how long it would have taken me to find you if I hadn't matched her."

She told Jonas about Lucy, the mystery match on the other site. She gave him a sheepish smile. "I hate to say I stalked her, but I did. I thought she was the answer to everything. I still have no idea who she is, but she doesn't match Sasha. She must be a match to me on my birth father's side. Unfortunately, it doesn't seem she has much information to offer."

"I'm still impressed you figured us out. You're going to have plenty of new leaves on that family tree of yours. You already talked to my Aunt Bonnie." Jonas let out a groan. "I guess she's your Aunt Bonnie too. I have to stop doing that."

"It's okay. I know this is a lot to take in."

"Anyway, Aunt Bonnie is awesome, as I'm sure you realized. She and my Uncle Jeff have three kids. Sasha, who started this whole DNA thing as you know, is the oldest. Bella is about to graduate college, and Charlie is in his last year of high school. You better look out come football season. He's been accepted to UF."

"Oh no, not a Gator," Jules clutched her chest dramatically.

"Charlie's a great kid. My aunt and uncle live about an hour away on a big piece of property. She works for the golden retriever rescue, so their house is always filled with the sweetest pups you can imagine. She has a heart of gold, which is why I'm sure she had quite a lot to say to Mom about coming clean about everything and doin' what's right. You'll love her."

Jules nodded and hoped she could keep this all straight. Secretly, she wished it was appropriate to take notes. She couldn't wait to start her own tree.

Jonas continued. "Then there's my Aunt Enid. She and my Uncle Bill live nearby. They have two kids, both in high school. See, there's a lot of cousins for you to meet and don't think we're not going to plan a big reunion so everyone can meet you. When we all start having kids, I can't even imagine how big the family events are going to get. The holidays are insane when we all get together."

Jules pursed her lips. He hadn't mentioned Barb. It would be odd to think big family gatherings could happen with the rest of the family if her birth mother didn't want any part of a reunion. Jonas was acting as if he expected it would all work out. Jules swallowed past the lump in her throat. She couldn't even imagine this big family welcoming her and including her in family gatherings as if she belonged there.

In a flash, she thought of her parents. The mention of spending the holidays with this large, extended family left her excited but also overwhelmed. She couldn't imagine telling this all to her parents. They hadn't even asked about her DNA test. In an ideal world, she would want both families to meet, but she didn't know if that would ever happen. She felt happy and conflicted all at the same time.

Jonas watched Jules's face turn serious. "Too much? I swear you'll love 'em. Our family's a little nutty, but you'll never find a better bunch of people."

Jules shook her head. "It's not that. It's my parents. They were nervous about me searching. Scared about having to share me. I'm just trying to figure out how I'm going to tell them all of this."

"Ah. Yeah, there's a big adjustment period on both sides, I guess. Not for me, though. I couldn't wait to meet you."

"Me either. I was so focused on finding my birth mother, I hadn't even stopped to think I might meet a brother first. My parents were older when they adopted me, so I never had a sibling, but I always wanted one. My best friend Becky is the closest thing to a sister I have. She's been so supportive in this whole DNA thing. I was so nervous about the whole thing I made her do a test too." Jules laughed.

"So, what did she find out? Was she adopted too?"

Jules averted her gaze and stayed silent for a moment. "No, she's not adopted. I was going to try to do a family tree for her baby ..." her voice trailed off. "She was trying to have a baby, but they had to do IVF. She had a few embryos—they all died before they could transfer any of them. It's been really hard for her. I was going to be the baby's godmother, and I thought a tree would be a cool gift." She cringed as she remembered Becky's reaction. "Now I feel horrible about it."

"It's not your fault the IVF didn't work."

"No, I know. She wanted to be supportive. She did the DNA test and gave it to me to mail in, but then she changed her mind. She was convinced it would be bad luck." Jules hesitated. "She wanted to wait until she was actually pregnant. She left me a message—asked me not to send it—" Jules looked down for a moment at the table. "I didn't get the message in time. I had already dropped it with my test into a mailbox."

"Oh." Jonas winced. "Was she mad?"

Jules scrunched up her face. "I didn't tell her. I know, that's awful. I figured it wouldn't be bad luck if she didn't know. I've been so obsessed with my search that I never even looked to see if her results came in."

Jules drank the last sip of her coffee. "I can't wait for you to meet her. She and her husband Bryan have had some issues lately with this whole baby thing, but I know they'll work through it and be okay. They are one of the best couples I know. Gives me hope that someday I might find someone. What about you? Love life?"

Jonas's face lit up. "Engaged, and she's amazing. I couldn't stop raving about you after our call last night. She's excited but maybe a little nervous that things are going to change."

"Becky told me not to find a sister to replace her," Jules said. "She'll be thrilled you're a brother."

As Jonas glanced at the time on his phone, Jules felt her pulse quicken. This breakfast had been incredible. He had made it sound like they would continue to spend time together. Still, she had to ask him while she had the chance. Just in case.

"I know you said your mom needs time to sort through this, and I can respect that. Don't get me wrong, I'm thrilled about this." Jules gestured with her hand between the two of them. "Would it be too soon to ask for a favor?"

"Don't be silly. I'm your brother. Ask me anything." He paused and eyed her. "Not money, right?"

She smiled. "No, not money." Jules began cautiously, hoping it would all sound okay when the words came out. "My whole life I've wondered about who I really am. My adoptive parents are great, but there was always something missing, something I felt like I couldn't define until lately. Meeting you today—" Her voice wobbled until she wasn't sure she could even get the words out of her mouth. "Meeting you today was a dream come true. You know you have my nose and my chin, right?" Jules asked as she tried to regain her composure. "Until you, I've never seen anyone who has a resemblance to me, a face that looks like mine. All these years, I've always wondered about my birth mother. Tried to picture in my mind what she might look like."

Jules squirmed in her seat. "Would it be weird if I asked if you had any pictures of her on your phone? I just really want to know what she looks like. I'm sure that's probably hard for you to understand."

Jonas picked up his phone from the table. "It's not weird at all. Of course, you'd be curious, and oh, you're gonna see a resemblance all right."

He scrolled through his photos and selected one, and then handed his phone across the table to her. Heart pounding, she took it from him. She caught her breath as the woman on the screen looked out at her, wearing the same oversized smile usually found on Jules's face.

Jules caught her breath. As her eyes welled up, she stared transfixed at the woman who shared her very essence. She didn't even need the DNA test. There was not a doubt in her mind that Barb was the woman who had given her life.

She dipped her head to him in grateful acknowledgment. Without words, she handed the phone back.

"I've got to get to work." Jonas stood up and dropped cash on the table to cover the bill. "We need to try to make up for lost time. Let's plan to get together for dinner. You bring your friend and her husband, and I'll bring my fiancée."

"That would be great. I'll check my calendar and text you some dates." Jules slid out of her seat, stood up, and hugged him goodbye.

As she watched him walk away, she felt complete. She had answers, and even if they might not be all the answers she wanted, her story was no longer a mystery. That alone was worth everything.

CHAPTER FIFTY

Becky

Becky had gone into the store that morning only to find Tonya was still giving her the cold shoulder. She had even called in Michelle as if she thought Becky wouldn't show up after their confrontation the day before.

"Morning," Michelle said with a smile as she twirled and her skirt flared around her.

"Morning. Hey, that's one of the new dresses we just got in."

"I know, I love it. I figured you and Tonya are always saying we should wear stuff from the store. I'm finally starting to get ahead with my paychecks so I figured I could splurge."

Becky narrowed her eyes but said nothing. All of a sudden, Michelle had extra money?

Michelle went to help Tonya, and Becky stayed out of her way until it was time to go. She was relieved to be leaving for the neurologist and slunk to the office and out the back door without saying goodbye to either one of them. As Becky drove to her appointment, her foot tapped the brakes when she saw Jules was standing outside a coffee shop with a handsome man.

Jules hadn't responded to her voicemail the night before. She still felt guilty it had taken her so long when Jules obviously had big news.

Becky would explain what happened at the store. Jules would understand. Her friend would agree that the notion that she would steal from the store was ridiculous. As the bag of jewelry under her bed flashed in her mind, she cringed. Maybe the idea wasn't so crazy after all. But, even though the jewelry had been in the bag, there was no sign of the cash Tonya had said was missing the day before.

Becky squinted out the window as she watched the man embrace Jules in a close hug. That didn't seem like a potential client. He held the door open for her, and they disappeared inside.

Normally Becky would have been the first to hear if there was even the inkling of a new man. Her best friend hadn't said anything at breakfast. She hated to think her problems had been so burdensome that Jules hadn't bothered to tell her she had met someone.

When Becky got to the medical building, she circled the small lot outside. Her stomach twisted—not a single parking spot. She waited to see if anyone would pull out as she glanced at the clock. She had promised not to be late.

With no other choice, Becky pulled her car into the entrance of the parking structure. Dread filled her insides. She tried to avoid them at all costs—too dark, too many places for someone to be hidden in the shadows. As she drove farther and farther down into the darkness, one level after another, she felt her palms dampen on the steering wheel. There were no available spots. Her phobia urged her to circle back up and into the daylight.

She felt caged in as she got to the bottom level. Thick concrete all around her would muffle any sounds she might make down here. Another glance at the clock. She would need to either forego her appointment or park down here in the darkest, dankest level.

Bryan's face flashed in front of her. Her breath stalled as she slid into a tight spot between two other cars. She didn't like this at all.

Her heart was racing. Wedged in so close to the vehicle next to her, she could barely get her door open. She exited sideways and slammed the door. After locating the quickest route to the elevator, she put her head down and dashed in that direction.

As she sat in the waiting room, her breathing gradually returned to normal. She wasn't even sure what she would tell the doctor. *I bumped my head and became a cheater and a thief and a terrible friend.*

When the neurologist appeared in the room, Dr. Summers was just as warm and kind as she remembered. Becky attempted to focus on the questions the doctor was asking her. Were there any chunks of time missing she couldn't explain. She told him about her bizarre nap in the stockroom.

"Any other instances where time went missing?" the doctor asked.

She shook her head. She wasn't late for work, and aside from the missing hours in the stockroom, she could account for every minute of each day.

He was taking notes in her file. "Do you notice yourself being unusually aggressive or subject to huge mood swings?"

"No more than usual," she said in a soft, wobbly voice.

His gaze swept to her stomach.

She acknowledged the look. "Nope, no baby in there," she said in a somber voice. "IVF didn't work for us."

The doctor dipped his head in acknowledgment. "I'm sorry. I remember how much you wanted that to work."

She blinked back tears.

He continued to quiz her. "Have you been getting headaches since the accident? Or are you noticing any other physical symptoms that you didn't have before?"

"No more headaches than usual and nothing else that I can think of except that the people all around me think I'm a different person."

She dreaded having to explain, but this was the real reason she was here. She told him about Bryan and saw the surprise in his eyes.

"I would never want to hurt him, although I guess I did after the IVF didn't work." She gazed down at her hands folded in her lap. "I was so wrapped up in my own misery, I didn't take his feelings into account the way I should have." The doctor studied her intently, and she brought her gaze back up to meet his. "I don't blame him for being angry with me, but I'd never cheat on him." She told him about Tonya and the boutique. "But that would make no sense either," she said, her voice shaking. "I own the store with her. It would be like stealing from myself, but yet the jewelry was there—in my house, under my bed."

She told him about smelling cigarettes and her perfume that she knew she hadn't sprayed, the candle that had been lit twice without her remembering, the mystery dresses, and looking for any other explanation for how the teddy bears had appeared or how her cat had gotten out and disappeared into thin air.

He offered her a warm, reassuring smile. "I know it doesn't seem like it, but there has to be a rational explanation for all these things."

He sounded like Bryan.

"Your husband is probably suffering just like you are at what happened with the IVF. He just saw someone that looked like you, and his grief made him jump to a conclusion that wasn't rational."

Someone wearing the same clothes at precisely the time she couldn't account for her whereabouts? That didn't sound like grief, but Becky stayed silent.

"Does anyone else have a reason to steal from the store and a key?" Dr. Summers asked. "It isn't logical that you would steal from your own store, so there has to be another explanation or another person you haven't considered. Maybe the other girl felt guilty and tried to return the jewelry to you at your house. Is it possible Bryan took it and forgot to tell you before he left? Does she know where you live?"

Becky scrunched up her face as she considered it. "She does know where I live. I guess it's possible. I haven't talked to Bryan, so he wouldn't have told me yet if it happened the night he left."

Dr. Summers addressed her other issues. "Sometimes the nose can play tricks on us and make us smell things that aren't there. Maybe somehow someone did leave the bears for you as a surprise. When the pregnancy didn't happen, they felt silly and didn't want to take credit. I'm sure you've had a lot on your mind between the IVF and the accident. It's probably not a stretch to think you forgot about buying the dresses or lighting the candle."

Did this go along with what Kim had told her? It still didn't seem possible that she simply had so much going on that these things slipped her mind.

The doctor continued. "And the cat probably wandered out an open door somehow. Maybe a neighbor is feeding him thinking he's a stray. The nap you took in the stockroom isn't completely unreasonable either. It would be shocking if you weren't exhausted after everything you've been through lately."

She started to object, and he held up his hand. "Maybe your partner just thought your car wasn't there. Maybe her memory went back to a different time when your car wasn't there when she pulled in. People have a lot on their minds these days. It's not surprising we run out of room to hold it all in our head." He tried to coax a smile from her.

Becky took it all in and sat quietly on the exam table. She knew her crestfallen expression relayed the disappointment she felt. Even though some of what the doctor presented made sense, no one else in her world thought so.

"What you're describing and what you're telling me doesn't seem to suggest a head injury. You did the right thing coming in today. Follow up can be crucial, but my professional opinion is that there are no lingering effects from the accident. I know you feel overwhelmed, but there has to be a rational explanation for everything that's happened."

The doctor patted her hand, and his tone turned personal. "The grief from what you went through could be very profound even though you weren't pregnant. My suggestion would be that you and your husband might want to think about some counseling to deal with the feelings you both have about the situation. My guess is a lot of these issues will fall away as you deal with the loss together."

Her expression glum, Becky nodded even though she wasn't sure she agreed. She had optimistically hoped the doctor could tell her that there was something wrong he could fix. She could tell everyone this wasn't her fault, take a magic pill, and put the splintered fragments of her life back together.

"Good luck," Dr. Summers said. "You'll find your answers, I'm sure of it. I'll give the nurse the names of a few counselors. She'll have them for you when you check out."

As promised, when she paid her co-pay, the nurse handed her a slip of paper with three recommendations for therapists. Becky took the paper and mumbled thank you. Bryan wasn't even speaking to her. It seemed unlikely they would be going to counseling anytime soon. She didn't know how she could convince her husband that grief had caused him to believe he saw something that wasn't real. It almost wasn't possible to convince herself.

She walked down the long hall of medical offices and pushed open the door that led to the parking garage elevator. She stepped in and pushed the button for her floor. As the door began to close, her thoughts drifted to Bryan. She had wanted to call him today, but if Dr. Summers didn't have any answers, then she was back where she started.

Becky silently bemoaned the fact that she had to go back to the bottom level of the garage. Her nerves were on edge. She wanted to get to her car and get back up to the sunlight. As the two metal doors drew within a few inches of each other, a hand suddenly appeared and prevented them from closing. Becky stifled a gasp as the doors automatically reopened. A man stepped in and she knew her face bore evidence of the fact that he had startled her.

"Sorry," he said. "It's always so slow. I didn't want to have to wait for you to send it back for me." He offered her an apologetic smile.

Becky swallowed hard and gave him a sideways glance to look him over. He hadn't pressed a button for a different floor. In that small space, it seemed hard to believe this man couldn't hear her heart beating, see her pulse throbbing at her temple. She clenched her hand into a fist and felt her nails digging into the palm of her hand.

The ding of the elevator announced her level, and she subtly glanced in his direction as the doors slid open. She stepped out, keys in hand. Her anxiety ramped up as he stepped out as well—right behind her.

She knew exactly where her car was located and walked swiftly in that direction. The sound of footsteps hitting the concrete echoed behind her. It was the middle of the day. Of course there would be other people in the parking garage. The feeling she was being pursued, hunted even, overwhelmed her.

She couldn't help herself. As she spun around ready for a confrontation, she frowned as there was no one behind her. Her senses were on high alert as she looked for any flash of movement that would tell her where he'd gone, but she saw nothing.

She took off running in the direction of her car. When she was safely inside, she slammed the button to lock the door. Sucking in a huge breath of air, she then exhaled loudly. No monsters appeared. No one was chasing her. So why did she feel like someone was?

CHAPTER FIFTY-ONE

Jules

As Jules reflected on the last twenty-four hours, she tried to reconcile her emotions. So much had happened. Not only finding Jonas but the unexpected call she had gotten from Tim on her way home. Anticipation and nerves caused tiny flutters in her stomach when she thought about seeing him again.

She shook her head and tried to focus on her breakfast with Jonas. Her birth mother hadn't welcomed her with open arms, and she wasn't quite sure how she felt about her birth father. Jules closed her eyes as she contemplated his role in her life. She wasn't sure she'd want to meet him, even if Barb or DNA told her who he was. He had known all about her. He just hadn't wanted to be a father. More precisely, he hadn't wanted to be *her* father. Lucy might need to figure out her own mystery when she was ready. Jules wasn't sure she needed to find her birth father. The dad she already had adored her.

At that moment, she appreciated her parents more than ever. Never had there been a moment she hadn't felt their overwhelming love for her. Guilt radiated through her that she had hurt them to seek out people who weren't necessarily looking to be found. Jonas had promised her it would all be okay in the end. She just had to go on faith that eventually he would convince their mother to meet her.

Her resemblance to her birth mother had stunned her. Part of her regretted not trying to get Jonas to forward her the photo of Barb.

Jules leaned back in her desk chair and closed her eyes. It felt odd to think her endless hours of searching were over. Her addiction to researching her family had taken over her life lately, and she'd been neglecting some of her clients.

As she logged into her laptop at her desk, her thoughts wandered to what Jonas had asked about Becky. Jules hadn't even looked at her friend's DNA results. Becky had agreed to the test, had handed it to her to mail. It wasn't her fault she hadn't gotten Becky's voicemail in time, but guilt nagged at her that she should have at least told her she'd sent it. Jules had been obsessed with her own search, but she couldn't deny she had tried to ignore Becky's results as if they weren't there.

She clicked on her friend's results, and Becky's ethnicity profile popped up. That was odd. It showed she was Greek and Italian. Jules had thought Felicia's side was from Scotland, but there was no sign of that. Becky hadn't mentioned either of her parents had Italian or Greek in their family, but then again, she hadn't seemed to know much about her grandparents.

Jules loaded the page with Becky's DNA matches. As she took in the information, she gasped. She blinked hard as she tried to comprehend what she was reading. She was new to DNA, but she thought she knew what this meant, except that it didn't make sense. Or maybe it made perfect sense. Maybe it explained everything.

CHAPTER FIFTY-TWO

Becky

Becky's fingers trembled as she jabbed at the numbers on the lock. It turned red and beeped. Her shaky fingers had hit a wrong number. As she stood on the porch, she tried to settle the knot in her stomach. She hadn't even bothered to go back to the store, not that Tonya would care. She was home now, and on the other side of the door, safety loomed.

The vibration of her phone buzzed against her hip. She reached into her purse. What would she say if it were Bryan or Tonya? Her appointment had yielded no answers, no way to fix everything. Her gaze drifted down and she saw Jules's name and picture pop up. She was returning her message from the night before. Answering the call, Becky brought the phone to her ear. She held her breath and concentrated while she pushed the numbers for the code. Success. She turned the knob to unlock the door.

"Hey, I'm just walking in the house. Sorry it took me so long yester—"

"Becky! I have to tell you—"

"I can't wait to hear all about what you found. And by the way, is there something else you haven't told me? Did I see you with a new boyfriend this morn—"

Becky's head jerked forward. She grimaced as an unexpected jolt of pain coursed through her skull and radiated down into her neck and shoulder.

From behind her, she heard the front door close with a deliberate thud. The metallic sound of the deadbolt turning announced she was being locked in.

As Becky moaned in distress, her legs refused to continue to hold her upright. She crumpled to the floor, her phone slipping from her grasp and clattering to the floor.

CHAPTER FIFTY-THREE

Jules

"Becky? Becky!" There was background noise but no response. Jules was sure she had heard whimpering. "What the hell?" She tightened her grip on the phone. "Becky, what happened?"

As the line went dead, Jules's panic escalated. "Shit, shit, shit!" She took in short stuttered breaths and redialed Becky's number.

Hey, you've reached Becky. I'm not around right now. Leave a message—

Jules didn't wait for the beep. She found Bryan in her contacts and pressed the number. Her heart racing, she waited for him to answer and hoped he wasn't in a meeting.

"C'mon, Bryan. C'mon!" she said out loud as her impatience inched up. Maybe she was overreacting. She tapped the side of her leg and then dropped her head in relief when he answered.

"Hey, Jules."

Jules erupted on the other end in a frenzied explanation about what she had found regarding Becky's DNA results.

"Whoa, Jules, slow down."

"There's no time for that now, Bryan! This could explain every-thing. Meet me at your house but be careful because I think someone might be there with her. I'm worried Becky could be in trouble."

She heard Bryan gasp. "Did you call 911?"

"I'm scared something might happen if they show up with the sirens blaring. Besides, I hope I'm wrong. I'm going to call my brother—he's a cop—and tell him to meet us there too. He actually works in your town, so he has to be somewhere close."

"Okay, I can be there in fifteen minutes. I just have to—" He paused. "Wait, your what?"

"I'll explain later. Just hurry."

Jules grabbed her keys and purse off the kitchen table. Racing down her narrow staircase toward the front door, she caught herself slipping and grabbed hold of the railing. Tumbling down the stairs wouldn't help her get to Becky.

As she turned to lock the door behind her, she dialed Jonas's number.

He answered on the second ring. "Hey, sis, what's up?" His hearty laugh came through the receiver. "That's so cool. I never thought I'd be able to say that."

"Hi. I hate to play the new sister card so early in the game, but I don't know what else to do. I need your help." She frantically explained what she had found on her computer and the call with Becky that had gotten disconnected. "I hope I'm wrong, but if I'm not, she could be in trouble."

"Okay, I'll head there now. Just give me the address, and I'll meet you. I'll call it in and tell them to be on standby in case I need backup."

"415 Winston Park Lane. Please hurry! This is all my fault. If anything happens to her, I'll never forgive myself."

CHAPTER FIFTY-FOUR

Becky

As her eyelids fluttered, Becky struggled to rouse herself. Weakness had settled over her and left her feeling numb, oddly detached from her body. She let her lids close, and a low rhythmic hum filled her head. It was oddly comforting, like the sound a refrigerator makes to prove it's working.

Finally, she mustered enough energy to force her eyes partially open. What she saw through the narrow slits was blurry and distorted. She took in the coffee maker, the checkered backsplash behind the sink, the sliding glass door to the porch. She was in her kitchen. She squinted and made out their fireplace poker leaned up against the chair next to her.

The haze was gradually lifting. Bits of memory flooded back like puzzle pieces. She struggled to figure out how they could all fit together to put her in her kitchen feeling like she'd been drop kicked.

Lifting her head only slightly, she winced. The bright light above her made her acutely aware of the throbbing in her head. As she tried to reach up, her hand wouldn't budge.

Looking downward, she attempted to focus. Terror coursed through her when she took in the zip tie around her wrist. Her frantic gaze flew to the other hand. She yanked her wrist upward, but it remained pinned, bound by plastic to her kitchen chair. Pain shot through her as the sharp edges dug into her skin. She took in short, shallow breaths as the reality of her plight hit her.

Her gaze dipped down, and her heart raced at what she saw. Strips of plastic had been strategically placed on her ankles as well to render her paralyzed. Fear rapidly replaced the confusion that had earlier muddied the gravity of her situation.

At least she finally knew she wasn't crazy. That feeling in the parking deck hadn't been her imagination. She was right. There had been someone chasing her in the darkness. She just hadn't run fast enough. Whomever it was had caught her.

Summoning a deep breath, she endeavored to think through her panic. She glanced around the kitchen in search of her phone. There was a purse on the counter. The bag wasn't hers. Did that mean the person who had tied her to the chair was still there?

She sat and listened. The air conditioner whirred as cold air blew through the vent, but she didn't hear anyone in the house. If she could get to the counter, maybe she could get a knife and cut herself free.

Blinking back tears, she leaned her body weight toward the side of the chair. As two legs of the chair lifted off the floor, she shifted in the other direction. The chair moved. She inhaled deeply and methodically leaned again. As the legs lifted, she heard hasty footsteps coming up behind her. Becky stiffened and held her breath. The presence of another person filled the space encircling Becky as she let the chair back down.

Becky's labored breathing was the only sound in the room. There would be no escape. Fear tightened her chest as her thoughts drifted to Bryan. The idea that she might never see him again—she clenched her eyes and stifled a sob.

The footsteps paced back and forth behind her as if she was being taunted. Becky was afraid to speak, afraid to move a muscle. Her mouth was dry, a metallic taste on her tongue. Even if she could scream, there was no one to hear her. No one except the person behind her who seemed to be contemplating her fate.

The footsteps continued, pacing back and forth until they finally stopped, and the person spoke. A female voice filled with contempt. "Oh, Becky. You couldn't have just made this easy and died in the car accident, could you?"

The woman's voice was oddly familiar. Becky tried to turn her head to look over her shoulder and grimaced in pain. She swallowed, her parched throat in desperate need of water.

"I don't understand," Becky said, her voice raspy and unfamiliar. "Do you work at the hospital?"

The faceless voice snickered. "Right. I'm a nurse, ready to save the world." Her voice was tinged with sarcasm. "I guess maybe I shouldn't have called it an accident. That probably implies I didn't cause it."

Becky flinched. "You—you caused my accident? Why?" Becky's mind was reeling as she tried to find any scenario this person fit into that would explain why she would have wanted her to crash her car.

The voice was devoid of any emotion when it responded. "I was hoping you would die."

If this person had tried to kill Becky in her car, what chance did she have now tied to this chair? "Why—why would you want me dead? I don't understand."

"Of course you don't understand. I had the ending all figured out, but you wouldn't cooperate. It's your fault I had to change my plan."

"Plan? Plan for what?" Fear stretched Becky's voice high and tight. It gutted her that she could die with Bryan thinking she had cheated on him. A pained whimper escaped her lips.

The air behind her stirred as the woman paced back and forth. If Becky's distress was noticeable, it seemed to be of little concern to her. "It didn't have to be this way."

Becky inhaled several stuttered gulps of air. "I don't know what I've done to you, but whatever it is, I'm sorry. Please just cut me loose."

"Let me think—" There was a pause. "Nope, can't do that. Not part of the plan."

Panic clawed at Becky's throat. "Please—please, just tell me what I've done."

Her plea went unanswered for several moments, and then the woman spoke. "Maybe you should ask your mother."

Becky flinched. "My—my mom? What does she have to do with this?"

There was a flicker of movement. Becky caught a glimpse of the figure as she stepped out from behind her and made her way around the side of the chair that held Becky captive. Finally, the woman came into Becky's view and stood in front of her. The voice was faceless no more.

A stunned gasp clipped the silence in the kitchen. As she struggled to comprehend what she was seeing, her heart pounded painfully in her chest. She opened her mouth and then let it close. Her gaze was anchored on the woman in front of her, but shock had cut off her ability to speak. She didn't know what to say.

The face that looked back at her was her own.

CHAPTER FIFTY-FIVE

Becky

Becky gaped at the alternate version of herself, her brows lifted in disbelief.

"What—how—are we—"

"Twins?" The woman smirked as if the stunned expression on Becky's face amused her. "Even I was surprised at how much we look alike. But we do, which will make this so much easier."

A thin sheen of sweat formed on Becky's hairline. "Make what easier? I don't understand."

Her twin paced back and forth in front of Becky, the soft sound of her footsteps on the tile interrupting the silence that hung in the air. After several passes, she stopped and crossed her arms as she turned toward Becky. Her eyes were cold and dark. "Some people will do anything to get a baby. Did you know that?" Her voice was filled with disgust.

Her twin picked up the poker leaning against the chair and tossed it on the table where it skittered across the wooden top. She kicked the legs of Becky's chair until it turned ninety degrees, and then yanked a chair from the table and settled into it facing her.

She leaned back and crossed her legs, her hands folded in front of her as if she was simply here to observe.

Becky covertly studied the woman sitting across from her. Her twin's hair was precisely the same cut and color as hers, almost as if she had taken Becky's photo to the hairdresser. She also had hazel eyes, but they were different. Darker and dulled like whatever she had gone through had dimmed the sparkle that should have been there.

Upon closer inspection, Becky realized there were other subtle differences. Fine lines around her twin's upper lip suggested she was a regular smoker, and a deep indentation between her brows remained even when she wasn't actively scowling. Becky tried not to get caught staring, but there was a long, thin scab on the side of her twin's face. Could that have been a cat scratch?

"Your mom was not a good person," Becky's twin said. "Well, the mom who raised you, anyway. To be honest, the one who gave birth to you wasn't much to talk about either."

Confusion washed over Becky's face. "Are you saying I was adopted?"

Her twin snorted. "Adopted? I'm not sure that's quite the word for it." Her eyes were angry as they bore into Becky's. "Money buys anything. Especially with a best friend who's a nurse at the hospital and a pregnant woman who's stupid *and* broke."

Becky's mouth fell open slightly. Ros. Her twin had to be talking about Ros who had been a nurse. Becky thought back to the day she had overheard her in the hallway at Tranquility. What was it she had said to her mother—Ros would explain something to Becky and she would understand. Now it seemed this is what she was referring to and not a made-up story about her mother worrying about her inheritance.

The alternate version of Becky pinned her with an icy stare. "Our mother didn't know she was having twins. Or so she said. Tried to convince me she would never have given her baby up. But two? Two was perfect."

Her twin sat tapping two fingers against her pinched lips as she leveled her gaze at Becky.

"Why—why was it perfect?" Becky already knew the answer she'd be given, but it was clear she was expected to ask.

"Why, one to keep and one to sell, of course," her twin responded with dramatic glee. "With a pile of money offered to her, our greedy mother cashed in. You went off to your happy little life. But me? I went off to hell."

"No, it couldn't have happened that way," Becky said with conviction. "I've seen pictures of my mom when she was pregnant."

Her twin leaped out of her chair so quickly the chair skidded across the floor behind her. "Not you in there. Probably not even a baby. Probably pulled it out and slept on it at night." She sneered at Becky as she leaned in until her face was just inches away. "Trust me."

Becky tugged subtly at her wrists, but they wouldn't budge. She needed to buy time so she could figure what to do. "Can I ask you what your name is?"

"Peyton. Not that it's any of your business, but I guess we are twins."

"Peyton, I swear I never knew any of this." Becky hoped her insistent tone was convincing. "I had no idea I was a twin. My mother never told me anything." Becky thought back to her birth certificate. It had her parents' names on it. Had Ros helped falsify that at the hospital?

Becky's mind drifted as she thought back to the day just recently when her mother had said, "I have something to tell you." Was this what her mom had to tell her—that she had bought her as a baby and separated identical twins. Is this what she and Ros thought she would understand?

Peyton stood in front of Becky, her hands on her hips. "Of course your mother never told you. How could she confess that your storybook childhood was all based on a lie? You did grow up to have a perfect life, though, didn't you? Friends, handsome husband, great job. You've got it made." Her eyes focused in on Becky. "I mean, you realize I can't let you have it all while I had nothing. I still have nothing." She smirked. "But that's all about to change."

With a sense of foreboding, Becky's body tensed. "I'm sorry, but can't you see it wasn't my fault? I was a baby. I didn't have anything to do with this. Wasn't there anyone who could have helped you and your mom?"

"Oh, after your parents' money ran out, it didn't take her long to find her way back to James, our daddy." Peyton taunted Becky with an expression of feigned sympathy. "Oh, are you disappointed you missed out on him while your other daddy was pushing you on the swing at the park?" Peyton smacked Becky across the face, leaving a hot sting on her cheek.

Becky recoiled, her face burning. "What the hell did you do that for?"

The corners of Peyton's mouth turned up into a cruel smile. "Because I can. Pretty much the same reason James did. It didn't take much."

Becky thought of the loving dad she had grown up with and shuddered to think about the father Peyton described. For an instant, she was grateful she had been spared. Maybe her mother and Ros had thought they were protecting her.

"Did James know about me?" Becky gritted her teeth and tried to ignore the stinging sensation on her cheek.

Peyton snorted. "Believe it or not, you can blame that one on your mother. Mine kept her mouth shut. I mean, how would she explain selling one of his kids and having no idea where you were or even what your name was."

Becky frowned. "So, my mom knew James? Told him I was his?"

"Not quite." Peyton shook her head, an expression of disgust clouding her face. "Those people who raised you—did they think no one would ever see you and notice you looked exactly like me?"

Becky gave a slight shrug. "Maybe they didn't realize we were identical when we were babies?"

Her twin picked up the fireplace poker in her left hand and slammed it down on the kitchen table. "Are you making excuses for what they did?"

Becky flinched and leaned back in her chair. Her gaze remained fixed on the poker in Peyton's hand. "No. I'm not making excuses. I'm just trying to figure this out."

"Well, figure this out. There's your mom coming out of the store holding your stupid little hand, but James is there too. Don't you think he was more than a little curious why another girl looked just like me? My mother told me he staked out that store for months until he saw the two of you again and followed you home."

Becky caught her breath. James had known where they lived.

"My mother told me he went right up to your front door, bellowing for his kid." Becky closed her eyes as a long-forgotten memory played behind her lids. Her mother had grabbed her arm and dragged her into the darkest corner of their closet. "Shh," she had said. "We have to stay quiet. This is where we stay safe."

The man yelling at her daddy was scary. Becky had wanted to escape the darkness of the closet but was worried the man would find her.

"Your father claimed he had no idea what James was talking about. James warned them that when they least expected it, he'd snatch back his property. That's all we were to him. Property."

This had to be why they moved so suddenly when she was in second grade. Pulled her out of school and just left. Whisked Becky away to someplace where James couldn't find her.

Peyton snickered. "I would have loved to see his face when he realized your parents outsmarted him. He kept your parents on their toes for years. Even showed up on your grandparents' doorstep."

"My grandparents?" Becky didn't understand what they could possibly have to do with this.

"James was as smart as he was mean. He thought they would know where you were. But then he saw the size of their house, and he saw dollar signs instead. He offered to stop looking for a sizable payment." Peyton watched Becky, waiting for her reaction. "Apparently, your parents had pulled a fast one. Pretended to be pregnant and never told them you were someone else's baby. Your grandparents told him they had no use for any child that wasn't their own blood, and they slammed the door in his face."

Becky shifted in her seat as Peyton laughed. The comment on the will, the broken relationship. It all made sense. She thought of the photo she had found of her parents with her grandparents. Maybe her mother really did fake being pregnant with her so they wouldn't know she wasn't blood-related. It wouldn't surprise her if her snooty grandparents had told her parents they wouldn't consider an adopted child part of the family.

"Such a sad story," Peyton said, pretending to wipe a tear from her eye. "James went out one night. Told Mom he was gonna get beer and cigarettes. I guess he was gonna pay for his purchase with his pistol plus take a little extra for his troubles. He pulled a gun, but someone else in the store had a gun too." Peyton's eyes bore into Becky as she continued. "Shot James dead right there next to the snack rack. He died in a haze of Twinkies and Devil Dogs. Not completely inappropriate, I guess." Her lips curved into a knowing smile. "But I guess you read all about that, right?"

Becky's mouth fell open. She closed it quickly and tried to cover up her reaction. The article in the folder. James must have been the subject the P.I. was following, and her parents had known he died. They should have felt free finally of the fear that he would find them.

"Peyton, I didn't—"

The sound of the doorbell echoed into the kitchen. Both women froze.

"Don't say a word," Peyton hissed as she grabbed the fireplace poker. Peyton cast a wary glance between Becky and the front door as she made her way closer to Becky and stood behind her.

Becky bit her bottom lip as anxiety coursed through her. This person might leave without knowing the danger she was in. She felt a twinge of hope when there was insistent knocking on the door as if the person was surprised she wasn't answering. This had to be someone she knew.

Becky agonized about taking her chances. But who would be knocking? Bryan wouldn't knock. Maybe it was someone who could save her. Her heart skipped wildly as they waited. Silently, Becky pleaded for this person to help her even though she knew her twin had deadbolted the door. Only she and Bryan had the code.

She needed to take the chance. It might be the only one she got. Becky opened her mouth to shout but was instantly silenced. Becky twisted her head violently, but Peyton's hand was firm and determined. She fought against the pressure being inflicted on her face as she struggled to find a way to get air into her lungs.

Becky realized this was it. This was going to be how she died. Just as the fight went out of her and she went limp in the chair, the hand fell away from her face. Becky gasped and drew in a huge gulp of air. She choked down a sob.

She was still alive, but in an instant, what might be her only chance to be rescued had vanished.

CHAPTER FIFTY-SIX

Becky

"No one's coming to save you, Becky," Peyton said, a smug expression on her face. "It will end eventually, don't worry. But I'm not done with you yet."

Peyton calmly opened the refrigerator and peered inside. "This is all making me very thirsty." She sighed dramatically. "All this diet soda." She turned, and her lips curved into a smile that seemed meant to torment Becky. "I'll have to start drinking it, I guess. I mean, that's what my husband expects, right? He's quite handsome, Becky. I appreciate that you picked so well for us."

Becky's breathing was still ragged. She swallowed hard. An icy chill ran up her spine and left goosebumps on her flesh. She didn't want to consider what her twin was planning.

"I did quite enjoy watching you fall apart." Peyton rubbed her hands together. "I mean, seriously, that was fun. I didn't even think you had any more crocodile tears in you, but you kept surprising me." She rolled her fists next to her eyes. "Boo-hoo. If I were your husband, I would have run away too." She cupped her hand around her mouth as if she was imparting a secret. "You're quite the Debbie Downer, Becky."

She clapped her hands in front of Becky to ensure she was paying attention. "As much fun as it was until you started to depress me. I've grown tired of following you around. What has to happen now is your fault. Now that I've seen how good you have it, I've decided I'd much rather enjoy your life and simply eliminate you from the picture." Peyton waved her hand. "Bye-bye, Becky."

As her chest heaved, Becky stared incredulously at Peyton. "Eliminate me? You mean *kill* me? What did I ever do to you? I didn't even know you existed."

"You—You got the life I should have had!" Peyton's eyes grew dark. "I've decided to just rid the world of you and step right into your place. Don't worry, I'll make up with that handsome husband of yours. That girl you work with won't find anything else missing, and I'll go to see your mother again and tell her I know all about her devious ways. But of course, she won't say a word and who would believe her anyway? Oh, and that fucking cat of yours? I wish I could say I skinned him alive, but he scratched the shit out of me and bolted."

Becky had been right about the scratch on Peyton's face. At least Sherlock had gotten away and could still be out there. Fear twisted her insides when she considered she probably wouldn't be so lucky.

Seething, Becky pulled hard against the zip ties, but it got her nowhere. "No one will ever believe you're me." She spat the words through gritted teeth. "You're nothing like me. Just because we look alike doesn't mean you can fool them."

Peyton tilted her head and gave Becky a withering stare. "No?"

She went over to the kitchen counter and reached into her purse. Pulling out a driver's license, she walked back and threw it on the kitchen table next to Becky.

"DMV didn't have a problem. I just told them I lost my license and showed them your passport." Peyton laughed. "Well, *our* passport. By the way, I'm so glad we have that. I'm thinking of taking a nice romantic vacation with my new husband. Maybe, like a second honeymoon. We can go back to Mexico, make passionate love as the warm breeze floats over our naked bodies. I hope he's ready for me." She winked at Becky. "Don't worry. He'll just think you've learned a few new tricks."

Anger consumed Becky. She narrowed her eyes and glared at Peyton. "And how will you explain to my husband that you're now a lefty?" She leveled an unrelenting stare at her twin. "His wife is right-handed."

A slow smile spread across Peyton's face. "You noticed that, huh? I think your mom did too. She may not be as out of it as you all think. It's weird though, right? Identical twins, but I came out a lefty."

Peyton put her face close to Becky's. The smell of stale cigarette smoke wafted off her. Becky held her breath.

"Listen to me," Peyton said as her eyes burned into Becky's. "I'll break my right hand if I have to, convince everyone I learned to do it all with my left hand because I had no other choice. They'll be in awe. Don't you worry your pretty little head about it." As Peyton pulled back, the necklace Jules had given Becky swung from her neck, glistening as it moved back and forth and caught the light.

Becky shook her head. "He'll catch on, you know. You don't know anything about our life together."

Peyton moaned dramatically and grabbed her head. "You know, I do think I was hurt in that car accident. Certain things I just don't remember anymore." She paused. "You just leave your husband to me." She laughed maniacally. "Like you really have a choice in the matter." Peyton's face grew serious. "I've been waiting for this for a very long time. All those fights our parents had about you, neither one of them ever told me the truth." Peyton tapped her temple with her index finger. "But I'm smart. As I got older, I listened when they started yelling. They planted the seed that I might have a sister."

Becky hadn't been as fortunate. All the lies her parents had told her had led to this moment, in this chair. There had been no inkling, no warning. Becky was going to pay the price for her parents' decisions. A lump grew in her throat at the idea that Bryan wouldn't know how much she loved him.

"I didn't have all the advantages you had." Peyton anchored her steely gaze on Becky's face. "I'll bet you got to go to a good college, didn't you?"

"Well, my dad died right before my senior year—"

Peyton smacked her on the side of the head. A jolt of pain shot through her, and Becky clamped her lips shut to keep from yelping.

"But you went to a good college, didn't you?" Peyton asked again, her tone indicating she already knew the answer. "Your mother made sure of it. Not me, I went to the school of hard knocks. Landed me in jail on more than one occasion. But I used my time there wisely to figure out how I could find you."

Becky gritted her teeth. How *had* Peyton found her? She had already admitted her mother had no idea where Becky was or even what her name was.

"When everyone first started talking about all this DNA stuff, I was intrigued. Stole the money to buy a test and sent it in. Imagine my surprise when, lo and behold, you finally showed up, my perfect DNA match. You weren't just a sister. You were my identical twin."

Becky caught her breath. Her DNA test. Jules must have sent it after all. That sick feeling she'd had in her gut about it hadn't only been because it was bad luck for the pregnancy. It was because someone evil was out there looking for her.

"I eventually reconnected with my mother, and we had an interesting little chat so I could share this all with you before you had to go. It's amazing what someone will tell you when they think you might kill them." She fixed an icy gaze on Becky. "That bitch deserved what she got."

Becky shuddered, and Peyton casually continued as if she hadn't just suggested she murdered their mother. "Of course, your test was guarded by that girlfriend of yours. I need to thank her for using her real name on her account. Once I figured out who she was, your photographer friend wasn't hard to find at all. The internet is amazing, isn't it?" She snickered. "And of course, she led me right to you."

Peyton paced back and forth in front of Becky. "My first plan was to commit some horrific crime and leave a little drop of blood with your DNA at the scene. We do share identical DNA, you know. Then I figured with your lily-white reputation and my record already out there, I'd probably just find myself back in the slammer."

Peyton glanced around the kitchen. Her eyes stopped on the scorched kitchen cabinet, and she shook her head. "That lovely smelling lilac candle. If you weren't so damn forgetful, I would have been successful in burning down your pretty little house."

Becky seethed as she realized everything that had happened to her had been Peyton's doing. She tried to move her legs, but they were bound just as tightly as her hands. She gritted her teeth in frustration.

Peyton sat in a chair and calmly continued. "Did you know twins don't share the same fingerprints? I made sure I didn't leave any in the boutique when I helped myself. No more time behind bars for me. My new plan lets me start with a clean slate." She pointed her index finger at Becky. "Well, it's actually your clean slate, but it's not like you'll need it anymore."

Panic rose in Becky's chest, and then she tilted her head. She was sure she had heard a noise at the front of the house. Maybe the person at the door had come back. She tried to listen but heard nothing else. Her eyes welled up. There was no way she was getting out of here alive. She thought of Bryan sleeping next to her twin, loving her because he thought she was Becky. Her heart sank when she realized he would have no legitimate reason to think otherwise.

Peyton tapped her index finger on her lips. "You know, I may even let your mom move back to that cute house of hers. Then I can take her out anytime I please. Can you believe I brought her cookies and she wasn't sure she wanted to go to lunch with me? What kind of nonsense is that? I mean, it's really your insult since she thought I was you. Or maybe she didn't." Peyton shrugged. "Yeah, that place is too expensive, even if they do make a mean tuna melt in the dining room. I mean, if she wanders away, that's just one less thing for me to worry about, right?"

Becky pulled urgently at the ties that were pinning her hands to the chair, but there was no slack at all. They just dug into her skin until she wanted to shriek in pain. Her mind raced. She needed to get free from this crazy lunatic. She glanced up at the time on the microwave even though it wasn't like Bryan would be home to save her.

It had been Peyton he had seen kissing someone by his office. Her blood boiled that her own sister could be so cruel. Yes, she did look like Becky, but how could Bryan have believed this evil witch was her?

Becky hung her head as the puzzle pieces fell into place. The dresses in her closet. Peyton probably had a matching set. She wasn't kidding when she said she had tried to take everything from her. The lit candle, the stolen jewelry, the mystery dresses, even the bears. Becky wasn't losing her mind. It had all been her twin.

Peyton picked up her driver's license off the table and stood. She smacked the top of Becky's head with her left hand and strolled back to the kitchen counter. She filed the license back into her wallet, reached into the bag, and pulled out a large set of keys.

"Oh, by the way, these have been very helpful. I tried to grab yours at the hospital, but you and that husband had to make things difficult. At least your nap the next day made it easy to grab yours so I could make myself a set. Really, you should lock that back door if you're gonna take a long snooze." She flashed a cocky smirk at Becky. "Of course, I'm the reason you were so sleepy."

Becky's eyes widened. "You drugged me?"

Peyton crossed her arms over her chest as her mouth fell open in mock indignation. "Oh, stop! Would I do that?" She dipped her head, and a satisfied smile spread across her face. "Okay, so maybe I did. But only when it was absolutely necessary."

CHAPTER FIFTY-SEVEN

Bryan

As Bryan made the last turn into the neighborhood, his heart was racing. Jules was here. She had gotten there before him and parked several houses down from his. As he jerked the wheel toward the curb to park behind her, he saw she was still in the driver's seat.

He glanced at his house as he turned off his car and got out. His anxiety wouldn't dissipate until he could see for himself that nothing was going on inside.

The breakfast he'd eaten was threatening to come back up. Maybe Jules was wrong. All this panic for nothing. At this point, he'd be fine with that. He wouldn't even be mad if they walked in and Becky was curled up on the couch watching television. He'd hug his wife, tell her he loved her, and what he thought he saw would be forgotten. None of that mattered anymore. All he cared about was that Becky wasn't in any danger.

Maybe this story of Jules's hadn't led down the path she thought it had. His mind drifted to what he had seen across the street from his office. He didn't want to admit Jules's explanation made more sense than anything he had come up with so far. Guilt stabbed him.

He had been willing to believe the worst about his wife. Nothing bad could happen to her. He needed to tell her he loved her and was sorry for ever doubting her.

As Bryan approached Jules's car, she rolled down the driver's side window. "Hey, I just got here too." She ran her index finger under each eye and wiped away tears. He watched as Jules took a deep breath.

Bryan nodded in the direction of the house. "Becky's car's in the driveway." His eyes scanned the length of the street. "I don't see anyone else's car. What do we do now?"

He spun around as a police car pulled along the curb behind his car, its siren and lights off. Bryan raised a questioning eyebrow and glanced back at Jules.

She hit the button to roll up her window and scrambled to get out. "That's Jonas. He carries a gun, and that's what we need."

Bryan flinched. He wiped a line of sweat from his temple. The idea that they needed a gun to deal with whatever Becky was facing had his gut twisted like a pretzel.

They hurried down the street together. As Jonas got out of the car, Jules hugged him, her face a mask of anxiety.

"Good call parking away from the house." Jonas looked over at Jules. "If you're right, we don't want to announce our arrival." He glanced at Bryan.

Jules made a hasty introduction. "Jonas, this is Bryan, Becky's husband." She gave a half-hearted smile. "Bryan, this is Jonas." She paused. "My DNA test found a brother," she said by way of explanation. "This wasn't exactly the way I wanted y'all to meet."

The men shook hands.

"So, what do we now?" Bryan asked Jonas as he took in a deep breath.

Jonas's gaze flitted between the two of them. "You two stay here by the car, and I'll go see if I can figure out what's going on."

Bryan shook his head. "No way. That's my wife. I can't just stay here." His voice cracked. "I need to make sure she's okay. Please."

Jules wiped away fresh tears. "Me too. This is all my fault."

Jonas exhaled as he contemplated both of them. "Why do I have a feeling you two won't stay put if I leave you here?" He shook his head. "Okay, but be quiet and be careful," he said, his voice stern. "Stay behind me. Until we see what's going on, we all need to err on the side of caution. Okay?"

Jules and Bryan nodded in unison.

As they made their way toward the house, Bryan glanced across the street. It was a rare occasion that Mrs. Ritter wasn't outside watering or weeding. Her front yard stood empty, and he was grateful he didn't have to stop to explain. They trudged along the sidewalk until they got to the perimeter of the house, then sidled up the side of the driveway and walked single file along the garage.

Jonas turned around and whispered to Bryan. "What can we see through that big window?"

"You can see the entire living room and into the kitchen. It's not a big house."

"Okay, see if you can get in between the shrubs and the house. Duck down. If anything is going on in the living room, we don't want to show up as an entourage in front of the window. Let's make our way down to the other end and see if we can peek in from the side."

They made their way carefully and covertly to the small porch. Jonas crouched down as he stepped off and made room for Bryan and Jules to follow.

"Crap." Bryan heard Jules mutter as she accidentally knocked into one of the flowerpots.

Jonas turned around and put his fingers to his lips.

"I know," Jules said in a whisper. "Sorry."

As they all made it to the other side of the front window, Jonas pointed to the grass behind him. Jules and Bryan ducked down and scooted around him.

Jules peered in over Jonas's head and emitted a strangled gasp. Her hand flew up to cover her mouth.

"What?" Bryan asked. "What did you see?" Nudging Jules aside, he looked in the window. He had a direct view through the living room into the kitchen. He squinted. Becky sat in a kitchen chair with a woman standing over her. She didn't seem to be able to move.

"Well, I'll be damned," Jonas said as his gaze went back and forth between the two sisters. His attention shifted to Jules. "You were right."

Bryan's jaw clenched. Rage bubbled in him for the woman who had done this to Becky. His immediate instinct was to storm the house and save his wife.

He whipped around to face Jonas. "We need to do something. Now."

Jonas held up his hand. "Let's try to remain calm. So now we know for sure there's a situation happening. Let me call in the backup. Let's not do anything impulsive that makes this worse for your wife."

As Jonas stepped off to the side to place a call, Jules backed away from the window, her head in her hands. Bryan wheeled around.

She looked up into Bryan's eyes. "I'm sorry, this is all my fault."

Bryan shook his head. "You didn't put her in that chair. You can't blame yourself."

Jules's eyes welled up. "Yes, I can. The DNA test. She only did it for me. She didn't want to, but I made her. And then she changed her mind. But I didn't get her message in time—I had already sent it. I didn't tell her because she thought it was bad luck because of the baby. I thought if she didn't know, then it couldn't be bad luck, but—" Her voice broke. "It was bad luck, Bryan. Really bad luck because that's how her twin found her. From the DNA site, it looks like her name is Peyton, and she found Becky because of me."

"Don't cry. We'll figure out how to get her out of there." His eyes skirted around until they found Jonas. He was on his phone, but he lifted his hand and waved Bryan over. With a glance at Jules, Bryan hunched down and scurried to where Jonas stood at the side of the house.

Moments later, Jonas crept back to return to his spot by the front window. Bryan was right behind him, his mouth set in a determined line.

As they all peered through the window, they could see that Peyton had picked up a fireplace poker and was moving it from hand to hand for effect. She was taunting Becky. A whimper escaped Jules's lips as Bryan moaned.

Jules faced Jonas. "Please, I'm begging you. She's my best friend, and I did this to her. We need to save her."

Jonas glanced back at her and gave a curt nod. As his eyes went between the two of them, he held his finger to his lips. He lowered his voice. "I need to go in. The sister doesn't look like she has a gun, but they're in the kitchen surrounded by knives, and I don't like that fireplace poker. With any luck, I'll have the element of surprise on our side while we wait for the backup to get here."

Jonas focused on both of them intently as he pulled his Glock from its holster. He wagged his finger between them. "Don't do *anything*. I mean it. Stay here."

Jonas ducked down and crawled toward the porch. Once there, he quickly inspected the door. He glanced back to ensure Jules and Bryan were still where he left them. He raised his foot and aimed the heel of his shoe. As the wood splintered and gave way, the door flew open with a thunderous crack.

Bryan ran up and in after Jonas, with Jules close behind. Jonas raised his gun after crossing the entryway, then paused for a moment. He kept his focus on the kitchen and whispered tersely without turning around. "Don't you two listen? Stay behind the man with the gun, do you hear me? No sudden moves. We have no idea what we're dealing with, and the last thing I want to worry about is the two of you."

Jonas made his way carefully through the living room and stopped when Peyton was in his line of sight. Bryan and Jules huddled side by side behind him. It was such a small area to cover. Bryan knew there hadn't been much time between the door flying open and Jonas standing there with his gun. Still, Becky's twin made no attempt to move.

Bryan's bottom lip trembled as he took in his wife. Everything in him wanted to run to her and cut her free. Jonas had said no sudden moves, but standing there doing nothing was torturous. His eyes met hers as he tried to send her a message. This would all be okay. They would save her.

Jonas looked over the barrel of the gun aimed at Peyton. "Police! Put down the poker and step away from the chair." His voice was calm and controlled.

Peyton turned her attention to the group encroaching on the kitchen as if they were arriving for tea. She plastered a fake smile on her face.

"Oh, look, Becky. The cheering committee is here. I guess they'll have figured it all out by now." She laid the poker down on the kitchen table and clapped her hands. "Bravo!" She fixed her gaze on Jonas as she slowly and deliberately picked the poker back up off the table.

"Don't do it." Jonas held the gun steady with both hands. "Put it back on the table."

Peyton met his unrelenting gaze. "Yeah, I don't think I feel like doing that." She tossed the poker from hand to hand as she stared him down.

Jules grabbed Bryan's arm, her fingers leaving white marks where she gripped him. "Seriously?" she whispered. "She's wearing the necklace I gave Becky."

Bryan glared at Peyton, his face contorted with rage. Her face wore a bemused expression as if having a gun pointed at her was of little concern. If Becky's twin had nothing to lose—Bryan couldn't bear to finish the thought.

Jonas hadn't moved a muscle. "Put the poker down. Don't make me tell you again."

Peyton moistened her lips slowly before responding. "Um, no." She smiled at Jonas sweetly, even while he had his weapon fixed on her. "What happens if I make you tell me again? Am I in trouble?" She pretended to pout. "Do you get to shoot me with your big, bad gun?"

As the lookalike spun around to face Becky, Jonas flinched slightly.

"Becky, what do you think?" Peyton asked with exaggerated interest as she turned sideways to face the group. "Do *you* think he should shoot me?"

Becky glared at the imposter, loathing flashing in her eyes.

"I mean, he *could* shoot me," Peyton said as she clutched her hands to her chest. "But Becky, how would it all end up if I died?" Her eyes drifted between Bryan and Becky, and she paused. "I mean, after all, I am carrying your baby." She brought her fingers to her lips and blew a kiss at Bryan.

Bryan's gaze moved quickly to Becky. The blood had drained from his wife's face. He shook his head back and forth, a frozen grimace on his face, his mind reeling.

Peyton snickered as she observed the non-verbal exchange between the two. "Oh, Becky, as much as I would have loved to have had a piece of that hunky husband of yours, I wasn't quite that lucky. I mean, we almost had Mexico, but that seems shot to shit now, don't you think?"

Bryan's shoulders relaxed, but his face still bore his confusion. Just what was Peyton talking about then? She had to be lying about being pregnant.

"Probably better anyway," Peyton said, her tone coy. "I'm not sure I could resist the margaritas. All that tequila probably isn't good for the baby."

The baby again. Bryan looked helplessly at Becky who stared at her twin with hatred.

Peyton mocked Becky in a high-pitched voice. "But I had three good embryos. How could this happen?" She went on to explain, her tone smug. "Well, according to Brenda—who is also yours truly—these things happen sometimes."

Peyton anchored her gaze on Becky, an evil smile spreading across her face. "Well, they happen to you anyway. No need to worry your pretty little self into a tizzy. I was happy to take your place at the embryo transfer."

She rubbed her stomach in a small circular motion. "And now, I have your baby tucked safe and sound inside me."

CHAPTER FIFTY-EIGHT

Becky

Becky started to shake as Peyton's words rang over and over in her head. *I have your baby*. Her face grew hot, the fury heating her from the inside out.

Fueled by rage, she lunged at Peyton, but the restraints kept her from reaching her intended target. From deep within her throat, Becky emitted a growl. "You evil bitch! I'll kill you myself when I get out of this chair!"

"Easy, tiger." Peyton snickered. "I don't quite see that happening. And besides, kill me, kill your baby. You wouldn't want to do that, would you?" With her trump card played, a satisfied expression crossed her face.

Becky turned her gaze to Bryan. He had his fists clenched. Fury radiated off him, contorting his face and turning it beet red. She gave him a slight shake of her head. She didn't want him impulsively charging forward.

Becky watched as the cop with the gun turned and whispered something to him. Hopefully he was telling her husband to stay put. She saw Bryan grit his teeth and nod.

The police officer turned his attention back to Becky's twin. "Listen—" He paused when he realized he didn't know this lookalike's name.

Peyton rolled her eyes and groaned. "Oh, geez, now you need to know my name too. What does it matter?"

Becky spoke up on her behalf. "Her name is Peyton, and as you can see, we're identical twins."

Peyton whipped her head around, an icy stare aimed at Becky. "Shut up, bitch! I'll decide what Rambo here gets to know."

"Hi, Peyton. I'm Jonas. We get it," he said in a low, calm voice. "You're in control. We're not planning to make any sudden moves. See, I'm putting my gun away." He holstered his weapon. "But as you heard Becky say, she didn't know anything about you, so why not let her go? I mean, you two are sisters. You can't really want to hurt her."

Peyton laid the poker back on the kitchen table, and Becky saw Jonas's chest deflate with relief.

Becky let out the breath she had been holding, but in the next instant, Peyton swung back around, her eyes narrowed to small slits. "We may look alike and even share the same DNA, but she is *not* my sister. Her mother made sure of that." Peyton paced back and forth next to Becky. "She's nothing to me. You all may have ruined my plan to take over her life, but trust me, there's not a chance in hell she's going back to it either."

Jules whimpered, her friend's chest heaving in and out as she stifled a sob.

Peyton stopped pacing and fixed her attention on Jules. "You. You two are like the sisters *we* should have been." She gestured at Bryan. "He was so easy to convince. But you? I knew you would be impossible to fool. Not that I didn't try to get rid of you."

Becky gasped as she recalled the incident by the deli. "You tried to hit her with your car."

Peyton shrugged and held up a hand. "Guilty. Although it wasn't one of my more successful moments." She turned her attention back to Jules. "I would have liked for us to be friends. I mean, eventually, I will need a photographer for my baby shower." She rubbed her belly. "For real this time."

Jules glared at Peyton, hate oozing from her. "Never," she spit out through clenched teeth.

"Well, that seems kind of harsh. I mean, without you, I might never have found my darling twin. I haven't had a chance to thank you properly for making that so easy."

Jules's bottom lip quivered as she pleaded for her friend. "Let her go. She never did anything to you."

"I'll go back to prison before I let her go back to her perfect life." Peyton's eyes flashed with anger as she scowled at Becky. "Why should *she* get everything? I got *nothing*."

With one quick movement, Peyton was at the kitchen counter, her body aimed at the wooden block with the kitchen knives. She reached for the biggest knife and yanked it out of its slot.

Now. Now was the time for this cop to shoot her twin. It was going to be either her or Peyton, but she didn't see how they were both going to come out of this alive. Becky cowered back in her chair.

Bryan turned toward Jonas and screamed. "No! Jonas, stop her!"

Jonas had already pulled his gun from the holster at his hip.

Knife in hand, Peyton glowered at him, daring him to pull the trigger. "Are you willing to kill their baby to save her?" Her expression hardened.

"It doesn't have to be this way, Peyton," Jonas had his gun steady in his grasp, aimed at her. "Let's talk about this. You don't need to hurt your sister."

"I'm done talking. And I already told you, she is *not* my sister." Peyton took her eyes off Jonas and leveled her gaze at Becky. With a single pivot, Peyton turned toward her twin, a guttural scream coming from deep within her throat.

As Becky sat, bound and helpless, it all seemed to happen in slow motion. Peyton raised the knife in her hand, and the sunlight streaming through the kitchen window reflected off the large stainless-steel blade that would end her life. Becky's only consolation was that at least Bryan knew she loved him. He knew she hadn't cheated on him.

Her best friend's wailing seemed to fill the room. Jules hung her head with her eyes closed as if she couldn't watch what was about to happen.

Becky's frantic gaze shot to Jonas who was still in position but hadn't fired. Why wasn't he shooting her? Maybe he *was* trying to protect Becky and Bryan's baby, but at this point, she was willing to take the chance her twin was a liar. There was nothing Becky could do to avoid the attack about to be inflicted upon her. She winced and braced for the worst.

A sudden flash of movement exploded in a frenzy behind her twin. In an instant, an officer had heaved his body against Peyton's until she toppled to the floor. Her face froze in a stunned grimace as her cheek lay flat against the tile, the officer's hand over her neck. Two additional officers were right behind the first. One held her wrist tight while the other wrenched the knife from her grasp.

A whoosh of air escaped from Jonas as his arm, held rigid with his gun aimed at Peyton, relaxed and dropped to his side.

Pinned firmly against the floor, Peyton couldn't move, but she spewed her anger in Becky's direction. "I hate you, you stupid bitch. I should let them kill me and take your baby to the grave with me. I hate you!"

"Shut up," one of the cops demanded as he forced Peyton's arms behind her and clicked handcuffs around her wrists. Standing her up on her feet, he shoved her toward the porch and away from Becky.

Becky exhaled with one deep breath, still not quite believing she was safe. She was still trembling at the vision she had of her life with Bryan ending in an instant.

With Peyton subdued, Bryan ran to untie Becky. He scrambled for the scissors in the kitchen drawer to cut the zip ties.

"I'm so sorry, babe. I'm so sorry." Bryan's eyes filled with tears as he fervently sawed at the zip ties with the scissors. He winced. "They're tight. I'm trying not to hurt you."

The adrenaline flowing through Becky slowed as she controlled her breathing and allowed herself to feel relief. She flinched at the plastic digging into her wrist as Bryan cut through it. "I was never so happy to see anyone as that cop behind her. But how did they get in through the back door?"

"Ah, that." Bryan glanced up for just a moment and then returned his attention to the zip ties. "I guess Jonas kicked in the front door for effect, but I gave him the code for the back door. He texted it to the backups. They must have been hiding in the laundry room until they had a clear shot at her. Your birthday saved your life today."

Becky cringed. "Peyton's birthday too. No wonder she was able to get in after we changed the locks." Bryan finally freed her from the ties binding her wrists. She rubbed her raw, irritated skin while Bryan went to work on the ties around her ankles.

He got one ankle free, and Becky rolled it in a circle to get feeling flowing back through it.

"Got it," he said as the second tie broke to release her remaining ankle.

Becky lifted herself from the chair and unsteadily melted into his embrace. As she hugged him fiercely, he held her up against him until her legs regained their strength. She didn't want to let go. Her cheek against his chest, she could hear the thumping of his heart. Fresh tears pricked her eyes. These were happy tears of relief, to replace the ones that had fallen when she thought she might never see him again.

She finally pulled herself back from his embrace. "She wanted me dead—the bright light, the car accident. That was her. She tried to kill me, and when that didn't work, she tried to ruin all the good things in my life, including you. That was her in front of your office."

Bryan looked down for an instant, and his eyes were wet when he brought them back up. "I'm so ashamed that I believed you would do that." His face fell as his bottom lip quivered. "You were vulnerable because I left and wasn't here to protect you. There's no excuse, but she looked—she looked just like you. We were fighting. I didn't know what to think, but I should have known there had to be another explanation."

"I get it." Becky reached up and cupped his face in her hands. "She had me convinced I was losing my mind and I know I took it out on you. So much was my fault. I didn't know what the hell was going on, but I should have told you everything that was happening. She was very smart. I'll give her that."

Bryan gazed into his wife's eyes. "But you were right that I should have had more faith in you—in us." He kissed her again and again. "I love you. Can you ever forgive me?"

"You need to forgive *me*. I was selfish when I thought the IVF failed. I thought it was my fault, and maybe you were disappointed in having me for a wife."

"Never. I told you a long time ago I intend to grow old with you."

Becky shuddered. That almost hadn't been possible. "If you hadn't shown up to save me, she was going to kill me today and steal my life, including you, my friends, my job. I have no doubt she would have done it. She practically admitted she killed her mother."

"I would have known right away it wasn't you. She's an angry, ugly version of you. She may look like you, but the essence of you isn't in there. She's pure evil."

Becky glanced in the direction of the porch. "She's my genetic duplicate. How could we be so different? She learned to be a horrible, hateful person while I learned the opposite." She paused. "I guess I have to figure out if what she said about my mother is true. It seems a large sum of money changed hands, and I'm not sure any of this was even legal. Who knows if my mom will remember exactly what happened. Although it seems Ros might be part of this too."

Bryan looked at her quizzically. "Ros?"

"Peyton said my mom's best friend was involved and she worked at the hospital. That has to be Ros. She's the only one who could have helped pull this off, maybe even gotten me a birth certificate. It explains all the hushed calls and conversations I heard between my mom and her, even when I was little. Maybe they really thought they were doing something to protect me. I hate to say it, but they may have spared me from a horrible life."

Bryan dipped his head. "And you probably wouldn't have me." His lips curved up into a small smile.

Becky's mind went back to Peyton's declaration about being pregnant and felt her stomach twinge. "Do you think it's possible she's pregnant with our baby? Could she really have shown up for my appointment and the doctor would have taken her?" She recalled the driver's license Peyton had shoved in her face. "She has ID now with her picture on it and my name." She hesitated. "The office told me Dr. Levine was out of town for my transfer, but that call was from her. Probably another lie to keep me from following up and finding out what she'd done." Her eyes searched Bryan's. "Wouldn't Dr. Levine have known it wasn't me?"

Bryan took her hands in his and sighed. "I don't know, Beck. She does look like you, and the office would have had no reason to doubt her. I mean, who would suspect you had an identical twin trying to steal our embryo? She fooled me, and I'm your husband. We'll call Dr. Levine in the morning. Without all the drugs you were taking, I doubt the implantation would have stood much of a chance. When we talk to the cops, we'll make sure they insist on a pregnancy test."

Becky suddenly had a flashback to the news story about the stolen fertility medicine. Could that have been Peyton? What if she had researched how to be a gestational carrier and tried to prepare herself. Becky couldn't even imagine their baby having to grow in that monster who would no doubt be going back to prison.

Bryan put his hand on her shoulder. "We'll find out how many embryos we had on day five. She couldn't have had them all trans-ferred, and we signed papers to freeze any that were high quality." He leaned over and kissed her tenderly. "I love you. We'll get our baby somehow. I have no doubt."

Becky nodded as she gazed up at him. "Getting pregnant seemed like the most important thing in my life until I almost didn't have one." She wrapped her arms around his waist and pulled him close to her. "I have a new perspective on things. As long as I have you, we can deal with whatever is ahead of us together. I love you."

"I'm not going anywhere ever again. No matter what happens, it's you and me."

Becky turned and faced the living room. Jules and Jonas were huddled with the police officers who had saved her.

As she stared, Becky was sure this was the same man she had seen her best friend with at the coffee shop. She turned back toward Bryan. "Is that cop Jules's new boyfriend?"

Bryan laughed. "I don't even think I know the whole story, so I think we should probably let Jules tell you. I'll give you two a minute so you can get caught up." He called into the living room where she was standing with Jonas. "Hey, Jules."

CHAPTER FIFTY-NINE

Becky

Jules hugged Becky tight and then pulled back and frowned at the gash on her temple. "Beck, you scared the shit out of me!"

"Yeah, I was more than a little nervous myself for a while there. You have no idea how relieved I was to see you all show up."

Jules wrapped her arms around herself. "This is all my fault. I'm so sorry. I never got your message in time that day. I sent in your test." She hesitated. "Obviously." She looked down at the floor as tears fell from her eyes. "I should have told you, but you thought it was bad luck. I figured if you didn't know, you wouldn't think you were jinxed. And then, everything happened with the baby ..." her voice trailed off.

"I know. I did think it was bad luck. Maybe it wasn't even because of the pregnancy. My gut just told me something wasn't right. But I gave you the test. I told you it was okay to send. It's not your fault I didn't change my mind in time. I mean, Jules, I wanted to be supportive. I wanted to do anything that would help you in your search."

"I was so obsessed working on my stuff. I didn't want to look at your account. I felt guilty. It didn't even require any detective work." Jules's voice wobbled. "If I had just opened up your matches, she was right there the whole time. As soon as I saw that you had an identical DNA match, I knew it could be only one of two things. Either you sent in another test, or somehow you had an identical twin."

Becky shrugged. "I'm not sure I would have even known how to send in another test."

"You didn't even want to do the one I got you, and I led her right to you. Everything she put you through. Can you ever forgive me?"

"You didn't know. Hell, I had no clue." Becky reached for Jules and took her hands. "Don't cry. There's nothing to forgive. You thought I might be a princess. Not quite, huh?" She let out a small chuckle. "That little tube should come with a warning label to spit at your own risk."

Jules sniffled. "No kidding. I was so excited about finding answers. I went in a little blind about what could happen."

Becky hugged her again and gripped her shoulders as she stepped back and looked her in the eyes. "We're good. Hopefully, I can leave all of this in the past. So, tell me about this hunky new boyfriend of yours."

Jules furrowed her brow. "New boyfriend?" She leaned in and whispered. "There's no one new, but I did get a call this morning. From Tim."

Becky tilted her head. "Did he see you at the restaurant that night?"

"He did. He said he thought he just imagined I was there, because he couldn't stop thinking about me." A flush crept across Jules's cheeks. "He said he stopped by the store a couple of times to ask you how I was, but you weren't there, so finally he just called me."

So, Tim had been the mystery man from the boutique. "And..." Becky raised an eyebrow.

Jules shrugged as if she was indifferent, but the hopeful glimmer in her eyes told a different story. "I'm not sure. He wants to have dinner and talk."

"Well, that seems promising." Becky paused. "Wait. So, who's that?" She pointed her chin at Jonas. "I saw you at the coffee shop this morning with him."

"You did? Well, we were planning a formal introduction at a time when you weren't being held hostage by a crazed identical twin. I guess it's a little too late for that." Jules led Becky into the living room where Jonas was talking to Bryan. "Becky, I'd like to introduce you to Jonas." She paused for effect and added a fake drumroll. "My brother."

Becky squealed and hugged them both. "Oh, so that was the message you left me." She stepped back and studied Jonas. "You know he has your nose, right?"

He smiled and held up his hand in protest. "I think it's more like she has *my* nose. But it's pretty incredible to have a sister."

"So, DNA brought you two together, and I got *that*?" Becky turned and gestured toward the porch where Peyton was still sitting on the tile. "That hardly seems fair and—"

The conversation halted as Mrs. Ritter came barreling through the open front door. She stared up at the broken door frame and paled. "What in heavens is happening here? You kids had me scared to death. After I saw your door was kicked in, I called the police. There are news media trucks pulling up outside. Can someone please explain what's going on before I have a heart attack right here?"

"Hey, Mrs. Ritter." Jules patted the older woman on the back. "Well, the guy who kicked in the front door is a cop, but I see how it would worry you."

Jonas dipped his head at Mrs. Ritter.

"Someone please tell me what's going on," the older woman said as she tried to catch her breath. Her eyes drifted to the gash on Becky's head and the blood dried on her temple. "Becky, honey, you're hurt. Oh, dear. Are you—"

A commotion in the other room diverted her attention as her gaze drifted toward the porch. One of the police officers had stood Peyton up, and she was about to be taken away. The color drained from Mrs. Ritter's face as the older woman gaped at the two versions of Becky.

"Oh, heavens." She swayed on her feet, and Bryan grabbed her arm to hold her up.

Becky reached for the other arm. "Yeah, it's a long story, but the good news is I'm not crazy. And it would seem I'm a twin, an identical twin, although the other version of me is not that charming." Becky glanced toward the porch. "I'm pretty sure I'm disowning her."

Mrs. Ritter took one last look at Peyton who sneered in her direction. She turned her attention back to Becky.

"Oh, honey, I never thought you were crazy. I knew there had to be an explanation, and oh, in all this chaos, I almost forgot. I came over earlier, but you didn't answer the door. I went out to water my flowers in the back this morning. Guess who was on my deck chair all curled up on the sweater you left behind the other day? He must have smelled your scent and been confused about where he was."

Becky's hands covered her mouth. "Really?"

Mrs. Ritter smiled at her. "Yup, there's a certain orange cat who is desperate to find his way back to you. I had a feeling he might have been eating the food I left out."

Becky let the tears fall, this last token of relief opening the floodgates. "He's okay?"

Mrs. Ritter nodded and patted Becky on the arm. "Yes, darlin', he's okay, and I won't let him go anywhere until you come to get him. I used the food and lured him into the house. Your boy must be hungry—worked like a charm. I'm sure he's hiding somewhere in the house now, but he's safe till you're ready to pick him up yourself."

Two other police officers came into the circle. Becky wiped away her tears and looked over at the porch, but it was empty. Peyton was gone. She glanced out the front window and watched as her twin was loaded into a police car.

The lead officer leaned into Becky and tapped her on the arm. "Could we ask you a few questions?"

When Becky nodded, they led her back into the kitchen. She assured them she believed Peyton had acted alone but turned her head when she saw Tonya storming in the front door. Becky watched as she ran to Bryan and wrapped him in a hug.

Tonya then stepped back and raked her fingers through her hair. "When Becky never came back to the store this morning, I got worried. I should have called you, but she's just been acting so strange. I had to put up surveillance cameras to find out what was going on."

"Tonya—" Bryan tried to interrupt her.

"I felt awful about the fight we had yesterday, but Bryan, she was *stealing*. I couldn't even believe my eyes." Tonya started to cry. "I didn't want to call the police on her, but now I just watched them take her away. Oh my god, what happened?"

Bryan glanced over and nodded as Becky came up behind Tonya and tapped on her shoulder.

Tonya whipped around, and her mouth went slack. She stared at Becky and then gestured at the front window. "Wait—how? I just watched them pull away with you in the police car."

Becky offered a half-hearted shrug. "Not me. Apparently, I have an identical twin. Those cameras I didn't know about? They captured *her* stealing."

Tonya's face fell as she let out a strangled sigh. "Oh, Beck, I'm so sorry. I should have known there had to be another explanation, but when I saw you on the footage, I was shocked. I—"

One of the officers patted Becky on the arm. "We hate to interrupt, but we should take you to the hospital to get that head checked out. You've got a nasty gash. Probably needs stitches. Then we'll need you to come to the station to give us a statement."

Becky nodded and reached for Bryan's hand. She turned to Jules. "The neurologist said there had to be a rational explanation for everything that happened. I'm pretty sure he never considered DNA and an identical twin."

"DNA can be a good thing, but it's like opening Pandora's Box, People lie. Stories lie. But DNA? That's where the truth hides." Jules hesitated. "Sometimes the truth is better off staying in the past. The problem is you don't know what you'll find until you go down the path. My Pandora's Box had quite the find in it. Yours was like one of those scary Jack in the Box clowns."

Becky gazed off into the distance. It startled her to realize she was okay with knowing the truth. After a moment, she turned her attention back to Jules. "You know, not that I would want to go through this again, but I'm not sorry I know about Peyton."

Jules cocked her head in surprise. "Really?"

"Yeah, really. It answers questions about things I never understood. As crappy as it is, it's still my story. It's my truth. Now my job is to make sure it makes me stronger and doesn't break me. That would be like letting her win."

Jules shook her head. "That would never happen. You're stronger than anyone I know. Today proved it."

"What about you? You've obviously found some answers. How do you feel?"

Jules smiled at Jonas. "Amazing. Like a huge weight's been lifted off me."

Becky nodded. "DNA's pretty powerful. We both proved that. I'm going to need you to teach me a little more about how to use it. This time I promise to pay attention."

Jules laughed. "I have more to learn too. I feel like I want to help other people find what I've found. You know, pay it forward."

"I'm in. People deserve to know their story if they want. Good or bad."

Becky dipped her head at the police officer. "Okay, I'm ready to go to the hospital."

"You mean we're ready," Bryan said as he reached for her hand and intertwined his fingers with hers. "You and me, remember?"

Becky gave his hand a gentle squeeze. "I wouldn't have it any other way."

As they walked away, Becky stopped and spun back around. "I'm serious about the DNA stuff, Jules. It's not like Peyton is my only relative." She raised an eyebrow. "You just never know who else might be out there."

THE INHERITANCE

Coming in early 2021.

Becky and Jules spend the summer learning from a renowned DNA expert and then open the doors of their DNA Detective Agency. As they take on their first official case, DNA and good old-fashioned detective work uncover much more than their client ever expected. Unfortunately, it seems someone else is determined to get to the answers first and will stop at nothing to eliminate anyone who gets in the way. Can Becky and Jules solve the case before they're silenced?

ACKNOWLEDGEMENTS

There were days I thought this book would never make it into anyone's hands but mine. Many times my son Ben would ask, "Are you still writing that book?" I was because I knew I had a story to tell. Ben endured many nights of take-out while I wrote and revised and wrote some more. To be honest, I use the word "endured" lightly. I'm pretty sure he prefers it to my cooking.

They say it takes a village ... (oh wait, that's for kids not books). It should be for writing a book as well because there are so many people who helped me along the way.

More than anyone, I thank Jonas Saul, who went from being a favorite author to a mentor to a friend. They say people cross our paths for a reason, and I can't appreciate enough that you crossed mine. Mere words can't convey the appreciation I have for your knowledge and generosity in helping bring this book across the finish line.

I thank Amy Sue Nathan for putting the wind back in my sails that I had something people would want to read. You helped me stay the course just when I needed it.

Poor Kelli Martin. She took on the first manuscript for this book, and it was a doozy. With her guidance, it started to take shape, and I thank her so much for the OMGs in the margin that brought a satisfied smile to my face and kept me going.

My obsession with DNA and the emotions around searching for family and adoption came from CeCe Moore and her amazing Facebook group, DNA Detectives. If you are trying to figure out the puzzle of DNA, this should be the first place you go.

Every girl needs their "person," and Stacy Ostrau is the Jules to my Becky. I thank her for providing a good deal of my character inspiration. Go Dawgs.

They say your hairdresser knows all your secrets. Peyton Regaldo knew all the book's secrets too. She supported this book from a mere thought until the end. She was always my most enthusiastic beta reader, even when the book was twice as long! (She said nicely she didn't think I needed to cut a single thing. Sweet but so not true.)

I still remember disclosing the plot to Michelle Roache over garlic rolls and wine. I can't thank her enough for gasping in all the right places as she said over and over, "I see this as a movie." I'd be okay with that! With her expertise, we won't be the only ones who read it.

For taking the time to read my book while it was a work-in-progress, I thank Woody Kamena, Bonnie Mikoleit, Valerie Riuli, Ken White, Brenda Staton, Donna Good, Deborah Carlon, and Brittany Schroeder. You all read different iterations of the book, and your feedback was appreciated and invaluable in shaping the final product.

Lastly, I thank Liz Cordero for sending an endless parade of sweet foster kittens through my office while I wrote this book. Who can be stressed with tiny kittens frolicking around your feet, right? The work Liz does is simply amazing. (Please consider adopting a forever friend or making a donation at www.loveforcats.org.)

ABOUT THE AUTHOR

Photo by Bill Ziady

Liane Carmen lives in Florida with her teenaged son and a houseful of pets. After solving her own family mystery, she became passionate about helping others and writing stories about the secrets DNA can hold. She works full-time for a large corporation and spends her spare time reading, writing and researching her family tree. This is her first novel.

Contact Liane Carmen
Website: https://www.lianecarmen.com
Facebook: @LianeCarmenAuthor
Twitter: @liane_carmen
Instagram: @liane_carmen_author
Email: lianecarmen@icloud.com

Made in the USA
Middletown, DE
18 September 2020

20067076R00196